Nicholas and Alexandra:
Soul Mates

Book II: The Soul Searcher's Series

Clydene Rae Brandt

PublishAmerica
Baltimore

ISBN: 1-4241-2850-1
PUBLISHED BY PUBLISHAMERICA, LLLP
www.publishamerica.com
Baltimore

Printed in the United States of America

Dedication

This book is dedicated to those who are truly in love...and to those who have acknowledged that God's plan of waiting and abstinence prior to marriage is the best...no matter how difficult. It requires obedience and trust...in God, in yourself, and in the other person. Above all, it requires a love that is worth waiting for...a love of incomparable worth...no counterfeit love here...but a life-giving love.

To all who believe, or have already found their "soul mate," this book is dedicated to YOU and to your faithfulness to the Lord of our Joy...Christ Jesus!

"Seal me in your heart with permanent betrothal, for love is strong as death…"

—The Song of Solomon 8:6, *The Living Bible Paraphrased*

Acknowledgments

To my friend, Pat Mason, who has helped me "stay the course" and never give up, I thank you. To my church, Victory Christian Center, in Oklahoma City, bless you for all those prayers and words of encouragement. To my friends and family, I could not have done this without you, and to my Lord and Savior, I could not have tackled this difficult and timely message without Your help and love. To all who believe in soul mates, this is for you…

—Clydene R. Brandt

Foreword

Readers of *Saint's Hospital* requested knowing more about the characters, Nicholas and Alexandra Stewart. The truth is, they fell in love with these characters and asked for me to share their story. Of course, I longed to tell it. It is a love story, but it is much, much more.

It involves a sinister plot to destroy our nation and other nations of the world. It is a mystery that covers two continents, involving a puzzle that endangers the lives of Nicholas, Alexandra, their friends, and their family. As their love for each other grows, so does the danger—and the sexual tension. It will test the pledge that they have made to each other—a pledge to wait— a pledge of abstinence.

Join us as the mystery unfolds, and as Nicholas and Alexandra each seek their soul mate.

Chapter One

Evil arrived in Westville at 9:00 a.m. on a sunny Thursday morning. The black sedan seemed to appear from nowhere. It entered the small town square at the same moment that one lone cloud drifted over the sun, hiding its brightness for just an instant. It was like an omen of what was to happen. As God and His angels looked down, they prepared for war.

The car pulled over to a curb, directly across the street from the high school. Its darkened windows remained closed, and the engine was left running, as a tall, dark-haired man, wearing a black trench coat, swung his long legs out from the back seat.

"Wait here," he demanded as he got out. He slammed the car door and crossed the street, heading in the direction of the school.

The driver and a second passenger remained inside the sedan. They watched as the third man entered the school and disappeared into the reflections made by the glass panes on old, oak doors.

Peering out from inside the auto, the driver of the sedan noticed several police cars parked just up the street at a small brick building marked "Sheriff's Office." He frowned, and then turned back to watch the happenings at the school.

Stretched over the doors of the school auditorium was a banner that read, "WELCOME TO WESTVILLE HIGH." Sweaty kids in band uniforms gathered at a side parking lot near the school, practicing a Sousa march. Their director, apparently frustrated with what he was hearing, stopped them by tapping his baton on a music stand.

"Stop—stop! Let's try that again," he shouted.

The music faded. Off-key horns stopped playing, and a noise from the drum section resonated in the air. The sound that lingered was a rather sad and mournful whine. The director muttered some stern instructions to his students and once more he raised his baton.

As the music started again, the driver in the sedan remembered another school in another town. It was a sunny day, much like today. He remembered the calm and innocence of that place, just before peace was replaced with havoc and gunfire.

The thought of it made the driver shudder. Beads of sweat broke out on his face, trickling down his balding forehead and getting lost in his thick, brown, eyebrows.

What will happen if Quentin misses his mark, or worse, if he's caught? There are more police near the school than we planned.

He consoled himself by remembering how professional Quentin was. Quentin would *not* put them in jeopardy, even if he had to delay this. He thought of all the other killings in which they had played a part. It was true. The "Organization" had sent their best man for this.

Nothing will go wrong. Quentin's too smart.

Just then, he noticed a slender young woman, who was crossing the street. She was right in front of the car. You couldn't help but notice her—attractive, blond, and wearing one of the high school uniforms, but too old to be a student.

She must be one of the actresses who are at the school today—either an extra or one of Nick Stewart's cast members.

The driver nudged his partner.

"Look at that," he said to the second passenger, who nodded and whistled in response.

The driver smiled as he checked his gun holster. The thoughts of the woman brought a smile to his soft, pudgy face. He felt better. It would all go as planned. No one would prevent it.

Alexandra Andrews stepped from the curb in front of a black sedan, hurrying across the street to the school. She had to hurry. Her alarm clock hadn't gone off this morning, throwing everything out of kilter.

"Today, of all days—Al will want to choke me."

She ran up the steps, took a deep breath, and opened the doors to the high school. Her short skirt blew up in the wind, showing shapely, girlish, legs.

Relax. Everything will be fine.

This was a big day for the town. It was also a big day for Alexandra. She would be interviewing actor Nicholas Stewart later in the day. She *would* have to be dressed in this ridiculous school uniform.

"What's he going to think, when a twenty-five-year-old woman does an interview with him, dressed in a high school uniform?"

Surely, the "Great Editor of Public Relations" must have it in for her! It was necessary, however, for the later rehearsal she had. She smoothed back her strawberry-blond hair, forced a smile, and walked swiftly down the main hall and into the auditorium. She was determined that nothing would make her feel bad today.

A crowd of teachers, actors, and security personnel had gathered in the school auditorium, and people were waiting for their "now favorite" celebrity. Alex looked around for her boss, newspaper editor, Alfred Moffet. She scanned the crowd, but didn't see him anywhere.

"He seems to be late too." She smiled, breathing a sigh of relief.

Alexandra walked toward the front of the auditorium, where the stage was set for Nicholas Stewart to address his fans.

No one paid much attention to the tall man standing in the back of the room. His forged pass had made it past security and into the main auditorium. Quentin Smith was intense as he surveyed the room. He checked the pocket of his trench coat one more time, feeling the hard metal so familiar to him by now.

Almost one year ago, Alexandra Andrews climbed her way to the top of her public relations firm. Then, everything seemed to fall apart. She burned out, almost as fast as she claimed success. Her relationship of two years failed when her fiance found a wealthy, younger socialite. He left Alex with an uptown apartment that she couldn't afford, a job she grew to hate, and a broken heart. It had almost destroyed her. That was when she decided to take another look at her life, and what she saw, she *didn't like!*

Her decision to move to a smaller town turned out to be a good one. She moved to Westville over eight months ago, rented an older brick house in the historical section of town, and found a church with a pastor who listened to her without making her feel any worse than she already did. Counseling with Pastor Dan Braddock helped her get over the numbness of what had happened to her. She wanted to work again, and she wanted her life back.

Searching the classifieds one day, Alexandra answered an ad from the local newspaper. They were looking for a part-time events editor. She had an appointment the next day with Al Moffett.

"You'd be responsible for covering all of the local arts and entertainment events in our town, Alex," Alfred Moffet told her.

Al Moffett, editor, photographer, printer, and "one-man show" for the newspaper, took an immediate liking to Alexandra Andrews. He knew that she was over-qualified, and he told her so, but when he saw the disappointment on her face, he hired her anyway. To Alexandra, the job sounded fun, and it seemed perfect.

To Al, who was nearing retirement age, Alex appeared to meet all of his expectations and more. It was through the job that Alex later learned about Nicholas Stewart.

Stewart was a wealthy film actor, and he was going to do a segment of his newest movie in Westville. When Westville town officials learned of this, they planned a large welcome, and an even larger public relations campaign. Al and Alexandra were notified of their upcoming duties and put on alert.

Al took over the photography, while Alexandra concentrated on the advertising campaign—interviewing local cast members hired as extras, avid Stewart fans, and nearby business owners.

She reviewed most of Nick Stewart's films, and had to admit that she considered him a fairly decent actor. This, from Alexandra, was a high compliment, as she didn't rate many films these days worth viewing.

She also noticed that in most of the roles he played, there was a quality that was likeable in the man. It may have had something to do with his looks— dark hair, almost turquoise-blue eyes, and his grin—a kind of half-smile that melted most female moviegoers' hearts. He was Italian-American, and originally from New York City. During her research on him, Alex found out that he was a widower with a young child. His wife died over a year ago, after a long illness.

"That must have been terrible for them," she told Al Moffett one day. "His child was just a toddler when her mother died. She is almost five-years-old now. I wonder what kind of father Nicholas Stewart is?"

"A rich one," grinned Al. "He's worth a mint."

"The media, for the most part, has spared his private life. There's not much information on the child, Sabrina Stewart."

"He's lucky there."

Alex noticed in the press clippings that when Stewart's last film grossed the studio a huge amount of money, his face was everywhere, and more attention had recently surrounded him.

It wasn't easy for Alex to get Al Moffett to give up the interview with Nicholas Stewart and let her do it. She begged, pleaded, and wheedled.

"You'll be taking so many pictures for the paper, it will probably take up all of your energy, Al."

They both smiled at each other, knowing that wasn't exactly true, but Al finally agreed that Alexandra could do the interview. She had suggested to him that she join the cast as an extra, so she could get an up-close and personal perspective.

"I believe it will be a good way to cover the event, Al."

When she asked him if she could try out for the one crowd scene in the film, she held her breath.

"Rehearsals would be on my own time, and it would tie right in with my job," she pleaded. "It isn't much of a scene—just getting into a limo with several actors, and with Mr. Stewart. I could do some interviews with the cast right after that."

It was no surprise to Alex when Alfred agreed to let her do this, too. These days, Alfred found himself usually agreeing with Alex. She seemed to be searching for ways to be helpful to him. Besides, he thought she would be good at the interviews. People always seemed to open up with Alex, and she enjoyed meeting and talking with them.

"Alex Andrews would have made a good investigative reporter," he told one of the town council members. "She's just a natural at interviewing people."

Al knew that she had burned out at her advertising agency job, but she seemed to enjoy her work on his newspaper, and she was excited about the upcoming film.

He also knew a little about her past love life. If he had learned one thing about Alexandra, it was that she *didn't trust men.* Her fiance had really done a job on her.

Nick Stewart was due to arrive at any moment. Alex looked around at the crowd. She was surprised at the large number of people that turned out, and credited Alfred Moffet for doing a good job publicizing the event. Al, in turn, would have given her praise. She had placed stories in major magazines, as well as the local newspaper. She had mailed out press releases to every publication, TV, and radio station that she remembered. As she surveyed the audience, she noticed that some of the big boys from the networks were there today, too. Nicholas Stewart should be very pleased!

Alex moved closer to the stage. Nick Stewart was to give a welcome to the cast and the locals, then do some photos. He had some interviews scheduled for today and tomorrow, when he would shoot both of his movie scenes. Alexandra saw a friend, Carol Lane, in the crowd.

"Carol? Hi."

"Hi, Alex. Are you ready for all this?"

"Yes. Al's here somewhere, and he's going to get the pictures taken. He's to find out when I can interview Mr. Stewart, too. I guess our group is going to rehearse our scene later. I hope to get some feedback from the cast on what they think about all of this. Hey, maybe I can interview you, Carol?"

Carol Lane grinned, muttered an "okay," and asked Alex what she thought about the heavy security that was at the school.

"Just look at this place," she said. "It's crawling with security, isn't it? Besides our local police, there are a lot of new faces—news crews, and some of Mr. Stewart's people here too, huh?"

Alexandra nodded, and as she turned to look, she was pushed into a large man in a black trench coat. He glanced down at her, but he never moved out of her way or cracked a smile. In fact, he looked so irritated that she moved away quickly, excusing herself for running into him. She had felt the hard object hidden by his coat. It had to be a gun.

Alex could tell a lot about people by looking into their eyes, and this man's eyes were the color of steel—cold and threatening. The color merged into his dark gray shirt and the black trench coat. Alex watched as he walked across the room, closer to the front, near the stage. He checked under his coat more than once. She saw that he was not surveying the crowd at all—as a security guard might. He kept his eyes focused on the stage where Nicholas Stewart would soon be addressing his audience.

There was a sudden buzz and a squealing noise shrieked through the sound system. The school's principal adjusted the microphone on stage and began announcing the agenda. People drew quiet, and a whisper began to grow in the auditorium. Alex watched as the crowd parted to either side of the room. They formed an aisle near the entrance, and for the first time, Alex saw Nicholas Stewart walking toward her, through the doors, and into the auditorium.

"Just like Moses parting the Red Sea," she smiled.

He was more handsome than he appeared in film, and he was taller than she would have guessed, well over six feet. Some of the female cast members were already "oohing" and "aahing." Alex, despite trying to remain calm and professional, found that her face was warm, and she knew it was slightly flushed.

As he entered the center of the room, Nicholas Stewart passed close to Alexandra, shaking a few hands, and waving to the crowd. When he was directly in front of her, he paused. He was gazing right at her, and Alex stared back, unable to say anything.

His eyes are the color of my turquoise bracelet. What's he looking at? Keep moving, Mr. Stewart. This is getting embarrassing...

Nicholas Stewart looked at Alex for what seemed a long time to her, and just for an instant, everything seemed to be in slow motion. He moved on toward the stage, but then turned back, once more, to see her brown eyes looking up at him. Alex swallowed hard, and she felt a little lightheaded. Perhaps she was making more of this than she should. He probably just recognized her as the reporter who was to interview him later.

"If anyone had ever looked at me like he just did you," interrupted Carol, "I would have done anything he asked."

Alex smiled at Carol and shrugged. She turned back to view the stage, and watch Nick Stewart. He was, in a word, mesmerizing.

Nicholas Stewart moved to the small auditorium stage. Cheers and clapping from the small town crowd seemed to please him, and he appeared to be relaxed and friendly. The crowd pressed in to hear what he had to say to them.

Alex noticed that his "security man" had been pushed further back in the crowd. She watched as the man said a curse word under his breath.

He's probably annoyed that he won't be able to protect Mr. Stewart from that far back.

Thank-yous were made, and photos were taken. The hometown press, meaning Alfred Moffet, suggested taking a picture of the cast with Nicholas Stewart in the middle. Alexandra began to move to the stage along with the other cast members. It was then that Nick Stewart did something no one expected. Looking directly at Alexandra, he went over to her, and pulled her up, into the center of the stage, next to him.

"Mr. Moffett, is it?" he questioned Al. "I have a suggestion, if I may."

Al looked befuddled, but nodded.

"I think a picture with just *one woman* might make a better composition."

He told Al that he would pose for another picture with the rest of the cast too, but he was sure that Al would like this one better.

Alex wasn't certain why he chose her. She felt genuinely surprised, and very uncomfortable. After all, she was staff. She worked for the newspaper. It should be someone else who posed with him. She decided that Nick Stewart just wanted to be seen with a woman on his arm and considered him an egotistical male!

It will make better press for him. You have to be a star, huh?

But, when he smiled down at her, Alex could not argue, stay angry, or remain indignant. She couldn't refuse Nick Stewart, even if Al didn't use the picture. Her knees gave way, and her pulse pounded. She suddenly felt like an awkward teenager again.

Both said hi to each other. Nick Stewart's half-grin affected Alex, just as it had all those other women in the room—she melted!

Those eyes—Stop this! You're a grown woman, Alexandra Andrews. Begin to act like one.

Nick told Al and the rest of the photographers in the room that he was ready, and while the cast was lining up on stage for their picture, he put his arm around her waist and pulled her closer—so close that she could feel the warmth of his breath on the back of her neck. Alex thought she felt him smell her hair, but she was so giddy by then, she could have imagined anything.

He leaned over her shoulder and said, "I hope you don't mind all of this. They have to do these publicity things. I just thought I might as well pick the prettiest girl in the room to be here next to me."

There it is again…his ego. It's just like a man.

Alex barely smiled. She wanted to say that it was not all right, but she found that she was unable to speak—not one word—she froze!

Idiot! Say something.

But, nothing came out of her mouth.

Then, it was over. He thanked her, shook her hand, and left to do something else. Alexandra glanced around. It seemed to her that everyone was staring. She was embarrassed, and she hurried from the stage and back into the crowd. She thought that she saw the man in the trench coat leaving the building.

Strange. Why wouldn't he stay to cover the other events?

She couldn't explain why, but she was relieved that he was gone. She turned and saw Alfred walking to her.

"The picture I took of you and Mr. Stewart should be good for your scrapbook, Alex. I have to run the cast picture. You know that, right?"

She nodded to him.

"I hope when I interview him, I'll actually be able to speak. Explain why I froze up there."

Alfred Moffet smiled at her.

"You'll do fine, Alex. Just don't look at his eyes," he laughed.

Alex gave him a shake of her blond hair.

"Not you, too, Al. I know that I'll only see him one more time today, or I'll have to wait until tomorrow, right after the limo scene. I need to get my thoughts straight about the questions I'm going to ask."

She moved away and into a corner of the room where it was less crowded. She scribbled down some of her questions, made some notes, and then absentmindedly began chewing on her pencil eraser.

Which will make the most impact for the column? What makes Nick Stewart tick? Surely there's more to the man than shows on the outside? Although…the outside isn't hard to take! What about his child? Maybe that's off limits.

Alex wanted to ask questions that wouldn't feed his vanity. He seemed to have enough of that. Alexandra Andrews wanted to be the reporter to find out who the real Nicholas Stewart is. That was her job, and she was good at it.

The cast extras stayed for one final rehearsal, when Carol came over to see how Alex was doing.

"Gee, Alex, what was *that* between you and Nicholas Stewart? It was as if you two knew each other."

"I'm not sure," Alex answered. "He is nice-looking, but he certainly knows it. I don't know that much about him. I just hope I can get a good interview that will tell us more."

She and Carol joined the other actors on stage for some final instructions, but Alex's mind was elsewhere. She had been lonely since her fiance left her. After that happened, she closed herself off from most of her friends in the city. She swore that she would not be hurt like that again. She was surprised at how she reacted to Nicholas Stewart, and then she remembered his eyes. They seemed trustworthy, somehow. They had looked directly into hers and never wavered.

Her ex-fiancé could never look Alex straight in the eyes, especially that last month. She took him at his word, and he had lied to her, over and over. Alexandra hated being this bitter. She needed to forgive—even him. Pastor Dan had told her that. She knew that he would be disappointed in her. She was disappointed in herself.

Quentin Smith was angry. He couldn't make his move in this crowd. There were more people in the small town than he had planned. He remembered the woman who bumped into him. She might have felt the concealed gun, but of course, she thought that he was security.

When he had the gun pointed at Stewart, the crowd shoved him back, and then the actor had pulled that same woman right up in front of him. It would have been messy to shoot then, and Quentin didn't like messy jobs.

He would have to kill the actor tomorrow, as his orders stated. He hoped that contact hadn't yet taken place between Nick Stewart and Ed Percy, Stewart's old army buddy. Percy had to be taken care of tonight. Quentin and his friends in the Organization were going to be busy making certain of that.

He walked across the street, through the remaining band members, and stepped back inside the dark sedan. As it pulled away, the engine let out a slight hissing sound, much like a viper, slithering away.

Alex could not believe that by the time the group rehearsal ended, she had missed today's opportunity for her interview. Nick Stewart had spoken to Alfred and told him he had to leave.

"Don't worry, Alex. You can interview him tomorrow."

That wouldn't give her as much time as she would have liked.

"How in the world could I miss him?"

"He seemed anxious to talk to you, Alexandra. He even asked your name."

Alex felt her heart skip more than a beat. She couldn't explain why she was this fascinated with the actor. She had done public relations at her other job for much bigger celebrities than Nicholas Stewart, and had never reacted in this manner.

"He asked my name?"

"Yep. From what I saw going on up there on stage, it looks like he's interested in more than an interview, too. You be careful, Alex. Those Hollywood types are all alike."

She nodded. It was what she had thought once, but somewhere in the back of her mind, she was hoping that Nicholas Stewart was not just one of those Hollywood types.

"I'll be sure and get my interview tomorrow, Al, even if I have to hog-tie Mr. Nick Stewart."

That thought made her smile.

Alexandra would have been surprised to know that Nicholas Stewart—underneath all of the publicity and all the fame—was a one-woman man, and that meant finding a love that would last him a lifetime, a love he believed he no longer deserved.

Driving back to his hotel, Nick jotted down the things he still had to do. Publicity appearances and promos were getting to be tiresome for him. He still had to talk to some town dignitaries tonight. He also had to call Sabrina and tell her good-night. Later, he had to phone his old army buddy, Ed Percy.

Ed had sent him an e-mail earlier this week, telling Nick that he had a temporary assignment in Westville, and had heard Nick was going to be there. He also told him that it was urgent that he speak with him. Nicholas wondered what it was about. It had been years since he had seen Ed.

I wonder what could be so urgent?

He thought again about the young woman at the school. He found out from Al Moffet that she was a reporter on the local newspaper and an extra in his film. She was slightly older than the rest of the cast members who were swooning around him. He couldn't seem to take his eyes off her. What was it about her? He felt flustered and awkward, and a twinge of something that he had not felt in a long, long time.

Why now?

He had a good career, more than enough money, and numerous women who wanted to share themselves with him whenever he wanted. The trouble was, he didn't want them. He never had. There had been only one woman in his life—Megan, and now, she was gone. Sabrina's mother, his wife, had died and would never return. Tears moistened Nicholas Stewart's eyes as he thought about her.

Meg had been so ill for such a long time, and she hated his career toward the end. She asked him to stay home more, but he hadn't, and he could never forgive himself for that.

He took Sabrina for a holiday, just to get her away from the illness and all the doctors. It had been the wrong time to do it. Meg got worse. Her cancer spread so much faster than it was supposed to—and then, she was gone. The thought of it saddened him all over again. He had little left that really mattered to him, except for his child.

He was too tired this past year to even try for a new relationship. The studio had been on him to date. That didn't tempt him. He hadn't met a woman with whom he had anything in common, and certainly no one he was attracted to—until today, when he saw *her*—*Alexandra Andrews*. He found out she wasn't married. That was good news.

Nick realized he acted the fool when he practically dragged her onto the stage with him for that photo. He could barely think of anything to say to her.

What a dope I was!

"Alexandra—Alex," he said her name, letting it linger on his tongue. He liked the sound of it.

His driver pulled up to the hotel and he went to his room. He called his daughter, Sabrina, to tell her he loved her. After dinner with the mayor, he tried to call Ed Percy. There was no answer. Later, the phone seemed to be out of order. He would have to try again tomorrow.

Nick was tired, and it had been a long day. He fell asleep in the recliner, still wearing the same clothes he arrived in.

Chapter Two

Alex couldn't relax after the late rehearsal. It was almost 8:00 p.m. She decided to stop for a few groceries and walk home. The cool night was pleasant, and it took her mind off the day's activities. She walked past a car parked at her neighbor, Ed Percy's home and when she arrived at her house, her dog met her at the door.

She had rescued Sandy from the shelter about one month ago. He was half-lab and half-golden retriever. He had been trained by someone to *sit, stay, and protect.* He had become her best friend.

Ed Percy had moved into the neighborhood a little over a month ago, and she didn't know him very well. The first time that she met him, the dog got between both of them and growled fiercely, until Alex had to remove him and put him into another room. That was one of the few times she ever saw Ed outside his own yard. He had received some of her mail by error. Since that time, they had only nodded in passing.

She guessed that Ed Percy was around thirty years old. He always appeared to have a worried frown on his face. Even when he smiled, the frown didn't go away. Alex felt sorry for him, thinking he must be lonely. She never saw anyone go to his house and was glad someone was finally visiting him.

Ed's house was on the corner, and on the other side of Alex lived the Rogers family, who seemed the exact opposite of Ed Percy. Emily Rogers, her husband, and two boys, were the first to show up at Alexandra's doorstep after she moved in. Emily Rogers welcomed Alex with a warm apple pie, and told her about everyone in the town who might be of any interest.

Finding out about Alexandra's fascination with history, Emily told her about the story of the tunnels that helped slaves from the South escape to the North.

"Did you know that we have quite a bit of history right here under our houses, Alex?"

"What do you mean?"

Emily and her husband repeated the tale of the tunnels to Alex.

"There are tunnels that connect some of our homes. Such a tunnel connects yours, Ed Percy's home, and mine. My gate is always left open to your gate, Alex, in case we ever need an escape route for an emergency, such as a fire or a storm. Have you found your tunnel, yet? I'm surprised your realtor didn't show it to you."

"Most of my papers were signed long distance by fax. I just took their word the house was in good shape. I guess they forgot."

Alexandra was intrigued by the story, and Emily showed her where the tunnel was. It had remained hidden from her, and she would never have guessed it was there in her basement, behind the furnace. Alex had to squeeze to get in through the old entrance, but when she did, there it was—a long, musty, tunnel. It was still solid, and old candle lanterns still hung on the walls. It came up to Emily's back door, right into the back of her garage.

"Mr. Percy blocked off the door to his section of the tunnel. You can't go up there, anymore. He hasn't opened it back up since he moved in. I don't know why."

Emily looked at Alexandra in the dim light. Alex was thinking how secretive and isolated Ed Percy had been. Maybe he liked the solitude, or had a reason to live alone.

Alexandra's dog loved the tunnel. He found he could go through it, up the steps of the Rogers' garage, and out their door into the back woods. He and Sugar, Emily's terrier, could now run and explore together. Sandy also liked the Rogers family. When Alex was working, he was at their home almost as much as his own. Alex felt a small twinge of jealousy. To be such a smart dog, he'd give it all up for Sugar—no question about it.

"Men! They're all alike," Alex once told Emily.

Alexandra went to her fridge and put away her groceries. She fed Sandy and started a pot of coffee. It had been a long day, and she needed a shower. Alex left the uniform that she had been wearing in the gym's locker at the school, and then, she changed into her sweats in the gym before walking home. Her blond hair was tied up in back, and for all her twenty-five years, she still looked like a girl.

Sandy greedily ate his kibbles and wanted outside. Alex fixed herself a TV dinner, which was all she could muster up, drank her coffee, and went to take her shower. When she tried to find a robe, she remembered she had hung the wash out on the clothesline in the back yard. Her robe and pajamas were still there.

NICHOLAS AND ALEXANDRA: SOUL MATES

"Nuts!" she whispered.

Putting her sweats back on, she went to retrieve the clothes and called for the dog. Sandy was there, in an instant. As she gathered the clothing, she noticed a strange, shadowy figure that appeared in Ed Percy's back yard. A chill went through her. She first thought it might be a burglar, and then recognized a familiar trench coat.

Alexandra hurried back inside her home, with Sandy at her side. She used her cell phone to call the Sheriff's Department.

Emmitt Clark had been the Westville town sheriff for years. He knew everyone in town. When Alex contacted him, he told her that he would be right out.

"Alexandra? Lock your doors and turn off your lights. If you see anything else, call me on my mobile phone."

Emmitt gave her the number, and then told her that he would be over as soon as possible.

After Alex turned off her lights, she tried to look through the slits in the blinds that were near her bedroom. It was then that she noticed a strange orange glow outside, and she heard a crackling sound coming from next door. Alex and Sandy both smelled the smoke. Ed Percy's house was on fire!

She opened the wooden blinds wider—wide enough to see three men outside the house. There was a dark sedan parked in Ed's drive. She couldn't see the tag, but she recognized the car. She had passed right in front of it earlier in the day. It was parked near the high school.

Then, everything seemed to happen! Ed Percy's house exploded—first in the front, then in the back! The force of the blast knocked Alex down, beside her bed, and away from the window.

"Oh, Lord, please help us," she cried out. "Sandy, come here. Here, boy."

The dog ran over to Alex and licked her hand. She used him to lean on and to help her stand back up. Then she pulled him by his collar to the cellar door, and they ran!

"Sandy, I think they saw me as I gathered the clothing. We have to get out."

Alex and the dog ran down the steps of her basement. She was about to use the old tunnel and go to the Rogers' home, even though she knew the family was gone tonight. They told her earlier that week that one of the children had a program at the church.

She and Sandy felt their way through the darkness until Alex found the box of matches that she had placed by the lantern. As she struck the match, the candle glowed eerily.

"Please, God," she prayed, "let Emily remember to leave the gate open tonight—and please let the stairway door be unlocked."

Sandy ran ahead of her, certain that he was on his way to see Sugar. Alex found the gate and the door both open. Her prayer was heard.

"Thank you, God," Alexandra whispered.

When she and the dog ran outside to the safety of the Rogers' backyard, she heard a motor start up. She was sure the men must have been leaving. She could hear Emmitt's siren in the background. Sandy and Sugar ran toward the woods, as Alex opened the Rogers' backyard gate.

"Where can I hide, just in case?" she pondered.

Alex saw Sugar's doghouse, and she climbed in, curling up inside the small space. She wished she could be invisible for just an instant, and at that moment, she heard a scraping. It was her neighbor's back gate opening!

"Someone's out here," a voice shouted.

Alexandra froze. She huddled closer to the side of the doghouse. There were footsteps at the Rogers' gate. The men were still there, and they were looking for her!

"Come on, Emmitt," she pleaded. "Get here."

The siren of the police car grew louder. All of a sudden, she heard the men running away and a car engine start up. Tires squealed as Alex took a deep breath.

Alexandra could still smell the gasoline and the smoke drifting over from Ed's house. She was afraid to crawl out of Sugar's doghouse, and that's where Emmitt and his deputy found her, still cringing in the back of Sugar's home.

Alex Andrews was still shaking, and it wasn't from the strong cup of coffee that Emmitt handed her. She gave the sheriff her statement of what she thought happened, but she was still bewildered about what was going on.

"Why would anyone blow up Ed Percy's home?" she asked Emmitt.

"I don't have any idea, Alex—not yet. I'm certain of one thing. You're not safe in your house tonight. I think you better stay with someone."

She agreed. She asked Emmitt if the police could go back home with her to get her overnight case. When she got there, she filled the case with makeup, a pair of jeans, a shirt, and other essentials. She was going to spend the night in *jail*, and it was at her request! Emmitt promised he would patrol the streets by her home all night.

Later, Alex phoned the Rogers family to let them know what happened. She told them that Ed Percy's body had been found in the debris. He was dead. She asked them to care for Sandy, as he was still with Sugar. They promised her that the dog could stay in the backyard for as long as she needed.

Alex had an unlocked cell and full use of the facilities, such as they were. She told Emmitt earlier about the man she had seen at the school. She decided that she was still going to go to the film screening in the morning, even though Emmitt warned her not to go.

"I'll be watching you the entire time, Alexandra, if you don't change your mind."

The thought of Emmitt and his police being close to her was a comfort. She told Emmitt that she would feel safer in a crowd than back at her house— alone. She wasn't sure how she would do the interview with Nicholas Stewart, but she had to complete it.

Alexandra was glad she had showered earlier. She climbed into the cot that was to be her bed tonight, and she fell asleep, dreaming of black smoke and a man in a black trench coat. His gun was pointed at Alexandra.

What Alex Andrews did not know was that the men who blew up the Percy house had added her name to their victim list, and they were making their own plans for tomorrow. Their targets now were Nicholas Stewart *and* Alexandra Andrews. The closer the two of them were together, the better. They planned ending both problems tomorrow.

Tonight was a success for them, and for the Organization. Ed Percy could no longer identify anyone in their group, but if he had told Nick Stewart what their real purpose was, then Stewart was still a threat, and the girl had seen them at Percy's house. She was becoming a big problem, too.

The three men decided that one would stay in the car tomorrow, while Quentin and the other would watch every move Alex and Nick made. When it was time for them to strike, they would. It would soon be over.

Alex awakened to the sound of a police radio. She smelled fresh coffee that one of the deputies was brewing. When he noticed her, he grinned.

"Coffee, Miss?"

"I'd love some, but I need to freshen up first."

She went into the small, bleak restroom, splashing her face with warm water, and drying it with a paper towel. Alex opened her makeup kit and applied blush and lipstick. She combed her short blond curls, and changed into clean clothing. She winced as she hit her elbow in the small space. When she came out, she took the black, fresh brew. It was strong, and it tasted good to her. The deputy offered her a doughnut, which she eagerly downed.

"I need to be at the high school auditorium in ten minutes," she said.

"Emmitt's already there, but I'm supposed to escort you over there, Miss."

The deputy showed her out the door, and they left in a squad car. He drove her less than a block to Westville High.

Alexandra stepped out of the police car and went inside into the locker room to change into her uniform. Other actors were already there. Carol Lane came over to Alex as she was dressing.

"Alex, are you ready for the scene?"

Alex nodded, but she had the uneasy feeling that she was being watched, although she saw no one. She was afraid, and she didn't want to go back home. In fact, she wanted to get away from the town altogether, for a while. In the back of her mind, she was hatching a crazy idea of how she might get out of town without anyone knowing, or preventing it—just until this blew over.

Nick Stewart was getting dressed when he caught a local news show on TV. That is how he learned about Ed Percy. He had tried to phone the night before, but there was no answer, and when he tried the second time, the line was out of order. Now, he knew why he was unable to reach him.

"Why? Why did that happen?" he asked the person on TV, knowing he would get no answer.

Nicholas wondered if anyone was arranging for a funeral. He was stunned by the news, and it was difficult to know what to do. He phoned the local police attempting to get more information, but the deputy was no help. He told Nick that he would have the sheriff call him later.

It was hard to concentrate on what he was doing. He and Ed had been in the service together. They were friends, back then. When Nick was sent home, Ed Percy had signed up for some type of special mission and had stayed in the service. Neither had made much contact since.

Why had Ed called him? The thought spun through his mind.

Nick had the limo pulled around to take him back to the high school. The filming of this scene should not last long, and then he would go to the

Sheriff's Office. If no one else had done anything about Ed's funeral arrangements, that was the least that Nick could do. He couldn't remember Ed having any family.

The last time they had been in touch, Ed lived in Paris, France, and was on assignment. He still had an apartment there.

Why would he move to Westville, a small town right in the middle of the heartland?

Nick thought again about the filming today. He had to do his first scene alone. The crowd scene would be next. That scene involved picking up the actors playing the students, putting them into his limo, and then driving off. They would be dropped off, and then they wave good-bye. It would be a short scene.

He thought briefly about Alexandra Andrews. Ed Percy's death had spoiled any plans he had to arrange meeting her alone. He needed to go see the sheriff, and that meant skipping a long interview. She would probably be in the second filming, but how could he say much to her in front of all the other actors?

He might be able to get a phone number, if he were not so distracted by this awful news. Nick wondered if Ed knew what was going to happen. Perhaps, that was why he wanted to talk to Nick. Nick walked over to the phone. He had to get ready for the movie shoot right now, so he called for his driver, Mac Timmons, and had his limo pulled around to the front of the hotel.

Alex borrowed some notepaper from Carol. She had a rather outrageous idea and was in the process of writing a note to Nicholas Stewart. If his limo could take her to the airport after this scene, without being noticed, she could take a flight out of Westville to California for a couple of weeks. Her aunt lived there and would let her stay with her, but she didn't want anyone else to know that, especially not Emmitt. He might not want her to leave yet.

She didn't know if Nicholas Stewart would go along with this, but she grabbed her cell phone and called Emily Rogers anyway. She made arrangements for Sandy to stay there for a couple of weeks, and then she finished her note.

It was time for the actors to go and wait on the curb, and then they would get into the limo with Nick Stewart. If she could just stay in the limo without getting back out, she could have him drive her out of town to the airport. No one would notice. After all, she was supposed to get an interview with him. The other actors would think she had stayed in the car with him for that.

That was certainly not what her note to him said. It was not asking for an interview—it was asking him to help save her life!

What if he says no and makes me get out of the car? Well, she would have to think about what else to do, *when and if* that happened!

The group scene was beginning. Actors were waiting on the curb by the high school as the limo approached. Alex saw a couple of the deputies observing her, and she felt a little better. No one in the crowd appeared suspicious to her, and she didn't see anyone that she didn't recognize. Alex still could not shake the feeling of being watched.

The actors crowded into the limousine, and Alex climbed in beside them.

She wanted to sit closer to Nicholas Stewart than where she was, but a giggly crowd of young actors ran ahead, pushing her out of their way. She noticed that he glanced her way a couple of times, but it felt nothing like their meeting before. The limo was slowing down to let the group out. If she was going to give him the note, she had to do it now!

Alex leaned across the seat and handed him a small folded message. He looked at her, took it, unfolded the note, and read it. Then, he smiled at Alexandra and nodded, and she knew he would help her. She had written the following note.

> *Dear Mr. Stewart,*
> *I'm the editor who was to interview you today. This is going to sound strange, but someone may be trying to do me harm. Could you give me a lift to the airport, so I don't have to leave your limo? I would not ask if it was not a matter of such great risk that I fear for my life.*
> *Sincerely,*
> *Alexandra Andrews*

The other actors left the limo. Alexandra didn't. For the first time, she was alone with Nicholas Stewart. He didn't say anything, but he tapped on the driver's window and told him to head for the airport. It was Alex who broke an awkward silence.

"Thank you," she said. "I know you must think this is very strange, Mr. Stewart, but you don't know what I have been through the last twenty-four hours."

When she told him about the explosion that was next door to her, he reacted in a manner that surprised her.

30

"You were there? Did you know Ed Percy? What happened?"

Alex explained what occurred after she left the school. Nicholas Stewart was leaning forward, across from her, listening intently. She asked him, "How did you hear about it?"

"I heard the news report on TV. Ed Percy was an old acquaintance. He tried to contact me just prior to flying to Westville. We weren't close friends recently," he continued, " but we were close years ago. I tried to get through this morning to the police and find out what happened."

Alexandra was amazed that he knew the man who had been her neighbor. She sat facing Nick Stewart and was about to tell him about Emmitt, when she noticed a black sedan pull from a side street behind their limo. It was familiar.

The sheriff's car was a long way back. Emmitt must have noticed that she didn't get out of the limo with the other actors and he was looking for her. The sedan was now between his police car and the limousine, and it was catching up to them, full-speed. Alex saw the passenger window roll down slightly, in the back of the sedan, and then, she saw the glint of steel.

She cried out to Nick Stewart, "Get down!"

The sedan had already pulled up to the driver's side of the limo. It was at that point, Alex heard the pop-pop-pop of gunfire. She pushed Nicholas Stewart out of the way, onto the floor of the limo. He, in turn, pulled her down under him as he tried to reach the microphone that went to the limo driver.

"Mac! Get out of here!" he shouted. "Don't worry," he shouted to Alex, " if anyone can lose these suckers, he can. Do you know who that is in the sedan?"

She was sure it was the men from last night, and told him. Nick Stewart's reassurance about his driver didn't make Alex feel much better.

The gunfire stopped, but the cars were going faster and faster. Alex was not only worried about getting killed, but now she was worried about involving Nick Stewart in this. She didn't want to lose him in a round of gunfire when he was trying to help her!

Nick Stewart, on the other hand, found himself afraid for Alexandra Andrew's safety. She could be hurt by a bullet or by the swerving of the car. He continued to hold her down in case the glass did break, and a bullet came through the car. He hoped that whoever was shooting at them didn't rip out a tire with one of the bullets. That would run them off the road, for sure.

Just then, his limo swerved, and the sedan hit the side of the limo. The sedan swerved to the other side of the road. His driver slowed down and purposely ran into the side of the sedan, not once, but twice. Mac was trying to run them off the road before they were able to do the same to the limo!

Alex was thrown first one way, and then to the other side of the limo, with Nicholas Stewart sliding over her and hitting his head—hard—on the back door. She gasped when she saw a small trickle of blood run down his forehead.

"Oh! Watch out," she screamed.

She slid into him, and then both of them slid back the other way. Alex heard a screech as the limo pulled ahead at breakneck speed.

"Boss!" the car intercom squealed, "are you two all right back there?"

Alex found the intercom to answer, "I think we are."

She asked if there was a first-aid kit in the limo, and told the driver she needed one.

"Can we get up now?" she asked the driver.

Mac Timmons told the girl that he thought it was safe. He saw that the police had caught up with the other car and that it was pretty banged up. He passed a first-aid kit back through the window. Nick Stewart slowly got up, pulling Alex back up on the seat with him.

"Are you okay?" both asked each other, at the same time.

"Your head, Mr. Stewart, is bleeding."

" I'm okay," he said, getting out a handkerchief and wiping blood from his face. "By the way, you may as well call me Nick, Alexandra."

As he spoke her name, Alexandra saw him smile, despite the circumstances. She managed to smile back at him as she handed him a bandage from the first aid kit.

"You were sure right when you told me you were in danger. Alexandra, I insist flying you wherever you want to go."

Alex was surprised that he appeared to be more worried about her than himself. She didn't expect anyone to think of her first, and certainly not him. Although Alex was grateful to him, she knew they had to contact the Sheriff first.

"I have to call Emmitt," she replied.

"Is that the local sheriff?"

"Yes."

While Alex called Emmitt on her cell phone, Nick Stewart was giving Mac instructions to give to the pilot and staff on his jet. Emmitt told Alex that the police car had seen enough to "book these two guys."

"You and Nick Stewart need to come back by the station and file charges. I want to see if you or Mr. Stewart can I.D. any of them."

Alex told Nick Stewart what Emmitt had said, and he asked the driver to turn around, back to Westville, and to the Sheriff's Office.

Mac Timmons was concerned about his boss's safety. He wasn't so sure the girl could be trusted. All this stuff about Nick getting a call from Ed Percy made him even more suspicious.

Why would anyone drive after a celebrity's car to try and kill one woman, unless the celebrity was a target too? Mac had experience with mobsters when he worked for Danny Zero. This wasn't a typical kind of attempted hit. It was right in front of police. Why would these guys do that, unless they were going all-out to stop the girl from identifying them? It seemed they didn't care if they killed Nick Stewart in the process. Mac was to learn later that he was not far off base.

Nick Stewart had hired Mac Timmons about eight years ago. Mac was grateful that anyone would hire him. He had lost his job with the governor long ago, and then got into the mob situation as a driver who had seen too much.

Danny Zero was a cruel man, and cruel men have enemies. Danny met up with his, face-down, in cement. Mac had turned snitch to the FBI. He was a source that sent many of the gangs to prison. Mac, in turn, went straight. Problem was, no one believed him—no one, but Nicholas Stewart.

They had an instant connection that no one understood. Nick was a gentleman, and he was a very generous person. He was part Italian, dark haired, and good looking. Mac Timmons, on the other hand, was a huge man with a broken nose and an ugly scar on his face. Nick called Mac his "gentle giant."

In the years that followed, Mac became the father figure that Nick needed. Nick's own father had died when he was young, but he had an Italian mother who expected much of him, raising him alone with two sisters.

Nick had worked hard, volunteered for the army, and then was lucky enough to get into films. He continued to help his family financially, especially his mother. Mac had seen the hurt in Nick's face when his siblings appeared to want his money and gifts, but left little in family love or loyalty. He still adored his mom, but he seldom saw his sisters anymore.

Nick's first marriage—that was a bad deal. Nick loved Meg. Mac knew he blamed himself for her death. Mac didn't know if Nick would ever forgive himself for being away from home when her condition worsened.

He worked harder than ever to keep his private life private now. Mac knew it was for the sake of his daughter, Sabrina. Nick devoted himself to her, whenever he could get away, and the child responded to him with the love that

Nick had not received from his sisters, and the love he no longer received from Meg.

"He's a good father," Mac whispered to himself.

Mac still was not too sure about this young woman whose life they had just saved. He would have to keep an eye on her. She seemed innocent enough, but why would she choose Nick's limo to be in when the gunfire started?

Although it looked as if both she and Nick Stewart might just be innocent victims, Mac would protect Nick Stewart with his own life, if need be—even from this young woman!

As soon as Nick asked him to call his plane crew, Mac phoned Nick's pilot, John Cabe, and told him what had happened. John was also Nick's best friend. Mac could always depend on John being there for both Nick and him.

John was a former Air Force pilot. He had been with Nick Stewart long before Mac was hired. There was little about planes, computers, or engines that John did not know. He told Mac he'd have the jet ready to take off whenever they were ready to board.

"Hey, Mac," he chuckled over the intercom, "this new chick coming aboard—what's she like?"

Mac grunted a reply. "She looks okay, I guess. She's pretty. She's in an awful lot of trouble, though. I haven't made up my mind if we can trust her."

Mac pulled the limo up to the Westville Sheriff's Office and Nicholas Stewart and Alexandra Andrews got out. Both went into the office, while Mac stood guard outside. Neither of them could identify anyone in all that confusion. Even Mac didn't get a good look at the men, except for the sedan, and the police had that.

Later, the couple returned and got back inside the limo.

"Mr. Stewart, we're so close to my home. Could I make a quick stop by my house to pick up more clothing and a few more personal items?"

"Of course, Alexandra—and it's Nick, remember?"

When they arrived, Nick saw what was left of Ed's house and where the explosion had rocked the neighborhood. He got out and walked over to the police tape, surveying the damage.

"My God...why?"

"I wish I could tell you why. I've asked myself that."

Alex went into her home and packed a few more essentials. She picked up the newspaper on the front porch and headed back for the limo. Mac helped her inside and called to his boss.

Nick appeared drawn and tired. He had arranged for Ed's funeral with the sheriff. Nick knew now why the girl was so afraid. He could not help feeling uneasy. Ed had tried to contact *him*. If only he had called him earlier. He felt somewhat responsible for what happened. He nodded to Mac, and the car finally headed for the airport.

Nick's pilot, John Cabe, had the jet ready to go when the limo drove up. He wasn't sure what was going on in town, but he had a whale of a story for Nick and Mac, when he received a report from CSI in California.

It was during the routine check that John had found a small silver cylinder. It had some type of liquid inside and had been well hidden underneath one of the wings.

John believed it could be some type of explosive, so he had sent it to his buddy, Joel Martin, who worked in the lab of CSI. It shouldn't be much longer before Joel called him back. John Cabe had the jet checked over with a fine-tooth comb after that, but found nothing else.

John was ready to get the plane in the air and out of Westville. He grabbed the luggage for Nick and the girl and put it in the jet. When Nick introduced Alexandra Andrews to John Cabe, he could see John's face lighten up. John saw that Mac wasn't exaggerating when he told him the girl was pretty. She was more than that. She was stunning.

Alex had changed her costume for jeans and a long-sleeve pink shirt. Her blond hair was held back, away from her face, with a pink headband. She had a clean natural look, which was refreshing for John to look at. As she climbed up the steps of the plane, he noticed that her figure wasn't bad either, but it was something in her dark brown eyes that made John look twice. She looked you square in the eye, and he liked that. She was someone John Cabe would trust.

She smiled at him, as they were introduced. "How do you do, Mr. Cabe," she said.

"Hello, there, beautiful," he replied.

When Alex glanced back at Nick, he just grinned and told her John always hooked up everyone with a nickname.

"That's all it is, Alexandra," Nick said, trying to excuse John Cabe. "He doesn't mean to be rude, although the name is quite fitting, in your case."

She laughed at both of them. They reminded her of a couple of schoolboys teasing one of the new girls in class.

John punched Nick in the shoulder, and gave him a nod toward Alex's back, as she climbed into the plane. It was as if to say she was okay with him. Nick smiled at John and followed Alex into the jet. He knew exactly what John Cabe, the ladies' man, was thinking.

Mac asked John to get out of the town as soon as possible and to watch for anything or anyone that looked suspicious. John Cabe thought about what Nick said to him earlier on the phone—almost the same thing! This was something new for Nick Stewart, who usually argued to all of them about having *too much* security.

He could hear the tone in Nick's voice, and he knew that Nick was on edge about something when he asked John to check out everything twice. John had a feeling that something bad was about to happen, but he didn't know what. Then, he found the vial.

"Let's get out of here!" he said to his co-pilot.

He went into the cockpit and started the engines. Shortly after, as the plane left the ground, he got the call from Joel Martin, and John's bad feeling turned into reality.

He called for Mac and asked him to get Nick up front, as soon as possible. When both men were there, John told Nick and Mac about the container he had found. Joel Martin had reported it held a chemical that was a bomb.

Someone had cleverly hidden it on the plane, where most of the crew wouldn't have discovered it. They just didn't know how John babied his planes, or how well he followed Nick's orders.

"The small vial could have blown up all of Westville." He watched Mac and Nick's reaction.

Nick Stewart had just learned that the danger they were in was more deadly than he had reasoned. He also knew that Alexandra was not their only target!

No one had noticed the dark figure at the edge of the airstrip. Quentin was watching the party board the plane, and he checked his watch as the jet left the runway. He looked disappointed as the plane flew away. Evidently, they had found his bomb. He would have to find out what flight plan they had filed.

This was far from over for the girl, or for Nicholas Stewart. Quentin walked slowly back to the small airport.

He muttered under his breath, "They caught my two partners. Someone is going to pay for this. They're going to pay very, very soon."

Chapter Three

Alex had flown in many company jets before, but she could not remember being in one as luxurious as this one. It had dark mahogany furnishings, and a well-stocked kitchen in this section. There were bedroom quarters further back, and another compartment that housed a bathroom, complete with shower. Alex had a chance to look around when Nick Stewart went up front to speak with Mac and his pilot. She was standing with her back to Nick, looking at some paintings, when he returned.

When Alex turned, she noticed for a brief moment the concerned look on his face, even though he tried to hide it.

Nick Stewart didn't want her to see how worried he was. The girl had already been through a lot. Who would want both of them dead? This was one piece of acting he had to do right now! He took a deep breath, tried to relax, smiled at Alex, and then motioned for her to sit down. Alexandra sank into one of the club chairs.

"Your plane's beautiful," Alex said.

She watched him as he sat down in the chair next to her. She still couldn't believe he had agreed to take her with him.

"It's time we get better acquainted, Alexandra," he said. "May I offer you something to drink or eat?"

Nick got up and went over to the bar. She noticed there was coffee, juice, and some soft drinks, but no wine or hard liquor. That was interesting. Most movie stars would have had wine, at least.

Alex accepted a soft drink but avoided glancing up at her companion. She still felt guilty involving him. Taking a sip of her soda, she took a deep breath.

"I guess you think this is all pretty strange. What must you think of me?"

"After what we've just been through and after seeing the mess that used to be Ed's house, I don't know what to think. He tried to contact me, but I never found out why. I think he was going to tell me he was in trouble, and the reason."

Alex handed Nick the newspaper that she had picked up and motioned to the front page. It described what police knew of the bombing, which was very little. It went on to say that both Alex and Nick 'were acquainted" with Ed Percy.

"I think they saw me last night and thought I could identify them, but the truth is, I only saw dark figures and heard the car. If it hadn't been for the tunnel between my house and the Rogers' home, I could be dead right now.

" I did see a man earlier at the school who looked suspicious. I thought at the time that he was one of your security people. Now, I think that he was one of the men at Ed's home."

Nick looked surprised and told her he didn't have any security there, except the local police.

"I reported it to Emmitt," she said. She tried to describe the man to Nick Stewart. Nick told her that he would let Mac and John know.

"Maybe they can trace the guy."

"I am so sorry for getting you involved in this," Alex said.

"I think I may be more involved than you are. These men may think that Ed already contacted me and told me something. Both of us have been put into a dangerous situation, and it seems that neither of us really knows why, Alexandra."

He still didn't tell her about the bomb John had found on the plane.

She shook her head, trying to make sense of everything that had happened. Could Nicholas Stewart be the *real target,* and could she have just fallen into this mess? Both of them were in it together now, whether they liked it or not!

"How is your head?" she asked him.

Nick hadn't thought about the bump on his head since the shooting. It had ached a bit, but it was only a slight cut. He raised his hand toward his brow and tried to feel where it was cut.

Alex came over to look at the wound more closely. She brushed his hair back, removed the bandage, and lightly touched his forehead around the wound. He flinched slightly the closer she got to the wound.

"I'm sorry. Does that hurt?" she asked, knowing the answer.

"No, it will be okay."

Alex knew it was painful, but *like most men*, he wasn't about to admit it to *her.*

Her closeness made Nick forget the pain. She smelled good—like outdoors. In spite of all the recent excitement, as she bent over him to touch his forehead, he caught his breath. She was too close to him, too close for him to think. Her hair brushed his face, and he found himself almost reaching for her, but he moved back.

What am I doing?

He wasn't sure why she made him so lightheaded.

After checking his bandage and assured that he was all right, Alex sat back down and smiled at him. Nick looked at this young woman. Maybe it was just the movie hero in him, but he was convinced that he had to protect her.

"When are we arriving in L.A.?" she asked. " I have some relatives nearby. I have an aunt in California that I think I can stay with for a while. I really appreciate your taking me there. I'll pay you for the flight, of course…"

He had meant to tell her, but had forgotten. They had another stop to make before California, and in all the excitement, he forgot.

"Alexandra, I apologize. I have a stop to make before I take you to California. I'm sorry. The studio just called John a few minutes before we boarded. I have a speaking engagement in the morning that I can't postpone. We should be able to leave around noon, the next day. I hope that's all right with you. I'll pay for your room, of course. If it weren't for such an important cause, I would have postponed it."

Nick believed that it might actually be a good thing that they changed the flight plan, just in case there were any more surprises like the one John found on his jet.

Alex started to object about flying elsewhere, and then thought about it. After all, he was already going out of his way to help her. It had been a long time since anyone had tried to help her or had been as kind as he had. He had obligations too. He couldn't help the delay.

Nick continued. "I insist taking you to dinner tonight, Alexandra. The hotel where we stay is brand-new and beautiful. The restaurant is on the top floor. You can see all of New York City from…"

Alex interrupted, "New York? We're going to New York City?"

Alex's mind was spinning. She should not be going by herself with a complete stranger, all the way to New York City. This was getting more complicated than it should have been.

"Oh, I'm not sure, Mr. Stewart. I didn't bring anything to wear to dinner. Don't worry, I can stay in my room, and order in."

It was the truth. She had only stuffed casual clothing into her suitcase. She had packed so fast. The idea of going to a city with a movie actor and two other men she didn't know, and then spend the night in a hotel that Nick paid for, just didn't sound right. She glanced toward him, and Nick Stewart smiled at her.

"I wouldn't dream of being denied dinner with you, Alexandra, after all we've just been through."

He said he would take care of finding a dress for her, and not to worry—to just sit back and enjoy the flight.

Alexandra, despite her hesitancy, found herself believing him. This was new for her—believing a man again. Pastor Dan would have fun with that and so would Al Moffett. If she was going to New York City, and it seemed she had no choice, she was determined to relax and have some fun. Besides, who in their right mind would refuse dinner with Nicholas Stewart?

She closed her eyes for just a moment and yawned. She was very tired. Her conscience bothered her slightly as she wondered what Pastor Dan would say to her.

Nick Stewart watched the girl as she fell asleep. He asked John Cabe to phone the hotel boutique and ask them to select a dinner dress, in about a size six. Nick smiled. She was Meg's size. He asked for flowers to be sent to her room, too—yellow roses.

Perhaps after dinner, I can show her where I grew up—my part of New York.

He had never done that, not with any of the women he dated, not since Meg.

Alex had curled up in the softness of one of the recliners. She looked very small and vulnerable to Nick. He hoped that they were safe now. Maybe both of them could breathe a little easier and relax, at least for tonight.

Funny, he believed when he first saw her that somehow he would meet her again, but not this way. What a crazy day it had been. He covered his mouth and yawned. He was getting drowsy too. Nick looked over at Alexandra and wished he could put his arms around her, like he did Sabrina, and tell her everything was going to be all right.

It was as if she heard his thoughts because she turned over in the seat, smiled at him, and then went back to sleep. He continued to watch her, until he dozed off too. It was the pilot's voice over the intercom telling them they were getting ready to land, that awakened both of them.

Alex couldn't believe that she had slept for over two hours. She felt slightly embarrassed as she awoke, but she saw that Nick Stewart had fallen asleep too. He had a slight beard and needed a shave. He looked a little rumpled but he was still handsome. He had been so nice to her that she forgot she didn't trust men. She had also forgotten, for a while, that he was a celebrity. He had been so easy to talk to, and it appeared that he had been exhausted, too.

She hoped that they could have some downtime at the hotel to prepare for dinner. She needed to wash her hair and shower. She certainly hadn't counted on landing in New York City, but now she was becoming excited. She had never seen the city before. Now she was here, and with a famous actor!

John Cabe landed the plane and helped Mac get the luggage into the waiting limo. They drove into the city and onto the hotel. Mac checked all of them in and then got their keys.

Alexandra saw a couple of reporters turned away and soon the group headed for the elevator and the reserved rooms. Nick explained to Alexandra that John and Mac had booked a room together but that his suite had several rooms plus two large bedrooms, and he wanted her to take his suite. He said that he would take the single room they just rented. That way, she would have all the privacy that she wanted.

Alexandra didn't expect him to offer her his suite. She refused. He insisted. She argued. He wouldn't take "no" for an answer. Mac and John grinned at each other during this exchange between them. Nick Stewart showed her where his room was and where Mac and John would be, dropping them off on the eleventh floor. Then, he took her up one more floor.

The elevator doors opened to a suite of rooms that might have only been found in home decorating magazines. The rooms were painted in soft white and beige, and the living area was surrounded with windows from ceiling to floor. It looked out on a large patio, which had its own hot tub.

There were plants, expensive paintings, and magnificent furnishings. There was even a grand piano. A plate of assorted cheeses, breads, and fruits was placed on the coffee table, and a selection of soft drinks was on the bar.

Alex's bag was put into the larger of two bedrooms, and yellow roses welcomed her. They were placed on her night table. When she saw them, she stopped, and leaned down to smell them.

"How beautiful," she whispered.

Nick Stewart stood back and watched, almost entranced by her. The suite was huge.

"I can't take this, Mr. Stewart. It's too much."

With a warm smile, he handed her the room key and after excusing himself, said that he would see her later for dinner.

After he left, Alex wandered into an enormous closet and bath. She put her overnight bag in the closet and saw a gown hanging there. It was an ankle-length black dress, with a sequined halter-top. The skirt was made of chiffon. Alexandra remembered what he had said to her earlier, not to worry about a dress. It had to be the dress that Nick Stewart had chosen for her to wear tonight. Alex was astounded that it was in her size.

There was also a pair of silver sandals on the closet floor. She slipped them on her feet.

"They fit!" she said. "How in the world did he know my shoe size too?"

Nick walked back to his room. It didn't matter where he stayed, as long as she was near. She was delightful, so serious at times, but so honest. He liked her smile, and he knew he wanted to make her laugh. He knew he'd like her laugh.

"She's as excited as Sabrina was on her first trip to New York City," he said, under his breath.

He caught himself humming. He hadn't done that in a long time. He was looking forward to their evening together. He had to shower, shave, and change clothing. Later, he would meet her for dinner.

Alex went into the bathroom and ran the water for a bath. She lit the candles on the tub, slipped out of her clothes, and stepped into the warmth of the tub. She thought of the dress she would be wearing tonight.

"It would have been the exact dress I would have chosen."

She would have to give Nick Stewart credit for a great ending to this awful day. She sank into the warm water and wiggled her toes in a tiny dancing motion.

This just had to be a dream. She was going to have an evening with a man she had only seen in movies. Nick Stewart could have any woman in the world that he wanted. He didn't have to choose her, except he had. He had picked her out of the crowd at the school. She couldn't help think about what had happened before, when he first saw her, and when she first saw him. She also remembered Alfred Moffett's warning. *You be careful, Alex. Those Hollywood types are all alike.*

Alex combed her hair, put on the black dress, and slid into the silver sandals. She glanced in the mirror. The dress looked good on her, she had to admit. She sprayed some of her cologne behind her ears. The scent was a mixture of jasmine and roses. She looked at the clock, and then heard the door chimes ring. It was time. She walked into the living area and opened the door, where Nick Stewart was waiting for her.

When she saw him, clean-shaven and dressed up in his tuxedo, she blurted out, "Boy, do you clean up nice!"

Alex clapped her hands over her mouth after she realized what she had said, but he laughed, took her hand, and spun her around.

"You're not so bad, yourself, babe."

She liked the nickname he had given her. "Babe." It didn't sound rough, when he said it. It was nice.

"I love the dress. It's going to take me awhile to pay you back for it, but thank you so much, Mr. Stewart. It's beautiful."

Nick was surprised that she would offer to pay him for the gown. He meant it as a gift, but he had to admire her morals. This was new, too—a young woman with morals?

"One more little surprise," he said.

After her last comment, he wasn't certain that he should do this. He pulled out a small box and handed it to her.

"What is this?"

"This is a thank-you for the first aid and for saving my life. And, remember, it's *Nick*, Alexandra."

She opened the box and found a pair of earrings. They were delicate silver flowers, with a small diamond in the center.

They're perfect. So is he. This evening is perfect.

The earrings were definitely a "Nick Stewart" kind of gift, a gift she knew she couldn't accept.

"They're beautiful, but…"

He sensed her start to refuse them and told her, "I'm glad you like them. I took a chance. I really want you to have them, Alexandra."

"Nick, I can't accept these," she said.

He looked disappointed, and then, he took another stab at it.

"Hey, Alex, this is strictly for fun, and besides, you have to look gorgeous to be my date tonight. It's what people expect. Wear them for me tonight, okay? If you want them later, they're yours, but if that makes you uncomfortable, you can give them back."

He had partially lied to her, and now *he* felt guilty. He wanted her to accept the earrings without feeling she had to repay him. Funny, his money meant nothing to him, right now. What was happening to him? She was driving him crazy, and he'd only just met her.

Did he really mean that, when he said, "It's what people expect"? Surely, he isn't that shallow.

Alex decided that she would return the earrings to him after dinner.

"Okay," she agreed, "I'll wear them, but just for tonight."

Alex realized if she were going to remain firm, she'd better start now.

He's smooth, all right.

43

Alex knew that her new Christian values were going to get a workout tonight. No one would believe a twenty-five-year-old *virgin* had a date with someone as charismatic and charming as Nicholas Stewart!

Meanwhile, Nicholas was thinking that Alexandra Andrews must have cast some kind of spell over him. He felt like a teenager who was on his first date. He didn't make blunders usually, as he had with her. What was wrong with him? He had to regain control of his feelings. He extended his arm to her.

"Shall we go?"

They got on the elevator and went up to the rooftop restaurant.

Alex was glad that Nick had thought about the earrings, when she saw the elaborate jewelry that most of the women in the ballroom wore. A waiter escorted them to a table by a window. It overlooked New York City, and it was as beautiful as Alex knew it would be.

"Thank you for making me forget about what happened earlier today, Nick."

She had softened toward him again, especially when he told her that he had to give a speech for a charity brunch tomorrow.

"I apologize again for keeping you an extra day. You can pick out another dress for the brunch, if you need, and I'll buy it for you, Alexandra. The hotel boutique has some exquisite designs."

He knew immediately he had said the wrong thing.

What am I thinking? She doesn't want anything from me. Look at her eyes—they tell the story.

Alexandra's brown eyes brightened with a fire that burned right though him when he mentioned buying her another dress. Alex told him she might skip the brunch altogether.

"Alex, I'd really like to have you there, for support. I really need you to be there. It's important to me. I can't tell you how important it is."

"If I do go, I insist on paying for my own dress! You can't just buy things like that. It's like trying to buy me!"

She knew she sounded too sharp, but she continued anyway. He had to understand.

"I appreciate all you've done, but we barely know each other. I can't take all of these gifts…"

Nick was stunned, and more than a little humbled. He hadn't meant it like that at all.

"I'm so sorry, Alex. You are doing me a favor. I just wanted to show my appreciation. I really picked the wrong way to show it. Can we begin again?

I really want you there. It would mean a great deal to me, having you there. I've disrupted all your travel plans. I'm sure you expected to be in California this evening, and not sitting here with me in New York City."

Then, he smiled at her. He looked at her with those sparkling blue eyes and that famous grin, and like most females attracted to Nicholas Stewart, she just melted!

"How could I refuse after you delivered me safe from those maniacs that were shooting at us? It's been unreal today, hasn't it?"

"Yes, you could say that. But, at least I got to meet you."

Alexandra couldn't say anything. She was too surprised. He had apologized *and* paid her a compliment, a really nice compliment. She fumbled with her menu, and then reached across the table. She covered his hand with hers.

"Thank you, Nick."

Nick smiled at her and ordered dinner, realizing he had to take this slower. He had almost ruined it again.

The music from the restaurant's jazz band started a slow blues tune. The lights dimmed, as the city's performance began. From where they were sitting, Nick and Alex could see New York City from all sides of the restaurant, and it was spectacular!

When Nick asked Alex to dance with him, she realized that she had waited all of her life for a moment like this. He held out his hand to her and she got up, avoiding his eyes, but completely unable to prevent the feeling she had.

As they danced, she felt him pull her closer to him, and she could feel her own heartbeat. Alex shivered, but she wasn't cold. She was afraid. This time, it wasn't men in dark trench coats, or black sedans, that were a danger to her. It was how she was starting to feel about Nicholas Stewart. Alexandra realized that, while she might not know him yet, she wanted to learn everything she could about this man.

After dinner and dancing, Nick asked Alex if she would like to take a drive and see part of the city. She agreed and took his arm. Mac had the limo ready, and as they left, Alex slid across the seat and watched Nick as he undid his tie. He put his arm on the back of the seat, barely touching her shoulder.

She tensed up slightly. He was awfully close to her, but when he looked over at her and grinned, she felt herself relax. She rested her head back against his arm and closed her eyes. He asked Mac to drive them to a carriage stand near Central Park.

"To really see New York City, we have to go for a horse-drawn carriage ride. It's part of New York City's charm."

"Oh, Nick, it's a lovely idea!" she exclaimed. "I want to see everything!"

Alexandra found that she was having a good time, but she didn't want to get too carried away. She didn't really know this man. Still, she had to admit that he was a lot of fun, and that she had never done anything like this before. *What's the harm in having a little fun?*

Nick helped her into the carriage, and they started around the park. Alex took in all the sights that he pointed out to her.

She turned to him. "I will never forget this night in New York City. It's everything I thought it would be. Thank you."

I remember a night like this too, Alex. I was a lot like you back then. I was with Meg. It seems so long ago.

"Just seeing you enjoy everything makes it worth it," he said. "Look at those stars, Alex."

Alexandra looked up and moved closer to Nicholas Stewart. She realized that she did feel safer with him than without him.

Later, when they returned to the limo, Nick told her he was going to take her to see his favorite place in New York City. It was close to where he grew up. Nick told Mac to head for "Mama Rita's." Alex had a moment's hesitation, but she said nothing. She could take care of herself if she had to, and besides, she was feeling better about him.

They pulled up in an older part of town. It was in a section of town known as "Little Italy." They got on Mulberry Street and drove to the small restaurant, which turned out to be a partially hidden frame house. It sat behind a large oak tree.

"Mama Rita's" was a typical family-type restaurant. When Alex and Nick entered, the place exploded with excitement. It seemed that everyone there knew him.

"Nicholas, my boy! Why didn't you tell me you were coming?"

"Mama, meet Alexandra—Miss Andrews."

The short. plump Italian woman who owned the restaurant hugged Nick Stewart as if she were his own mother. Then, she almost smothered Alex with a large bear hug. "Mama" immediately showed her off to all the customers—to older men who embraced her, and to the younger boys who wished they were older. She was introduced to the females in the café as "Nick Stewart's girlfriend" and she didn't deny it.

With the music of an accordion and a guitar playing loudly in the background, Nick and Alex were shown to a small table near the back of the café.

Alex thought the atmosphere was wonderful; somewhere, in the back of her mind, she hadn't expected Nick to be so comfortable, but he was. She had not seen him so vibrant since she had met him. He was laughing and telling jokes to the old men in the café, and he was charming with the older women.

Alexandra found herself enjoying every moment and humming to the music. She knew the tune they were playing. It was an old song, "You Belong to Me." Nick smiled at her from across the candlelit table. He told her that he had grown up near this neighborhood and had known Mama Rita for many years.

When he ordered coffee, Alex was surprised. She knew most celebrities would have ordered wine or champagne, but it seemed that "her" Nicholas Stewart was not a drinking man. He did ask her if she would like some wine, but she stuck with the coffee. Soon, both Nick and Alex were talking and laughing, forgetting the earlier part of their day, and learning what it was to become friends.

Alexandra asked many questions about his life. He told her about his childhood and about his father dying when he was young. His father was alcoholic. Alex soon realized the reason he didn't drink.

He told her about his first wife, Meg. He went on and on about his daughter, Sabrina. He didn't seem to mind telling her anything. Alex was taken aback by his honesty. She hadn't quite expected that, and Alex knew she was finding out too much about him, things he might regret saying to a reporter.

When Nick asked Alex to tell him about herself, she spoke of her childhood, of favorite things, and about her parents. They talked for hours, each wanting to know all they could about the other. It was as if they were in a hurry to catch up with what they had missed earlier, before they met.

It wasn't the interview that Alex planned in Westville. It was two friends sharing their experiences, and it wasn't what Alex thought it would be. She could never write all of this down to give to a paper. It was about their personal lives and she wanted it to remain between the two of them.

Some fine reporter I am.

When the conversation slowed, Nick reached across the table and took both of Alex's hands in his.

"You know, Alex, it may sound like a line, but the first time I saw you in the gym, in that ridiculous school uniform, I knew I had to see you again."

She wanted to tell him that she felt that way too, but she held back. She wanted to say to him that she thought they were *meant* to meet each other, but she said nothing. What if the things he had just told her were just a line?

She didn't want to be hurt again, even though she wanted to believe him. Alex looked into his eyes, and for the first time, neither of them was smiling.

"After tonight," she began, " I think I know more about you, and I really like that Nick Stewart, the real person."

When she smiled at him, she knew that she had taken him off guard. She continued, "I really mean it, and I would never repeat what you've told me. I care too much."

She hesitated, alarmed at what she had just said. They both heard it, and she knew it, as Nick tightened his grip on her hands. She fumbled over her own words.

"I mean it's personal, you know?"

Nick was silent. Alexandra waited for him to reply. She knew she had said too much. She could kick herself! She was now wondering if he could read her mind and knew what she was thinking. He was looking at her so intensely.

"I'm sorry," she continued, "I've made you uncomfortable. I talk too much...." He stopped her by putting his finger across her lips.

"Don't say that, Alexandra. Don't ever feel that you have to tell me you're sorry for anything you say. I want you to know me, and I want to know you a lot better. I'm going to take you home now, where it's less crowded, where we can be alone."

Nick Stewart rose, took her by her hand, and led her out of the restaurant. It had only been two days, and she felt she had known him a long time.

When they returned to the limo, he opened the door, put her in the car, and got in the other side. When he reached across her to lock her door, he paused in front of her and gazed at her as he had in the school auditorium. Much to her amazement, he leaned forward and kissed her. Even more amazing, when his lips touched hers, instead of stopping him, she found herself responding to him.

It had been so long that a man had made her feel like this. She knew she should stop him, but she couldn't seem to move. She had wanted him to kiss her. Reluctantly, he drew back from her and told his driver to return them to the hotel. Alexandra could not imagine that this was actually happening to her.

Her mind told her where this could be leading, and she knew she needed to stop it, despite her feelings for him. She knew too, that after his kiss, she had crossed over from fun to a dangerous territory for her.

On the drive back, he held her hand tightly, never releasing it, until they were at the hotel. He had been quiet, saying little. He finally escorted Alex upstairs and back to her suite.

Alexandra was torn. Should she ask him in? The wise thing would be to say good-night at the door. She knew that, but she asked him inside. He led her outside, to the patio.

"Here we are, Alex. Do you like it?"

Candles had been added. They cast shadows like fireflies, bright, and then flickering again. Their glow and the lights of the city seemed to merge with the stars above. Alex noticed that flowers had been placed on the patio, and she knew he must have planned this before they left.

Alex knew she was letting this get out of hand. She could hear the music from the club on the floor above wend its way down to where they were standing. She was unsure she could prevent anything if she returned to his arms.

Blast my parents and their puritanical upbringing.

She also knew that she didn't believe in pre-marital relations, and it had turned on her twice. It was the main reason her fiancé had left her. She had told him "no." And now, Nick—so charming, too suave for a girl with her background. Surely, he had been with someone since his wife's death?

As if in answer to her thoughts, Nick took both her hands and drew her to him.

"Alexandra, you're the first woman I ever took to Mama Rita's since Meg."

Should she believe him? Alex knew she should tell him that it was late and ask him to leave. Instead, she took a deep breath and moved closer to him.

"I am?"

"Yes. You're the only one I wanted to share that with. I can't explain what's going on, Alexandra. I…I…"

He put his arms around her, leaned down, and kissed her again. The moment was electric and the closeness of him was intoxicating. Alex was astounded at her feelings. She could barely stand up, let alone tell him to go.

I have to stop this, right now. I can't seem to move. Please, God, help.

Then, as if it was an answer to her prayer, she remembered something Pastor Dan had said to her. She had poured out her heart to him months ago, blaming God for being so parental and asking her to withhold herself until marriage.

Her fiancé had left her because of that. Her fiancé had told her, "If you really love me, you'll come to bed with me." He left her for another woman, because she wouldn't. She couldn't.

Pastor Dan had smiled, taken her hand, and said, "He is parental, Alexandra, because He *is* your Father. He wants the best for his child, just as you will when you have a child. The man that he has picked out for you will wait. It may be hard for both of you, but he will wait, and you'll see...it will be worth it!"

"Alexandra?" Nick said.

She knew what he wanted—what she wanted. It took all of her strength to pull back. She couldn't let this happen, not like this! She prayed for the right words.

He will wait, and you'll see...it will be worth it!

Would Nick wait? Was he the one?

"Nicholas," she answered in a whisper. "I can't."

She took a step back.

Why is it so hard, Lord? If it's Your will, why is it so hard?

Nick lessened his hold around her waist, and she felt as if she had died. To her surprise, Nick didn't insist on anything. Instead, he kissed her lightly on her forehead and smiled down at her.

"It's all right, Alex. I'm sorry. I got carried away. I don't do this, either. Please forgive me. We have a big day tomorrow, and I'd better get home."

He said all the right things, but she could still hear the disappointment in his voice. She turned away and glanced up at the sky. It had begun to cloud over.

"I think it may rain."

Small talk just made it worse.

She turned to him and said, "Thank you, Nick. Thank you for understanding. I better say good-night now."

He took her hand and walked her to her bedroom door. He even kissed her good-night. At that moment, they were two of New York City's most miserable persons. The rain began to fall. Alex walked into her room and closed the door. She stood with her back against it, still feeling his presence on the other side. One part of her wanted him to open it and come in. Her spirit knew she wouldn't.

Alex sat down on the bed, removing the silver sandals from her feet. Despite being true to her beliefs, she was human, and she ached for him. Tears were at the brim of her eyes as she turned off her light and threw herself across her bed, still in her clothes.

Nick had waited for an instant just outside Alexandra's door, listening to her breathe, just out of reach. He had forgotten how painful love could be. He didn't know why he had pushed Alex so far. He never wanted to do that. What if she was afraid of him now?

His feelings were so strong for her. How long had it been since he felt anything for a woman? Maybe that was it. He had been so "dead" before.

He knew that he would wait for her, forever, if it took that long. He had to make her know that. He crossed through her living room, closed her front door, and headed back to his room.

The next morning, Alexandra slipped out of her room and went downstairs to the boutique. She found a floral dress. It was blue, with pale yellow and white flowers. It had a matching jacket that was solid blue, and it looked perfect for a brunch. She had some shoes in her bag that she thought would match. As she paid for it, she grimaced when she signed the credit slip.

"That's a whole month's salary," she whispered.

When she remembered last night, she wondered how she would face Nick this morning. Still, what would he have said if she had gone to bed with him? Alex believed in her heart that he would have left her. It would have been that one-night stand that men brag about. It had not been easy to turn him away. After all of those things they spoke about at Mama Rita's, she found that she trusted him. But she had to control her own feelings.

When she went back upstairs, she found him outside her door, waiting for her. His face lit up when he saw her. He went inside with her and made coffee for both of them, not saying much. He poured two cups of coffee, and then sat down beside her.

"Alex? Are you all right?"

Nick was concerned when she wasn't in her room this morning. "I was worried about how we left things."

"Of course I'm all right, Nick."

Lie number one.

"I bought a dress."

Change the subject!

"I hope you like it. The brunch is at 11:00 a.m., right?"

She tried to sound casual. Inside, she was gelatin!

"Right. Let's see the dress."

He could tell she didn't want to talk about last night. He had wanted to tell her how sorry he was.

She held the dress up.

"Is it all right?"

" It's beautiful. Anything you wear would look beautiful…"

He winced. He probably shouldn't have said that.

Dope!

He was going to scare her off, again.

She didn't react as he feared she might. She just told him she would be ready whenever he was. Both of them went to change their clothes.

As Alex and Nick entered the meeting room for the brunch, the crowd that had gathered, applauded him. Alex and Nick were seated at the speaker's table. He was to speak first, and then they would go through the buffet. Alex knew the audience wondered who she was. If they only knew…

Nick spoke to the group about child abuse. He told about his alcoholic father. He was eloquent and knowledgeable, and Alex knew that it was painful for him. Perhaps that's why he wanted her there. He had been abused—neglected by a father who kept leaving him with his two sisters, and who later had died.

Alexandra could tell that he cared about the other children who were still being abused, and so did his audience. It was a $500-per-plate fundraising event, and Alex could see checkbooks being pulled from pockets and purses. His speech had been a success.

Later, as they were in the buffet line, several women approached him. Alex knew they envied her, and she couldn't help feeling slightly protective of him, and just a little jealous. When they excused themselves from the gathering, Nick led her back to the elevator and up to her suite.

"I'm going back to my room, now. Why don't we go ahead and change our clothes, and get ready for the trip, Alex? The plane ride back to California will be a long one, I'm afraid."

It will be a long ride, all right.

She thought of the way she felt about him.

"Nick, I was proud of you, back there. You were wonderful."

She had to say it. He was wonderful.

He turned back to look at her, and then he went over to her and put his arms around her.

"Alexandra, thank you for going with me, for putting up with me. I…"

He stopped. He was falling in love with this woman. He kissed her on her forehead, wishing for more, but he knew he would never take advantage of her. She was vulnerable right now, and while he realized that he could make it happen, he wouldn't. He wanted her to trust him. More than that, he wanted to be able to trust himself. It was a moral issue for her, and it became important to him—that he earn her trust.

She leaned into him, making it very difficult for him not to kiss her again, right there and then! He could feel every inch of her so close to him. He pulled away as the doorbell rang, saving both of them from this impossible situation. It was Mac.

Nick went to the door. "Yes?"

Then, he saw the worried look on Mac's face. Something was very wrong.

" Nick, we have to get out of here as soon as possible."

It was not what Alexandra expected to hear. She saw the anxious look on Nick Stewart's face, and she looked back at Mac. He was just as worried.

"What is it?" Alex asked Mac.

"The crew at the airport in Westville noticed this guy. Later, he was asking questions about our flight. When our guys wouldn't tell him anything, he bribed one of them to give him our flight plan. He wanted to know where we would be staying in New York. He left about an hour later, they said."

Nick turned to Alex. "I think he's after us, Alexandra. He could be watching our rooms right now. He's probably one of the men that killed Ed."

"Oh, no!" said Alex. She could not believe this nightmare was continuing. "What are we going to do? We can't just keep running, Nick. What is going on?"

"I don't know," he replied, "but we're going to find out." Nick sounded determined, as he told Mac they would be ready to leave in about two hours, whenever Mac could make arrangements.

Mac left to rent a different car. He had several things to take care of before they could leave. He asked John Cabe to stay outside Nick and Alex's door as he gave John his gun.

Nick went over to Alexandra and tried to calm her. He explained that he would protect her at all cost.

"Alex, don't bother to pack. Just put on what you're going to wear, and we'll pick up the rest later, when we get to our destination. It would be very unwise to go to California. They'd be waiting for us there. Right now, we have to find out what Ed Percy knew, and to do that, we will be heading straight to Paris. That is where Ed Percy's apartment was before he moved to Westville. He still has an address there. The secret of what's going on could begin there. We have to know what it is, before we can fight this."

He wanted to say to her, "…before we can have a life together."

Alex could only answer, "Paris? We're going to Paris?"

She didn't tell him that she would have followed him to Mars if he'd asked. She realized he was doing this for both of them, and she loved him for that. They were both targets now, and she knew it wouldn't end until they were killed or until they uncovered Ed Percy's secret.

Alexandra felt she had no choice, but to place all of her fragile, newfound trust and faith in God, and in a man she barely knew, but had begun to love, Nicholas Stewart.

Chapter Four

Mac rented a beige sedan and left the limo in the hotel's parking garage. No one had checked Nick or Alex out of the hotel. Their clothes and personal items were still there in case anyone looked in the room. Mac would call the hotel later and check them out when they were on the plane and safe. The payment was taken care of, and he would change their cell phone numbers.

John Cabe was standing guard outside Nick's room. The four of them were taking a different flight later, chartered under Mac's name. It would fly them to Paris, France, this afternoon.

Nick watched as Alex paced back and forth. He wished there was something that he could do or say to calm her.

"Alex, please come and sit down."

He poured them a cold drink. Alex sat down next to him. She had changed clothes, and was wearing a soft, terry sweatshirt. He explained again that he would protect her. He tried to convince her why they *had* to go to Paris to find out about Ed.

She looked smaller to him and even more vulnerable than before. She had curled up on the sofa, close to him. He lost his train of thought. He stood up and began to pace too.

Nick was wearing slacks and a sport shirt, and he looked better than ever to Alex. She tried to bargain with God. If they were going to die, wouldn't He make an exception? She almost laughed out loud at that reasoning! They needed a diversion. At least she did, and it had to be something physical.

"Nick, I've got an idea!"

"Tell me." He leapt at her idea, whatever it was.

"They have a gym downstairs, don't they?"

"You've got it! I challenge you to—whatever it is they have down there!"

He needed this—something to take his mind off of her, and still be with her.

"I'll race you!"

Alex was up off the sofa and at the door, before Nick realized she needed to be careful not to be seen.

"Wait, Alex!"

She ran right into John Cabe, who caught her, before she slammed him.

"Whoa there, little lady," John grinned.

"I forgot. We have to be careful. John, want to go with us downstairs to the gym?"

"I guess if the three of us go together, that would be okay, wouldn't it, John?"

"Sure, I'm tired of standing here, anyway."

The three of them took the stairs so they wouldn't run into anyone on the elevator. The small hotel gym was empty. They surveyed the room. There were a couple of treadmills, some weights, and a bike.

"I'll race you!" said Alex. "You take the bike. I'll take a treadmill. I bet I can walk more miles than you ride!"

"It's a bet!" replied Nick.

John watched them go faster and faster. He couldn't understand what they were up to but he got the idea they wanted to take their minds off this situation. He went to the weights. Nick and Alex were sweating, huffing and puffing.

If they keep going at that pace, they'll kill themselves with a heart attack. Then the gunmen won't have any targets—just crazy people!

"Oh, I give up!" Alexandra could barely breathe. She was hot, dry, and about to throw up. "I've got to have some water."

Nick almost fell off his machine. Alex was watching him. She ran to the water fountain before he could get there. Nick was right behind her. He shoved her and she hit his arm. She was laughing as he caught her by her waist and dunked her in the fountain. He was grinning at Alexandra, as both of them stumbled and almost fell down.

"I'll be," said John. He was fascinated, just watching them. "They're in love." he muttered. "So, that's what's up."

Alex was wet and tired but the terrible tension was over. She felt great, and she was in love again! She knew that Nick was attracted to her. She didn't know if his feelings toward her were as serious, but it didn't matter right now. If it were meant to grow into something, it would. She just had to trust God about all of this.

The fact that he was taking her to Paris had to mean something. She had almost forgotten. They were going to Paris! She had even forgotten about the men who followed them. She just knew she would be safe as long as she was with Nicholas.

It was as if they both knew this had to happen, when they met in the school auditorium, and again when they were in his limo, and even on the plane. Nick walked over to where she was, and Alex reached again for the safety of his outstretched hand. She would never again let him know how afraid she had been. He took her hand, smiled at her, and the three of them headed back upstairs.

Nick was still trying to figure out what had happened to *him*. He had fallen head-over-heels in love with this woman, and it had happened almost overnight. He was one who didn't believe in love at first sight, but here it was, staring him right in the face.

He also realized that Alex didn't fully trust him yet but something had changed between them. They were able to forget all the tension from last night. He would have to be careful with her. He knew that. She was so fragile but Nick also knew that he could never let her go.

"I bet we don't have much time left before we have to leave," said Alex.

"It's nearly 1:30 p.m. Why don't you go ahead and shower, Alex. John and I can keep each other company until you're through. Later, I'll go downstairs and do the same. That should put us right on time."

"Sounds good to me," Alex replied. "You do know I beat you, don't you?"

He threw her a hotel robe and shook his head.

Alex was glad that he and John had left her alone for a few minutes. She had to think. She went into the shower, not noticing the peculiar pungent odor that had settled there. She undressed and stood under the warm water. She was in love. God had to be glad for her.

Her thoughts started to get cloudy.

What if he doesn't feel the same way? When will I learn? I must be demented when it comes to—to choosing men.

Still, when he looked at her, she knew she was the only woman in the world. She had a headache.

One minute, he loves me, the next…

Now, she was so dizzy…it was all too confusing. She decided she trusted him, after all. She tried to step out of the shower, get a towel and reach her robe.

This happened right before she passed out, with the shower still running.

Alex woke up on the cold bathroom floor. She had an awful headache. What was that odor? She grabbed her robe, tried to get up and stumbled out of the bathroom into the hall. She had to make it into the living area where Nick and John were. She faltered and she fell again.

Please, help me. What is this? What's wrong?

Nicholas had been talking to John when he noticed a stream of moisture coming from the vent above them. He pointed it out to John, who got on a chair and tried to see what it was. The closer he got to it, the stronger the odor.

"Nick, get Alex and get out of here, NOW!" cried John.

John Cabe started coughing and tears were in his eyes. He almost fell off the chair.

"It's some kind of gas…it could be lethal. We have to get out…" John Cabe crumpled to the floor in front of Nick.

Nick started to the shower, when he saw Alex in the hallway.

"My Lord! No, don't let this happen. Alex, Alex?"

He too, began to feel the sickening effect of the gas. He was nauseous. He picked up Alexandra and attempted to carry her to the front door. A blast of fresh air streamed in as he opened the door to the hotel hallway. He lowered Alexandra on the carpet in the hall and called for help.

Then, he started back inside to get to John. John had managed to crawl to the door and Nick dragged him the rest of the way outside. The three of them, Nick, Alex and John Cabe, were gasping for air.

The ambulance crew that arrived at the hotel gave the three friends some oxygen. They seemed to be suffering from the effects of some type of gas poisoning.

All three had come around, but the woman, Alexandra Andrews, was still fighting a terrible headache and nausea; Nick Stewart felt groggy; John Cabe told them that he felt like he had a hangover. None of the three would agree to go to a hospital.

Nick didn't say much but he knew this "accident" was intentional. It was a warning for them. Somehow, they had to get out of here, now!

When Mac heard what happened to his boss, he rushed to the front of the hotel where the ambulance was. Nick ordered him to get the car and pick them up in the back, as they had planned. Nick was insisting they leave now. Mac had never seen him that angry, or that determined, and he left to get their car.

Later, Mac called Nick on his cell phone and told him everything was ready. He told him to go through the kitchen, in the back. He would pick them up in the alley. Mac took out a revolver and rechecked it, then put it back in his holster. Mac wanted no more of what had happened in Westville and now in New York City. He drove into the service entrance of the hotel.

It was a few minutes later when Nick, Alex and John came out the kitchen door. John climbed in next to Mac, still feeling sick at his stomach. Nick and Alex got in the back seat and Mac watched as Alex put her head in Nick's lap. He could tell that she didn't feel well at all. They drove away, heading to a small airfield where their plane was waiting.

Mac knew that the three of them had a close call. They had to be more careful. Whoever was after them had come to kill them but he wanted to taunt them first. Mac remembered the mob. This was the most dangerous kind of killer.

Mac still wondered about Alexandra Andrews. All of their trouble had started when she appeared in Nick's life and now, both Mac and John saw that Nick was falling in love with her. It was just too convenient that she ended up here with him. Still, she had almost died up there, too. Mac no longer knew what to think.

John Cabe rested his head against the car seat and his mind tried to sort through what had just happened. This was meant to be a warning but it could have been deadly if Nick hadn't pulled them out. Nick Stewart, even in this mess, must be the luckiest male alive.

John's mind wandered to when he first met Nick. Nick had come up from the ranks. He had little money before he started in films and it had not been easy for him.

He remembered when Nick was a kid, back in New York City. Nick had his share of girlfriends back then. The ladies loved him, even then. He had settled down when he met and married Meg and when they had Sabrina. It was too bad about Meg. His first wife died too young and Nick Stewart hadn't been the same since.

All that Nick was concerned about was his five-year-old daughter. Nick was determined she would always be able to depend on him.

He must really care for Alex Andrews to risk so much for her.

John glanced in the rear view mirror at Nick and Alex. Alexandra seemed different than any woman Nick had met, since Meg. Any man would have been taken by her. She was beautiful and before Nick met her, he had been so sad. It was rare that he laughed, unless he was acting and had to do it for a scene. John Cabe noticed that, even with all the trouble they were in, Alexandra could still make Nick Stewart laugh.

59

When he saw them together this morning, it was evident to John that something had changed. He saw a man and woman who were falling in love. He watched, as Nick reached down to brush her hair back from her face and patted her arm.

"Aah, love!" John smiled.

On the way to the airport, they discussed how they were going to handle this latest problem. John mentioned that he hadn't been shot at, or gassed, since they were in the war together. Nick remained somber. He didn't say anything. Mac felt the gun under his coat and thought about the mob. Alex closed her eyes and tried to get over the nausea and the horrible headache she still had.

John and Mac discussed once more what they knew. The man who tried to bribe one of his crew had been described as tall, with dark hair and gray eyes and he appeared to be wearing a trench coat. He was known only as Quentin. From what Alex had told Nick, he was evidently at the rehearsal in Westville and he was part of Ed's murder. It must have been Quentin who had followed them to New York and he must have put the bomb on the plane.

Nick was still holding Alex's hand. She looked pretty scared since the hotel incident and she was really sick. The sudden trip to Paris had been a surprise to everyone but the three knew that Nick wouldn't be doing this unless he wanted something or someone pretty bad. They all knew now how much danger they were in.

The sedan pulled up to the airport. The jet was waiting for them. John and Mac boarded first, then Nick and Alexandra. The plane lifted off, en route to Paris, France.

Alex and Nicholas were seated in a private lounge, while John and Mac took two of the passenger seats near the middle of the plane. There was a stewardess serving a light lunch and Nick was surprised to find that he was hungry again. He offered Alex some juice, while he took one of the sandwiches and some coffee.

Alex took the juice but put it aside. She thought her head was going to explode. The sight of food made her even more nauseous than she already was. This last attempt on their lives had happened in broad daylight! That, along with hardly any sleep the night before, had left her both scared and ill.

Nick got a wet cloth for Alex's forehead then he covered her forehead with the cloth.

"You need to drink some water or juice—whatever you can keep down, Alex." He knew she would be dehydrated if she didn't.

Alex couldn't help but notice how well he was taking care of her. He ordered some tomato juice for her, made with something that he guaranteed would rid her of her headache. She took it and almost gagged but she managed to get about half of the nasty stuff down. It didn't seem to help her headache or her stomach but she took a deep breath and tried to relax.

Nicholas sat down next to her. He told her to try and nap, if she could. "I know you're frightened. On top of that, I surprised you with this trip."

He knew too that she was also sorting through her feelings for him. It was pretty evident that she didn't feel good this afternoon. He felt so sorry for her and he felt so helpless.

After a short time in the air, John Cabe was feeling better. He and Mac were making plans about how they were going to find out more information on Quentin. They were also talking about how they were going to protect Nick and Alex. John told Mac that he felt Alex could be trusted, even though Mac had some reservations. John told Mac that he thought both Alex and Nick were set up as victims.

"After all," reasoned John, "Nick was in the service with Ed Percy a long time ago and Ed had tried to contact Nick just prior to his murder. There must have been something that Ed wanted Nicholas to know and that must be the thing Nick is searching for. We need to get a background on Ed Percy."

In less than a minute, John got on his computer and Mac was on his phone. The men had to find out something or they would all be in even more danger than before.

John Cabe soon found out that Ed Percy was not your typical neighbor. He was a member of a group called the Organization, a nasty bunch of traitors to almost every country in the world. But, it appeared he also worked for the United States government. He wondered if the Organization had found out he was a double agent, or if Ed was ready to double-cross them.

Chapter Five

Alex wanted to talk to Nicholas alone about what happened with them yesterday but she still felt lousy and she was so tired. Nick was kind to her and it felt good to have someone who was as caring as he was but what had happened between them was catching up with her and seemed awfully fast for her.

Her mind was spinning and this gigantic headache that had returned didn't help. Somewhere, in the back of her mind, she wondered if Nick had been drawn to her just because of the events they were going through. It had been more like a movie script than real life.

What if he just got carried away and this is just like another movie part to him? Lord, please let me think straight. I need Your thoughts right now. Just take my hurting head and replace it with a new one.

Then, the tomato juice backfired. It wasn't going to stay down and Alex knew it. She got up, heading for the bathroom, holding her stomach. Nick had to smile, even though he felt sorry for her. He had seen that shade of green before. When she returned to her seat, she looked a little worse for the wear and she was very pale.

"Alex, how are you?"

"I think I'm a little better."

She drifted off to sleep as he put his arms around her. Hours had passed by the time Alex woke up. Nick had covered her with a blanket and moved her onto a sofa.

When she tried to get up, she was dizzy, very dizzy. Nick, who was reading just across the aisle, saw her weave as she tried to stand. He caught her just before she landed on the cabin floor. He helped her back to her seat and pulled the blanket back over her.

She heard him whisper to her rather sternly, "Stay put! I'm going to make the jet a little more private for us so that neither the stewardess nor any of the crew will interrupt us."

Nick asked the stewardess for some aspirin and water and then handed them to Alex. As she watched, he went to the front and spoke to the pilot. She noticed that he could be quite forceful when he wanted and she found that she liked it. When he returned, he pulled the curtains in front and then closed a cabin doorway that was between them and the kitchen, where John and Mac were seated. They were alone at last.

"Are you feeling any better, at all, Alexandra?" he asked her. His voice was gentle and he looked worried.

"How do you define better?" Alex replied, trying her best attempt at a joke.

Nick smiled at her and promised her that she "would live." Then, he leaned over and gave her a kiss on her forehead. He noticed that her forehead still felt clammy and hoped this wasn't more than a hangover from the gas.

Alex felt another wave of nausea hit. She hated asking him but she couldn't stand up without his help. "Could you help me walk to the restroom, Nick?"

"No problem, babe. We'll just take it real slow. If you need anything, I'm right here."

He was so good to her and she just wasn't used to it. Why was he so kind? It would be so much easier if she could be angry with him. He helped her to the restroom, as she held onto the tiny sink and shut the door. Nick waited just outside, telling her to call out if she needed him. She threw up, again.

When Alex finally looked in the mirror, she sighed. She looked like the proverbial *something that the cat dragged in*. Her eyes were glazed and she had dark circles. There was no color in her face. Her hair had tangles and it looked like someone had teased it but had forgotten to comb it out.

"Just kill me now!"

She leaned down, still feeling dizzy and splashed cold water on her face. Alex found a packaged toothbrush and toothpaste in the small space above the sink and she brushed her teeth and gums with a vengeance. She tried to comb her hair with a small comb she found but she needed makeup, at least a lipstick. Her purse—where was it?

She finally stepped out of the restroom to a worried Nick Stewart, telling him she was feeling a little better and *demanding that he find her purse, fast!* Nick looked around and retrieved a small, black pouch from the floor. Alex grabbed the purse out of his hands, taking it, along with her sick self back into the restroom.

"Gee, she must really feel bad!" Nick muttered.

Alex had almost snapped at him. Alex knew that she was acting like a woman and she knew that Nick had forgotten some things about a woman. *A girl has to have makeup, especially after being shot at, gassed, falling in love, throwing up, turning green and being as dizzy as a Frisbee!*

She applied some lipstick and a little blush. It made her feel better—like she might live after all. The second time she came out from the restroom, she actually smiled at Nick and tried her best to be civil.

"Now, we can talk," she said.

Alex did not know if she was relieved to get these feelings out in the open or not. Lucky for her, Nick interrupted her.

"Alexandra, I know you're thinking about how fast this happened…uh, is happening…and that I tried to get you to…uh, you probably blame me for your hangover and this whole mess, because I do. I should have been watching out for you more and I know you have doubts about me."

Alex listened, amazed, as Nicholas Stewart refused to take a breath. He was talking so fast that he was actually stumbling over his words. His face and hands were sweating.

He continued, "I want to say to you that this isn't easy. But, here goes. If I had known you ten, twenty, or a hundred years, I couldn't love you more. I know it's fast, Alexandra but it's real and I'll wait as long as I have to for you…for you…to feel the same way. Just tell me you'll give us a chance."

He finally took a breath.

Alex didn't expect any of this! She suddenly felt like singing! Nicholas Stewart had just told her he loved her. He *loved* her and he said he would *wait* for her. Pastor Dan had been right and he was the *one!*

Alex had been swept off her feet from the first second they met. She had never felt like this about any man. Now, after Nick said these things to her—at that exact moment, Alex fell totally and completely in love with him, too. She got up, threw her arms around him and just grinned. As she looked up at this handsome man, he kissed her once more and it was a very good kiss.

Later, Alexandra told Nick that any man who could watch a girl go through a shooting, gas poisoning and still be there after his girl passes out and almost throws up on him, well, that person has to be a saint, or just plain crazy. He just grinned at her.

She tried to continue. "I have to tell you that I may still have some unresolved trust issues, Nicholas. I can't help it. I don't want to be hurt again, despite what I'm feeling. I want to be sure, Nick. I do. I'm still old fashioned enough that I can't go to bed with you, unless we're married. You must know how much I…." She knew she was rambling just the way he had. They both broke out in laughter and he put his arms around her.

"I did act pretty wicked, didn't I?" Alex asked.

"You kind of scared me, with that purse thing," Nick grinned.

"I'll try, Nick. I'll give us a chance. I owe both of us that much."

There—it was out. She might live to regret this but she wanted to believe in him and she wanted him to believe in her.

"I was so afraid," he said, "afraid that I had moved so fast you might think I…Alex, when I took you home last night, I just knew that you were…that *we* were right for each other. I know it more today."

Then, he said something that astounded her.

"Alexandra, do you believe in soul mates? Call me crazy. I guess I am but I believe I just found her."

You are my soul mate, love.

Alexandra could not believe what she was hearing. What he just said…it wasn't a movie script. It wasn't even smooth. He stumbled over his words. Both of them were talking ninety miles an hour! But, it was just plain spooky when he said that thing about "soul mates" at the very same time that she was thinking it.

It was what she had thought about too, the night before but couldn't tell him. Alex could not believe what she blurted out next.

"Nicholas Stewart, I love you. I love you so very much."

Alexandra listened to what that voice just said, the voice that sounded just like hers! It *was her voice,* although it sounded as if it were coming from miles away. Had she really said it? Had she told him out loud that she loved him?

She was almost afraid to look up at him but when she did, he looked into her eyes, breathed deeply and kissed her again. Neither of them said anything more. They didn't have to.

The plane had been in the air over two hours. Mac and John came into the cabin and sat down with Nick and Alex.

It was John who spoke first. "I hate to ruin this mood but we have to go over the details again of what happened and we have to talk about our plans when we reach Paris."

"Alex," Nick said, "there was one thing I didn't tell you yesterday. I didn't want to frighten you anymore than you were."

He told her about the bomb they had found on the plane before leaving Westville. He watched as Alex's face grew pale again. She was thinking that they all could have been killed, not just her and Nick but John and Mac.

"Don't be afraid, Alex. We're going to beat this. I'll take care of you. I promise you that. The reason we're going to Paris is to find out what connection Ed Percy had in this whole thing. We have to be ready and we have to be careful. I won't lose you now, Alexandra. I won't."

John and Mac looked at each other. Nicholas didn't have to say anymore. Alex had captured his heart. Even Mac had to recognize it. What Nick just said was more than enough to take care of the fear that was trying to overcome Alexandra. She just wanted to be safe and she wanted to be with Nick. More than anything, for the rest of her life, she wanted to be with him.

Nick and Mac moved to the table in the cabin of the plane and laid out a map of Paris in front of Alex and John. They pointed out where Ed's apartment was located.

"When we get there, you're going to be a married woman, Alex."

Alexandra looked up at Nick, quizzically, as Nick smiled at her.

"To John Cabe," he said.

Both John and Alexandra started to object and then thought about what he had just said.

Nick began to laugh.

"The expressions on your faces," he laughed. "Believe me, although you and John would make a real cute couple, I didn't mean I was going to push you into a real wedding—at least, not with John."

He smiled at Alex as if they had just shared a secret and she hoped it meant what she was thinking.

"It's just that the apartment manager might recognize me."

"I didn't think you meant that John and I…" Alexandra said, trying not to show her relief.

"Besides, I like John. I think he's…well, swell."

"And, I like you too, Alexandra." Now, John was making fun of her but she didn't mind his teasing. She liked John Cabe.

It was later, after they discussed exactly what they were going to do, that Nick asked to talk to Alex again, in private. He took her aside, in the back of the plane and he was very serious.

"Alex. This situation…when we get through this terrible situation, I want you to meet my daughter, Alexandra. I want you to meet my Sabrina."

It was the one true thing that he could give her now. It was a gift she could never refuse—to make her know how much he loved her, how serious he was and where it was leading.

Chapter Six

Paris is known as the "City of Lights," a city made for lovers, at least it should have been. For the small group just landing, it was anything but that. The group checked into a motel, waiting for morning to find Ed Percy's apartment. In all four rooms, the weary travelers slept fitfully, wondering what the morning would bring.

When Alex woke up the next morning, she heard a knock. It was a waiter from the motel's restaurant. He had a breakfast tray for her and the tray held a note from Nick. She poured some coffee and took one of the croissants. The bread was still warm and she was hungry, for a change. He had ordered her some fresh fruit and yogurt.

Bless you, Nick, she thought, as she opened his note.

His note told her that he had gone to a store to pick up a few things. He said he would be back soon and that John and Mac were right next door, if she needed them. She downed almost all of the food and went to take a shower. Alex dreaded putting on the same clothes, even though she had stuffed fresh lingerie in her purse.

She came out from the warmth of the shower with her damp hair wrapped in a towel. She put on the clean underwear and dressed in a robe from the hotel. As she picked up the newspaper, she automatically turned to the entertainment section. On the front page, there was a picture of Nick and Alex, at the charity brunch in New York City.

"No wonder they found out where we were," she whispered. "Nick, you need a disguise and a lot less press!"

Just then, Nick Stewart arrived at her door. He was clean-shaven and had a sack that he emptied onto the bed. He smiled at Alex, picked up a leftover croissant and then gave her a hug.

"Missed you," he grinned.

"Hi. I missed you, too. I was exhausted last night," she answered, feeling that she needed to explain why she didn't even kiss him good-night.

"I know. I was pretty worn out, myself. What are you reading?"

Alex handed him the paper. She noticed that he had bought them some t-shirts and a few personal items. She saw chocolates, toothpaste, brushes and a razor. She smiled when she read the slogans on the shirts.

"Viva Le France!" the logos read. They were going to look like tourists, all right!

"This picture—If they didn't know already, it's a pretty sure bet the bad guys know now we were in New York City. Alex, I'm so sorry."

"Sorry for being you? Never say that, Nick Stewart. Thanks for the clean t-shirt. I was dreading dressing in something I just slept in."

"We'll pick up more supplies when we get to the apartment. John just informed me that we have to leave in about twenty minutes. Mac already checked us out. Are you about ready?"

Alex went into the bathroom, slipped on the clean t-shirt and her jeans. She nodded to him when she came out.

"Meet Mrs. John Cabe, alias Mrs. Smith," she smiled.

Even in the gaudy t-shirt, she looked beautiful to him.

Alex got into a car with John Cabe and they drove to the apartment house where Ed Percy had lived. Mac and Nick followed Alex and John in a separate rental vehicle.

Their plan was for John and Alex to rent an apartment in Ed's building, saying they were husband and wife. Nick and Mac would sneak in the back way when they were certain that no one would see them enter. If they were very lucky, they would be able to get an apartment close to Ed Percy's apartment.

When they arrived at the apartment house, the landlord greeted Alexandra and John Cabe as "Mr. and Mrs. Smith." He spoke to them in French and since John didn't know the language well, it was Alexandra who spoke for both of them, in fluent French. She soon had the apartment rented.

She also found out in which apartment "her old friend," Mr. Percy, lived. Evidently, the Paris police had not yet heard of Mr. Percy's demise in the States.

John and Alex went up to their newly acquired apartment. It was one bedroom, simply furnished but clean. John went downstairs to let Nick and Mac know the room number and to give them a key.

When he returned, he told Alex that Nick and Mac would be up soon.

"I was impressed," he told her, "when you spoke French."

"Oh, I had French in high school. I always liked languages and managed to learn quite a few by the time I graduated from college."

John asked her how many languages she knew, thinking to himself, that she was not just some "dumb blonde." When Alex told him she had learned over twenty languages and spoke at least fifteen fluently, he nearly fell of his chair.

"What in the world did you do for a living?" he asked.

She laughed. She told him about being the public relations director for a little advertising firm in Chicago and later, an editor for a small newspaper. She feared if she told him how large the advertising firm really was, he might think she was bragging.

"When Mac and Nick get here, I'll go get groceries, supplies and more clothing for us," he told her.

Some of the items they needed had already been ordered from the jet and were waiting at a store near them. Alex looked out the window.

"It's not much of a view at all. This is no way to see Paris, John."

John had to warn her to stay back.

"Just in case anyone is watching the building, Alex, you shouldn't be seen."

As she turned away, she looked a little frightened. He hated to tell her that this was going to be their home for a while and that she probably wouldn't be going outside anytime soon.

Alex sat down on the sofa and wished for a cold soda, or hot coffee. She asked John to be sure and pick up coffee when he went for supplies.

"It's first on my list, Alex." He smiled at her. "We can't make it without our coffee, can we? Guess I'd better set up housekeeping and get a coffee pot too."

Alex borrowed a paper and pencil from him and began to make a list of things they might need. The apartment was partly furnished and did have a few dishes, pots and pans. There was a soft knock at the door and Nick and Mac came inside. As they entered, Nick hugged Alexandra and looked around the apartment.

"It's going to be tight," he said. "But, it shouldn't be for very long."

He asked John to pick up a sleeping bag for Mac and him. John could sleep on the sofa. The three of them were going to have to sleep in the living room. He told Alex that she would have the bedroom and he said that he'd divide the living room up some way, even if it was with just a sheet, so if she had to come out for anything, they would be hidden from her. Alex knew exactly why he was doing this and she smiled across at him.

"Hey, Nick, did you know the little woman also speaks over twenty languages?"

Nick turned to her and asked, "I knew that you spoke French but did he say twenty other languages?"

Alex just grinned and nodded. Nick tucked away yet another piece of trivia about his Alexandra. He just shook his head and smiled.

Mac nudged John. "Hey, I'll go with you to get supplies. Two people should be faster than one. We can leave in the two cars and meet up at that café we passed about a block back."

"I know the one," John replied. "I'll see you there in about an hour."

They both left with the list and Alexandra was alone with Nicholas. She was a little nervous as they sat down and viewed their surroundings.

"Ed's apartment number is 11-G," Alex said.

"How did you get that information so fast?" Nick asked.

"Oh, didn't you know? He's an old, old friend of mine. At least that's what I told the desk clerk. He was very talkative to an American who spoke fluent French."

"Especially, to a beautiful blonde with legs to die for," Nick grinned.

Alex hit him lightly on his arm.

"It got us some information, anyway," she said.

"This apartment reminds me of the one my mom and I shared in New York City for a while," Nick said, walking the apartment. "We had more than one bedroom but you should have seen it—my sisters living in one bedroom and me in the living room. Mom got the other bedroom. No one got in the bathroom! There were always hose and lingerie in the way and we were always running over each other but it was fun, for the most part. Our apartment wasn't far from Mama Rita's café," he related. "I was pretty young then, nine or ten years old."

As he reminisced, Alex relaxed. She liked hearing about the real Nick Stewart and she listened intently. So, he was just a boy from the Bronx, after all—just a real, live little boy.

"Nick, do you think we should go up and see if we can get into Ed's apartment or wait?"

"We'd better wait for John and Mac. They have some tools that will help us get in."

"Do you think this building is being watched?"

"I wouldn't doubt it, babe. My plane was to fly back to California, which should put the guy off our tracks for a while. Hopefully, they'll think that we are on board. Mac had a couple of friends who were going to get on that plane dressed like you and me. I just hope it worked. They should be home by now."

"I just hope they're safe." Alex shuddered.

She thought of how frightened she would be to get on that plane with those gangsters out there. She hadn't thought about others who would be watching Ed's apartment.

"They've probably already searched Ed's apartment," she said. "Do you really think we may find something that will help?"

"Darling girl, if I didn't think that, we wouldn't be in Paris, right now."

Nick grinned at her and put his arm around her waist

"Why don't we make the most of the couple of hours the guys will be gone and quit worrying about this right now?"

Alex smiled at him. "Nick Stewart, if you think I'm going to make out with you after we promised, you're mistaken."

"Trust me. I think even the Lord himself would agree that this apartment needs a little tender loving care. We need to clean it up and we need to figure out the sleeping arrangements."

She felt embarrassed. Maybe her mind was too much on what she *thought* Nick was thinking, instead of what he was really thinking.

"A neat freak, huh?" she replied. "I'm sorry. I'm just a little gun-shy, I guess."

" Forget it, babe. It's new to both of us. Now, the one bath and shower— it's cozy for four people. We need a schedule, I guess."

"Cozy is hardly the word," Alex replied.

She was thinking of the tiny bathroom that she had seen earlier. It only had a small shower stall, no tub, and a sink.

"It could be challenging," he insisted.

Alex rolled her eyes and threw her hands up. She was just giving up on this discussion. She and Nick started toward the small bathroom.

"You're right. It's filthy," said Alex.

"I'll clean this up," Nick said. "Is there anything to scrub with? A sponge, a cloth?"

Alex looked under the sink and found some cleanser and a sponge. She tossed it to him. She never thought she would see Nicholas Stewart on his hands and knees. She had to admit; he looked kind of appealing.

"Here, Sir Clean-a-lot," she laughed. "You take the shower and I'll get the sink. Hey, there are even some clean washcloths and towels in the cabinet. I can't believe it."

Alex scrubbed the sink but didn't dare look at the toilet. That had to be Nick's job, she decided. He finished the shower and looked up at her.

"As far as I remember, you're the only woman, other than my mother, who ever made me clean a shower stall. Now, for the dirty job!"

He tackled the stool like a pro, as Alex wiped the floor the best she could with a cloth. She didn't see a mop anywhere. Finally, the bathroom was spotless.

"Catch, Alex!"

Nick threw her a bar of soap and of course, it slipped through her hands and into the hall. She ran after it and slipped, flat on her face!

"I'm not hurt," she said, as Nick came out to help her up, "just very embarrassed."

She had to laugh as she watched Nick slip on the same bar of soap and fall to the floor beside her.

"You're graceful," she chided.

"Oh, you want grace, huh?"

He got up and then pulled her up. He used to tease his sisters and he missed that. Alex started to get up and tried to leave as he tried to take her hand but only managed to pull her back down. Alex glared at him. Nick chuckled at her.

"Are you laughing at me, Nicholas Stewart?" This time, she sounded perturbed.

" No, not ever, love. I'd never laugh at you."

He watched as she slowly got up and was finally able to go back into the shower. Nick followed her. There was barely room in the small bath for one person, let alone two. He had to laugh. It was comical—Paris, this apartment and their situation.

"Nick, I'm taking a shower while this is clean, before I have to share this with three men."

"Okay but watch the showerhead."

As he said it, she turned it on. The showerhead was turned straight toward them. When Nick cleaned it, he had turned it outward and forgot to turn it back around. They were soaked!

"Oh, Alex. I'm sorry."

"Nick, turn it off! It's freezing!"

"Here, I'll get it."

She looked at him getting soaking wet and began to laugh.

"Alex, you'll have to put those wet clothes back on, unless I can find you something to wrap up in."

"I think you better try," she said, still laughing. "I can get back into these but I do not look forward to it."

He started for the bedroom closet, while Alex closed the door, got out of her wet clothes and hung them up on the back of the door. She turned the showerhead around and climbed back in the shower, turning the water to a warmer temperature.

"Now, this is worth waiting for."

Nick found a set of sheets in the linen closet and he called out to Alex.

"Babe?"

"Yes?"

" I found a sheet set. You could wrap up in them, at least until your clothes get dry. Want to take a chance? I think they're clean."

Alex dried off and stuck one hand out the door, as Nick handed her the sheets.

"Nick?"

"Yes?"

"Thanks for fixing the bedroom and the living room for me. It's difficult, isn't it, not being together, I mean?"

She would never know how hard it was for him—being that close to her and not being with her. He had to reassure her that he wasn't going to invade her privacy."It's hard." He paused. "I want you to trust me, Alex. That might take awhile. I know that. In the meantime, just don't stand too close to me."

He grinned when he heard her giggle.

When Alex came out of the shower, she was so totally covered that they both had to smile.

"You look like a mummy!" he said.

"Just remember that," she laughed.

"Oh, I will."

Nick had hung some blankets up between her bedroom door and the shower. It actually gave her more privacy than she thought it would.

"Just look at this!" he said, pointing to his accomplishment.

Alexandra smiled at him and nodded in agreement. She thought of all the young couples that believed in abstinence. She had not realized how difficult it was before this. You had to depend on God's Word. You had to trust that His way is best and you had to trust in the person you had chosen.

Chapter Seven

When John and Mac returned with the supplies, they couldn't help but notice that Nick's clothes were soaking wet and Alexandra looked like someone from a horror movie, wrapped up tightly in several sheets.

"What the…?" said John.

"Don't ask!" said Nick.

Alex just scowled at them.

"Got clothes?" Nick demanded from Mac.

Mac dug through the sacks and handed him some clothing that they had picked out. Alex grabbed the sack of women's clothing and raced off to the bedroom to get dressed.

"Guess I'll wait for a little while," grinned Nick.

The men broke out into laughter.

"It's not anything that you both are thinking," said Nick.

John and Mac quit laughing.

"Sorry, boss," they both said.

"I want you to know nothing happened…nothing will happen. She's precious to me. I want you to give her the same respect you gave to Meg when she was alive."

He couldn't believe he said that. Mac and John looked at Nick. He was serious. Alexandra Andrews commanded respect anyway but now Nicholas Stewart had confirmed it. They realized she meant more to him than they ever believed possible.

When Alex reappeared, she wore a pair of jeans and a light blue sweater. She felt refreshed and full of energy. The time she and Nick had together had been playful and it was easier—not as serious as before. She felt as if they had been together for years and she was glad that they had talked about their feelings for each other.

There was still some tension. That was a fact. But, they were both determined to wait and this time, she felt no guilt about telling a man that she would be worth waiting for!

Taking the grocery bags to the kitchen, she began to sort through the supplies. She asked Mac and John if they wanted coffee and sandwiches. They both answered with a resounding yes, and Alex started a pot of coffee. They had bought what she considered "the good stuff."

"Nothing cheap here," she said, as she went through the groceries.

They were used to buying for Nick, she mused and he must only get the best. Alex also found the packed surveillance supplies that the men had brought and she gave them to Mac.

"Guess you'll want to get started with this, huh?" she asked.

"Thanks," said Mac. He smiled at her.

He and John took two more bags and a box back to the bedroom. While Alex fixed lunch, Nicholas came out of the bedroom. He had dried off and was wearing a pair of expensive jeans and a soft flannel shirt. Alex smiled at him.

"You look great," she said.

He walked over to her and kissed her on the back of her neck and then asked her if she needed any help. Alex handed him some plates and silverware to set on the small table.

She fixed thick ham and cheese sandwiches made on homemade bread and opened a bag of chips. She asked him to help her cut up some fresh vegetables while she poured the coffee and then they called Mac and John into the kitchen.

When they sat down, Alex said grace. She noticed the men were very quiet. She told God that they were thankful to be alive and to be together. The men ate ravenously. For such a simple meal, it went over with a bang!

"The best steak in town wouldn't have tasted any better today, Alex," said Mac.

They all knew that they had to get to work after dinner, while Alex cleaned up the kitchen and made more coffee. The men sat around the dining table, planning something far more dangerous than the dinner they just had eaten.

"We need to go to his apartment as soon as it's late enough that the neighbors don't see us," said John.

Mac told them he'd get started on the camera and set the stuff up in this apartment and that John would get the bugs planted in Ed Percy's apartment as soon as they broke into it.

In the meantime, they needed someone to talk to the manager without rousing too much suspicion. They might be able to get some information from him—if anyone had been in that apartment and what might have gone on before Ed was killed.

"Alex could do that," suggested John. "She's already got him eating out of her hand and she's the only one who speaks French."

"I don't like it," said Nick. "What if he gets suspicious of her?"

"Man, we don't have a choice," said Mac. "I say we send her down to ask him for some sightseeing directions and then see what she can get out of him."

Alex walked out from the kitchen and all the men got suddenly silent.

"Did I miss something?" she asked.

"No, babe," said Nick. "We just need you to do something and I don't want you to do it unless you feel comfortable."

She walked over and took his hand.

"I'll do anything you want if it will help."

Mac told Alex what she needed to do and she agreed.

"I'll go down right now," she said. "See you later and don't worry."

She waved at the door to all of them. John thought Nick might try to stop her but he did nothing. Mac put the monitor and sound equipment up in the apartment. He had it wired and ready to receive sound and pictures from Ed Percy's apartment as soon as John could wire that apartment too.

When Alex showed up at the desk downstairs, the manager looked up over his thick glasses at this tall, slender blonde. He smiled and asked her if he could assist her.

She answered him in flawless French, asking for a map of Paris.

"My husband and I want to see the sights. My friend, Ed Percy, always told me that if I ever got to Paris with John, that he'd show us around. I guess I didn't count on him not being here."

The manager gave her a map and pointed out several points of interest. She was a pretty American and he found himself easily talking to her.

He said, "Yes, Mr. Percy has been gone on business for a couple of months now. He usually lets me know when he will return but I've heard nothing from him in a couple of weeks now."

"Do you have any idea where he went?" she asked.

"No, Madame," he said. "He left with another gentleman and he told me they had business in the States."

"Another man?" she asked. "Do you know who he was?"

"Oui. He was an American, a Quentin Smith."

Alex didn't say anything but she knew she might have just struck gold. *So, our friend Quentin did know Ed Percy. He might have made Ed go to Westville with him.*

"Did he happen to say what his business was in the States?" she questioned.

"No, no…only that it was very important. He didn't talk too much."

Alex remembered her rather quiet neighbor. She could understand why he would have been a good undercover agent, unless they found out that he was working both sides!

She thanked the manager for the map and mentioned she was tired from the trip and that she would see him tomorrow. He smiled at her and nodded.

"Good night," he said.

Alex waved to him and started up the stairs.

Alexandra started back to her rented apartment but not before walking down the hall to see where apartment 11-G was. It was only about four doors down from where they were staying. She stopped in front of it and out of curiosity, she tried the door. It creaked and swung slowly open. Did she dare? Nick had warned her not to do anything without him or John or Mac.

She peered inside to the living room. It looked like the same floor plan as their apartment. She took a step inside, when a noise behind her made her jump. Standing directly behind her in the hallway, was a man that she didn't recognize and he was holding a gun. He had it pointed directly at her!

Nick glanced down at his watch. It was time for Alex to be back. For some unknown reason, he had the distinct feeling that she was in danger and he asked John to come with him to see where she was. It was when he looked down the hall, that he saw the opened doorway. Could that be Ed Percy's door? He motioned for John to stay behind him. John had his gun and he had already taken the safety off, prepared for the worst.

Alex thought for sure that she had been caught by one of the hit men. She spoke to him in French, asking what he wanted and he replied he was a security officer for several apartments.

"What are you doing in Mr. Percy's apartment, Miss?"

Alex breathed a deep sigh of relief, telling him that she and her husband were friends of Ed's and they thought he might be home when she saw his door open. The man cleared his throat and told her that she should not be here and that Mr. Percy was out of town.

"I'm so sorry. I'll be glad to leave."

As she started toward the door, she saw Nick, with John right behind him, gun and all. It was evident they were looking for her. She tried to motion them away and turned back to stall the man that she mistook for a threat. She told him she was very sorry for trespassing and that she was staying with her husband, just down the hall. She told him that he could check with the manager if he needed.

When she saw that Nick and John had disappeared, she left, heading back down the hall to her apartment. The security officer watched her as she went inside, where Nick and John were waiting for her.

"Hi, guys," Alex said sheepishly.

They appeared more threatening than the gun that the man had held on her. She knew what they both were thinking. She had gone ahead and explored without even telling them and she had been wrong. She tried to apologize.

"Curiosity killed a cat, Alexandra. Didn't I ask you not to draw attention to us?" Nick said.

It was evident that Nick was very angry. In fact, she had never seen him that angry.

"I just saw the door open. I'm so sorry. You're right. I was scared to death. I won't ever do that, again."

She was so humble that Nicholas couldn't stay upset with her.

" I just don't want you to get hurt," he said, walking over to her, "and these men aren't playing games, Alex."

He put his arms around her. It was evident he was concerned for her and that was why he was so mad. She had been thoughtless to put him through that.

" I do have some good information for you," she said to him, trying hard to change the subject. "They knew each other. The man who has been trying to kill us left Paris with Ed Percy. According to the apartment manager, they were headed for the United States. He hasn't seen Ed Percy in over two months. He said the man that Mr. Percy left with was Quentin Smith."

She tried to remember everything that the manager had told her. She wanted to make up for the worry she had caused them.

"Good girl," said John Cabe. "See, I told you he'd open up to her." He glanced over at Mac.

Alex was glad that John, at least, forgave her for the stupid thing she had done. Nick squeezed her waist. At least, that was something.

Mac was scowling but he acknowledged that Alex had done something to help.

"Well, it's time to go see if we can get back into his apartment," said Mac. "Everybody ready?"

Nick told Alex to wait in the apartment until John came back to get her. By now, she felt thoroughly reprimanded. She had disappointed him and all she really wanted was to please him.

He saw the look on her face and explained, "Too many of us in the hall will really look suspicious. John's going to be our lookout, while Mac and I try to get back in, unnoticed."

"Be careful," she whispered to him.

The security officer had left their floor and was nowhere in sight. Mac slid the pick in the lock of Ed Percy's apartment. He had the door open in less than two minutes.

"Feels like old times," he laughed.

They walked inside and looked around the apartment. It was neat and everything was in order.

"What do you think about the way this looks?" Nick asked Mac.

"Too neat," Mac replied. "Someone's already been here. We may not find anything but look for a bug, first."

They were combing the apartment when John and Alex entered. Mac put his finger to his lips, making sure they didn't say anything.

After a couple of minutes he said, "It looks clean. I'll set up the camera and microphone. At least we can see if anyone enters or leaves after tonight."

Nick and John went through the desk, then looked over the sofa and the chairs, turning cushions and feeling underneath. Alex was looking at the pictures on the wall, when she saw one that showed a group of service men. She motioned to Nick. His face was among the group in the photo. When Nick moved beside her, he saw the picture and recognized it. He removed it from the wall.

"It's a picture of our old army unit."

"I recognized you," she said, pointing to Nick's face in the picture.

Then, Alexandra recoiled. "It's him," she whispered.

"Who?" asked Nick.

"Quentin Smith, I bet," she said, pointing to a tall dark male in the back row.

Nick took the picture and put it under a lamp, where they could see it better.

"How do you recognize him?" Nick asked Alex.

"He's the man that was in the school auditorium…the one I told you about. He was there!"

"That's not his name," he said. "At least, when I knew him, he went by Aaron White. He was an odd one, all right. He was a loner, even then. As I remember, he was a whiz in math and was an explosives expert. Well, Quentin or Aaron, White or Smith, we have your name and now, we can get a background on you."

Nick hugged Alexandra and she felt almost forgiven for her earlier indiscretion. He turned the picture over to see if there were any names written on the back when he noticed a small slit in the cardboard backing.

Pulling open the staples, he removed the backing. There was a small white envelope inside and it was addressed to "Mr. Nicholas Stewart, Confidential and Urgent."

Nick hurriedly opened the envelope and unfolded an old creased paper. On one side was a sort of map that had an arrow pointing north and to a picture marked as old airstrip. There were some other markings too and on the other side was a list of some kind of numbers.

"I don't make much sense of this," said Nick. "Let's take this back to our apartment and try to decipher it."

They left Ed Percy's apartment, turning on their camera and sound system that John had installed. They locked the apartment and headed down the hall. A woman appeared, as if from nowhere. She was coming up the stairs, heading directly for them and she saw the four people coming toward her. Nick tried to look down, so she could not identify him.

They passed her without speaking. Alex unlocked their apartment and the men hurried inside. The woman continued on down the hallway. She slowed down when she was near Ed Percy's apartment but continued to the next apartment. Alex watched, as she went inside.

"She's gone," said Alex. "She must live next door to where Ed lived."

Nick unfolded the paper from the picture frame and spread it out on the dining room table. The group gathered around to look at it. It was definitely a map of some kind.

"Where is it?" asked Alex.

"Does anyone recognize the landmarks?" John said, "It looks like a treasure map of some kind. Look at that arrow, pointing to an X, and notice the writing that says 'old airstrip'. It doesn't make sense. It doesn't give us a clue what country it's in or anything."

"I know exactly where it is," said Nick.

"You do?" asked Mac. "Where?"

"It was an old army base where we were stationed for a while. It's in England, near Cambridge. We were helping clean it up. They turned part of it into some type of historical WWII site. Ed would have known that I was the only one who would recognize it, besides the other members of our unit. That must mean Quentin doesn't know about this, yet."

"What would be at a deserted airstrip?" asked Alex.

"That's what we're going to find out," said Nick.

Mac and John looked at each other.

"Guess we know what that means," said Mac.

"Yeah," replied John, "I'll make some arrangements with the helicopter service I used to fly with. When do you want to go, boss?" he asked Nick.

"Let's try it day after tomorrow, or sooner, if you can get hold of them," replied Nick, as he turned the paper over.

"What do you make of these numbers?" he asked the group.

The four of them leaned over to look at the other side of the paper.

"A111, A113, A115.... goes all the way up to A199 and then it starts over with the B111, B113 and C and so forth..."said Mac.

"Could be a code," said John.

"Or a safe deposit box?" questioned Nick. "Although it doesn't see to make much sense."

Alex was quiet. In the back of her mind, she had seen the numbers somewhere but where? She couldn't remember what she associated them with, or where she had seen them, so she didn't say anything. She decided that she would think about it and talk to Nicholas when she remembered. He had so much on his mind right now.

She was suddenly quite weary. This had been another long day. Alex excused herself and went to the bathroom. She changed into her robe and pajamas that someone had picked out for her and then went into the bedroom and fell asleep. Later, Nick came into check on her. He felt bad, getting so angry at her earlier but he was so afraid for her.

"Alex? You asleep?" he whispered.

"Just resting," she lied. "Nicholas, what about your work in California? You can't go on chasing these criminals. Shouldn't we just turn this over to the FBI? I'm worried about you."

He sat down on the edge of the bed and told her, "I have to do this. I have a couple of week's vacation anyway. I called the studio and told them I was taking it. I don't want you to worry. We're never going to feel safe unless we find out what's going on. If I think we're in over our heads, I'll be the first to contact the FBI."

Alex was still worried about him but she tried not to show it. She sat up and moved to the edge of the bed, close to him, as he put his arms around her. They talked about the map and what it might mean. The last thing Alex remembered was Nick reassuring her again not to worry. She fell asleep in his arms, while he was still trying to figure out what the numbers might be. He was still talking when he looked down at her.

"Alexandra, sleep well," he whispered. He gently kissed her forehead, placed her on the bed, covered her up and walked to the doorway, turning off her nightlight. He knew that he had to get to sleep too but images of car chases and burned houses still filled his mind. It was early in the morning when he finally dozed off.

The alarm went off at 7:00 a.m. and woke Alex. She dressed and then went through the living room and into the kitchen, taking her make up kit with her.

Might as well let them sleep a little while, she thought.

She heard the shower running and realized that someone must be up. She was glad she had showered yesterday afternoon. She didn't want to share her shower with anyone but she still needed to wash her face and put on her makeup and the kitchen would have to do for that. She leaned into a small mirror from her case and combed her hair.

"Ugh, need toothpaste," she muttered.

She retrieved her toothbrush out of her make up bag, brushed her teeth and then washed her face under the kitchen faucet. Alex could hear John Cabe's voice singing in the shower and she realized that Mac and Nick must still be asleep in the living room.

If only she had a hair dryer, she could shampoo her hair out here, too. Alex was applying her lipstick when Nick came into the kitchen. He was still in yesterday's clothes and he looked so tired to her.

"Hey, beautiful, you're the only one I know who looks as good in the morning as they did the night before."

She turned around in her chair and grinned. "And you called me a sleepyhead," she grinned.

"I know. I didn't get much sleep. Must have been 2:00 or 3:00 a.m. before I got to sleep."

"I'm sorry I conked out while you were still talking to me. I was so tired. I think it just all caught up with me. Forgive me?" she asked.

He pulled her up from the chair and kissed her on her cheek. "We'll have plenty of time for us, when this is over," he said. "Don't worry, I plan to ravage you later."

She laughed at him. At least, he could still joke. Alex started for the coffee pot. "I have to start breakfast and try to get in the bathroom later, if John ever gets out."

He laughed and said, "I'll try and hurry him up."

Alex fixed them a big breakfast of bacon and eggs, toast and a pot of very strong coffee. She knew they needed a decent meal before this day started.

She was pouring some juice for all of them, when John Cabe walked into the kitchen.

"Morning, Alex," he said. "You disappeared early last night. Pretty hectic day, huh?"

"Yes, you could say that, John," she answered as she handed him a cup of coffee.

"Did you come up with anything new?" she asked him.

"No, I'm going to try and run the numbers through a decoding device I have. The map's our best bet and Mac has the camera and sound going in the other apartment. I guess we should check it out."

He left to see if anything was on the tape while Alex finished fixing breakfast. Then, she heard John call out to them.

"Hey, come and listen to this!" she heard John say.

As she went into the living room, she heard static. John had the sound turned on and the small computer screen showed the Percy apartment. It was empty but there was a sound directed from a heating vent. You could barely hear it but could tell that it was a woman and a man talking.

"Can you turn it up?" she asked.

"Yeah, everyone be real quiet. I think this is coming from that apartment next door to Ed's. This is pretty sensitive. We should be able to hear them."

It must have been the woman they passed in the hall. The voices were muffled but you could hear the woman speaking.

"They're here. I saw them yesterday in the hallway."

There was more static and then a male voice said, "Tomorrow. We'll see about that tomorrow."

Alex shuddered as she recognized the voice. It was the voice of the man who told her he was a security officer, only now she realized he wasn't. John and Nick glanced at each other. Alexandra could have been killed yesterday. It was in all of their thoughts.

"Oh, Nick. You were right. Now, they know we're here," she said.

Mac, for the first time, put his arm around her. He was calm when he spoke.

"And we know where they are. Don't worry, Alex. We'll be fine."

It was something her own father might have done and Mac had called her "Alex," instead of Alexandra. All of a sudden, she felt extremely calm and it was Mac Timmons who made her feel that way.

Nick smiled, seeing them together. He knew that Mac was beginning to warm up to her. That meant he was starting to trust her too and it was a confirmation he needed. He walked over to them.

"Mac's right. We may be targets but we know where they are. We can see them and we can hear them, something they don't realize yet. We have to get out of this apartment before they know we've left. When is the helicopter going to be ready, John?"

John explained that he couldn't get a flight out until late tomorrow. That meant staying around all day and not getting killed.

Nick shook his head in disagreement. "Look, we already know they don't care about how many people they take out. And, if they're waiting for Quentin or Aaron, this guy's a master at planting explosives. I say that we get out of this building now and we have to get out without them seeing us."

"That'll take a diversion," said Mac. "Maybe a little explosion or fire of our own? While the fire department is here, we could leave. John, we're going to need disguises, something—I don't know. Can you get out of here, without being noticed?"

" I can get out and still *be* seen but don't worry, they won't know it's me."

Like a magician, he pulled out a chef's hat from his sack of clothing. He went into the bathroom and when he returned, he did not look like John Cabe. He had donned a mustache, the hat. and a chef's uniform.

"What in the world?" asked Alex.

"John doesn't travel far without some kind of disguise," said Mac.

"Wish me luck!" said John.

"Be careful, you know that they're watching this apartment," Nick patted his friend's shoulder.

John went over to the window and looked out. The alley below was empty except for trash cans and the skinniest cat he had ever seen. He climbed out the window onto the fire escape and let himself down into the alley. The last they saw was John going down the alley, avoiding the gray, grungy trash cans and running into the street that was behind the apartment building.

"Oh, I hope he'll be all right," said Alex.

"He will. He's as smart as they come," replied Mac. "Why else do you think he already had a disguise in that bag? Let's eat, Alex."

Alex sipped her coffee and tried to get down some toast. She had long since lost her appetite. Mac ate, while Nick drank his juice and coffee. Nick didn't eat much either and Alex knew he was worried, too. She went to try and pack a few personal items in her purse. She knew they wouldn't be able to take any clothing with them again and she wondered where they would stay until tomorrow, if they got out of the building alive.

It had been over two hours and John had not returned. Then, the telephone rang. Mac motioned for Alex to answer it and told her to speak in French.

"Hello?"

It was the hotel manager. He told Alex there was a delivery for her downstairs. He told her that a chef from a bakery had left their "belated wedding cake" with him. Alex asked him if he would be good enough to bring it upstairs and he said he would.

She hung up the phone, saying, "I think we just got our uniforms."

The apartment manager brought up a large cake box. While Alex thanked him and paid him for his trouble, Nick and Mac hid in the bedroom.

The box was enormous. It looked like a wedding cake could be inside but instead, there were two fire department uniforms and a police officer's uniform.

"How did he do it?" Alex laughed.

"I told you he'd come through," said Mac, "Now let's get dressed. Keep your clothes on under these. Something tells me we're going to have a fire in the hotel in a few minutes. When the alarm goes on, both the fire and police department will arrive. That's when we have to leave. We'll go down the fire escape. John should have a car waiting."

Nick and Alex got into the two fire department uniforms, while Mac took the police uniform. Just as Mac predicted, in about ten minutes, the fire alarm went off. People in the building were yelling and there was a lot of disturbance. They heard sirens and then, the fire department was there, evacuating the building.

Alex, Nick and Mac climbed out onto the fire escape, down the alleyway and ran to the back of the building.

"Where's John?" asked Alex.

In all the confusion, Alex didn't see how they would be able to tell. Just then, a bakery truck drove up and a charming chef stopped the truck, just in front of them. He got out, opened the back door and the three climbed in.

Chapter Eight

The man known as Quentin Smith, alias Aaron White, was angry. He lost the young woman and Nicholas Stewart at the airport and it left him behind in his schedule. He received a report that the bumbling man and woman, who were hired to kill them in Paris, let them get away.

"If you want anything done right…"

He loaded a revolver and holstered it under his trench coat.

"Where are they now?" he asked the agents.

Those stupid disguises let them get away. They were smarter than he realized. *Where are they going to go? They have no place to hide. Nick Stewart's face would be recognized anywhere in the world and the girl is still with him. He wouldn't let her out of his sight. He's too much the hero for that.*

Quentin was on his way to the train station. He knew they couldn't hire a helicopter until later. He bet they were headed for the Euro Train. He would find them and soon. He had to. His own life was on the line now. The Organization wouldn't let him get by with any more mistakes.

Alex and Nick were out of the uniforms and sitting against the wall of the van. There were various confectioners' supplies in the van, as well as a large cake.

Mac yelled up to John, "Hey, whose cake?"

"Dunno," replied John. "All I needed was the box and the truck. A stop at the local costume shop was quite profitable, though. When I saw those firemen's uniforms and the police uniform, I knew they were the ones—something you could walk right out in and never be recognized. Then, I ran into the baker that we bought the fresh bread from earlier. He knew I wasn't a chef but he was willing to part with everything for the right price."

" I bet the price was high," said Mac.

"Well, you know, when you have lives to save, it doesn't seem to matter."

"Where to from here?" asked Alex.

"The helicopter couldn't leave until tomorrow," yelled John.

"Then, we'll take the Euro Train," said Nick, "the one that runs under the channel into England. We can rent a car from there."

"But, Nick, they'll recognize you," said Alex.

"Then, I'll have to do something so they won't. John, take off that mustache and give it to me."

Nicholas Stewart was used to playing parts. He put on the mustache and told John to find him a baseball cap and some sunglasses. He also asked for two wigs, one for Alex and one for him.

"I want something with long hair that I can tie back and Alex needs a change of color, maybe red."

"You don't ask for much, do you, boss?" laughed John.

"I know you, John. I know what your nickname was in the service."

"What was it?" asked Alex.

"The Scrounger," laughed Nick.

Mac grinned. "And, he earned every letter of that name."

Alex had to smile. John Cabe was invaluable. *He is a pilot; he can wire anything; and is a whiz at computers. Now, a master of disguise! What part of the service had he really been in, some kind of Special Forces unit?*

And, from the background she had learned about Mac, he had dealt with the criminal element long enough to have valuable contacts. Why had Nicholas hired them, really? She wondered if the term "old friends" was the entire truth. She knew that Nick had hired each of them for their skills, as well.

John pulled the van into an alley, behind the costume shop and took the uniforms from them.

"Back in a minute," he said.

When he returned, it was with an auburn wig for Alex, a dark-brown, long, wig for Nick and a baseball cap. In his pocket were some sunglasses.

"You want anything else while we're here?" he asked, taking a large piece of cake and cramming it into his mouth.

"This should do it," Nick said, as he grinned at John.

He put on the wig and donned the baseball cap. He tied the wig's hair back, with a rubber band and slipped on the sunglasses.

"He looks like a hippie," said Alexandra.

She was pleased with how much courage all of these men had and she had gained a new respect for them today.

The train station was crowded but no one seemed to notice the four people that headed for the train to England, except to notice an attractive auburn-haired woman with three escorts.

Mac acquired the tickets for a private car and the four of them boarded the train. They were early. None of them saw the last-minute passenger who got on the train in the car behind them.

John told them he had arranged for a rental car, when they arrived in England.

"We can drive to the airstrip from there. In the meantime, let's relax and enjoy this ride," said Nick.

They had been served a decent snack. It would have to do until dinnertime—whenever that would be.

"Here's to us," Nick continued, holding up a glass of water, "and to success in ending this nightmare that we seem to have stumbled into!"

As he held up his glass, the other three joined in the toast.

"This train is slick," said John.

"Yeah, can you imagine we're riding under tons of water, under the English Channel?" replied Mac.

"It's nice, alright," said Alex, "and our car is roomier than our last apartment!"

The group laughed. They all remembered the efficiency apartment with the small shower.

"It's a shame we didn't have time to grab all that expensive equipment we bought," said John.

"If they find it and watch our tapes, they know we're serious about finding them," Nick replied.

"Hopefully, before they find us again," said Alex.

"Hey, *red*," Nick chimed in, "enough of the bad thoughts. I want you to repeat after me, 'I am safe. I am with the best and brightest men I've ever known.' Now, say that at least five times."

He put his arm around her and she couldn't help but smile at him.

"That's better."

Mac and John glanced at each other. Although they knew Nick's promises of safety were just wishes, they felt better being together and on the train to England.

The passenger in the car behind them checked his revolver. He would meet another agent in England and they would finally take out this "problem" together. He wondered where the group was going. He would have to watch them more closely but he didn't want to give himself away, yet.

Chapter Nine

Just as John Cabe promised them, a car was waiting for them in England. They climbed in and began their drive to Cambridge. Mac was driving, with John in the front seat. Nicholas and Alexandra were in the back. The countryside was gray and it had started to rain. Alex noticed it was a pretty landscape, even with the bad weather. There were rolling hillsides with large, beautiful trees and the road ahead curved upwards. She noticed that the rain was starting to turn to sleet. It had turned much colder since they left the train station and it was getting slick outside. Alex wished for a coat, rather than the light jacket she wore.

Quentin Smith, who was in a truck about two cars behind the group, told his new partner from the Organization that he needed to catch up with Nick Stewart's car by the time they reached the curve that headed up into the hillside. The truck speeded up. It easily slid in behind the car, where four innocent passengers were about to be run off the road.

Mac was the first to see the truck. It was following too close.

"John, look in your rear view. There's a truck following us. In fact, he's following way too close."

"I see him. Be careful. It's slick out there. Slow down. Let's see if he'll pass us."

Nick and Alex heard what John said and turned around to look out the rear window.

"Mac, it's Quentin, I mean Aaron. He's in the passenger side," Nick yelled.

Just then, they heard the gun and felt the jolt. Quentin had shot one of the rear tires of their car. It swerved to one side and hit the stone wall that prevented traffic from diving into the ravine below. Then, the car swerved to the other side, where another car was coming from the other direction. It was headed right for them.

" I can't hold the wheel," yelled Mac.

"We're going to crash!" yelled John. The truck slammed into Nick's car as hard as it could, forcing it back over to the right side and over the wall!

Their car dove into the ravine below, hitting rocks, trees and anything in its path—until it came to a *dead* stop, wheels spinning, at the edge of another cliff. The front of the car hung over a boulder where it landed and precariously teetered. Smoke was coming from the engine and the doors on the left side were caved in. Mac was slumped over the wheel. There was no noise from the other three passengers.

On the highway above, a small crowd of onlookers peered down. Quentin and his driver left the scene, knowing that their job was finished. He knew no one could have survived that crash.

The first thing Alex was aware of was a strong smell of gasoline. Her head hurt and she noticed blood on her sleeve, near her elbow. Nick was lying across her and he wasn't moving. She panicked when she saw a small trickle of blood coming from his mouth.

It took her another moment to realize what had happened. Then, she remembered—Quentin! She tried to move her arm. She didn't think it was broken, which was a miracle. She tried to move. Her legs seemed to be intact. She slid her hand under Nick's head and she prayed.

"Nick? Nicholas, wake up," she called out.

She thought she saw his head move a little. She put her fingers on the pulse point of his neck and saw that he was still breathing. Thank God, he was still alive!

"God, please help."

She moved to the right side of the car but it creaked ominously. She thought she might get out the back door, so she unlocked it and slid over a little more, where she could see out the window. When she saw where they were, a wave of nausea covered her.

Even if she could climb out, she would never be able to get up the hill. It was too steep. She looked up at the front passengers and gasped. She honestly believed that Mac was dead. He wasn't moving and there was blood everywhere. John was covered up by an airbag. She didn't see him move at all but she called out to him.

"John? John, are you O.K.? Johnny, please wake up!"

John Cabe stirred. He thought that he heard someone calling his name. He ached and his body hurt everywhere. He found himself pinned behind an airbag but he was alive.

"Alex?" he called out.

"Yes, John, thank God. Are you all right?"

"I think so. I can't move my legs but I think it's because of this airbag. If I can get it to deplete, I can tell more."

"Here."

She somehow managed to find her purse and retrieved a long nail file. She gave it to John and he poked at the airbag. The smell of the airbag filled the space. It was awful!

"What about Nick and you?" John asked. "Dear Lord, Mac sure doesn't look good, Alex."

The airbag finally depleted enough for John Cabe to unhook his seat belt and try to get out.

" I seem to be all right, just lots of cuts," she replied. "Nick's still breathing but he won't wake up, John, and he's bleeding from his mouth. He may be injured, internally. Dear God, what can we do?"

"I've got to get out of here! Then, I can help you." John moved closer to his door.

"Watch it!" yelled Alex, "There's nothing holding up the front of the left side of the car but air."

The car rocked slightly but John was able to fall out of the front seat and onto the hard ground. He looked up from where they had fallen. It was steep and it was sleeting. It was a lot colder than when they had left. They'd never be able to get up the hill. They could never carry Nick and Mac very far without help.

On the other hand, John knew they couldn't stay in the car. He smelled gasoline. The car could explode any minute. He had to get the other three passengers out of the car.

He slowly opened the door where Alex sat and carefully pulled her out. Then, he got in the back seat where she had been sitting and tried to pull Nick outside. John couldn't tell how badly Nick was hurt and he hated to move him but he had to free him.

"Alex, I need some help. Come here and try and hold his head straight, or find me a board, or something, so I can get some leverage."

Alex looked around. The only thing she saw was a broken tree limb that their car had hit on the way down and it was too big. She tried to get her head back in the car and her hands under Nick's head. It didn't work.

She prayed another short prayer, "Please, Lord, I know I have no right to ask. If You can just help us out of this and give us supernatural strength and a way to escape…Amen."

"John, I have to get back in," called Alex. "That way, I can hold his head up while you pull him out."

John moved to the side and let her climb back in. Then, he pulled Nick toward the door, as slowly as he dared. Alex held his head and lifted it as gently as she could. They finally got him out the door and placed him a safe distance from the car. Alex tried to cover him up with her light jacket. She was freezing and she knew Nick was cold. They had not been prepared for this weather.

John yelled at Alex and told her he needed her help again. It was time to get Mac out of the car.

"John, the car is caved in on the left-hand side. I don't see how we are going to get him out."

"I'm not leaving him," he said, determined. You smell that gasoline? This car could blow up any minute. We have to get back up the hill and behind those rocks. With Nick unconscious, we're going to have to pull him and Mac up there."

Alex turned back to Nick. He was still unconscious but she knew John Cabe made sense. She looked at John and asked him what they needed to do first.

"If we're lucky, someone in those other cars up there has contacted police. They may be sending an ambulance or a helicopter. Until then, we have to survive. Let's try and get Mac out. I'll cut away his airbag and see if I can move him."

"John, the car's teetering on the edge of that rock, in the front. Is there any way that we can level it?"

"Maybe a tree limb wedged under the left wheel could help hold it up for a while."

They moved the limb that Alex had seen earlier and wedged it beneath the car and the ledge below. They put several large rocks on the end of the limb to try and hold it down.

"There, that'll help for a little while. Alex, I'm going to climb inside and see if there's anyway to get Mac out."

"Be careful," she said.

John saw that Mac was wedged in tight. He tried to cut away the airbag and then tried to move the steering wheel up. Mac wasn't moving and there was blood everywhere. John felt his pulse and found a weak, irregular beat.

"Come on, old man," he said, "We can't lose you now."

He saw Mac's arm. It was bleeding badly. He suspected a vein or an artery might have been cut. He tore off the sleeve of Mac's shirt and saw the large, open wound. It was terrible.

John removed his belt and tied it as tight as he could between the elbow and shoulder. He knew it would have to be loosened every few minutes. He had to get Mac out, or stay with him in the car—and the smell of gasoline was getting stronger by the minute.

John Cabe took hold of Mac's body and pulled as hard as he could. The car trembled. John thought for a minute that they were going right over the cliff but it stopped creaking and he had managed to move Mac over into the right side. He called out.

"Alex, help us!"

"I'm right here, Johnny. Tell me what to do."

Alex knew that her adrenaline had kicked in and she and John pulled on Mac until they miraculously had freed him from the wreckage. Panting from the strain, they both lay down alongside him, on the hard, cold ground.

"Thank you, Lord," Alex gasped.

John lay over Mac's body and released the belt, then tightened it again. He watched while Alex covered Nick, trying to warm him with her body heat. At that moment, the car teetered, groaned and fell over the cliff. It exploded into a million pieces as it dove down into the ravine below.

Alex and John both gasped at the same time. They couldn't believe how close they had been to still being in the car when it exploded. Then, miraculously, they heard a siren from the road above.

"Police!" yelled John. "We have to let them know we didn't go over with the car. Wave, Alex, wave!"

Police saw the smoke from the car below and radioed for a helicopter. They didn't see the four reported crash victims but they weren't taking any chances. If there were any survivors, they'd find them. It was almost an hour later when the helicopter pilot saw the four people on the cliff below.

The copter couldn't land but they could send down a line. Two of the survivors looked like they were able to stand but there were two bodies on the ground that appeared lifeless to the Emergency Unit. The pilot called down to the group with a horn.

"We're going to send down a stretcher in a basket gurney. Can you two get the worst guy into it?"

He watched as John and Alex waved back to him.

"I'll send down my partner," he shouted. He can help one of you into the copter. We'll have to come back for the other two but I'm sending down blankets and medical supplies. Okay?"

John waved a sign to them and the helicopter lowered the basket full of supplies and blankets. John turned to Alex. He knew she would be afraid to be left but they both knew the medics had to take Mac and Nick first. Alex made it easy for him.

"I think Mac needs to go in the basket. Then, they can lift Nicholas into the cockpit with them. You and I can stay here and wait."

John Cabe knew that she was frightened. He wished they could take her too. He hugged her and together they got Mac into the basket. Mac was raised, slowly, into the medical helicopter. An emergency technician was then sent down. He had to tie Nicholas to him. Then, he gave a sign to be lifted back up. He called to them, as he put Nick into the helicopter.

"We'll be back soon."

The helicopter flew off to the nearest hospital. Alex and John wrapped up in blankets and waited for their return. John Cabe pulled Alex next to him. She was in shock, he suspected. This last act from Quentin was nothing but attempted murder. They were out of their league. He decided, in addition to local police, he would contact Scotland Yard, as soon as he was able to get to a phone.

Alex put her head on his shoulder and John was glad he had been left with her. She could no longer hold back her tears. John held her, feeling her tremble from the cold. He wrapped another blanket around her and they waited. It was about an hour before they heard the sound of the helicopter returning. They were finally on their way to the hospital.

Chapter Ten

Alex and John were taken into the hospital's emergency room. Both of them were suffering from hypothermia, in addition to numerous cuts and bruises. They had been wrapped in an insulated material to warm them.

Their cuts and abrasions were treated, as both Alex and John tried to remember what had happened. John had a bad cut on his head. He was x-rayed first and then a doctor took an x-ray of Alexandra's arm. It was badly sprained, if not fractured, and they set it in a balloon cast, as a precaution.

The doctor told them Mr. Timmons was still in surgery. It was serious for Mac. He then told them Nick had a concussion and had not yet awakened. He said that overall, his other wounds were minor. He had a sprained ankle and lots of cuts…no internal bleeding, which was good…and he was also suffering from mild hypothermia.

"The concussion sounds serious," Alex replied. "When can we see him?"

"After we check you out, young lady. You've got quite a few cuts yourself and we need to see about that arm. It looks like it may just be a sprain but there was a bad cut and I don't want to take any chances. We'll know more when your x-rays come back."

"You do need to be checked out, Alex," John said. He looked terrible but he worried about the others. He was determined to stay with Alex, until they could see Nick.

"Mr. Cabe, we really need to treat you, too."

"I'm fine. What about Mac? You said he was in surgery."

"I don't know if he's going to make it or not. I have to be honest with you. He lost a lot of blood. We'll know more in the morning, if he makes it through tonight."

Alex said another prayer, thankful that they were still alive. She prayed that Mac would make it and that Nicholas would wake up. She thanked God for John Cabe. None of them would have made it without him. He had rescued them.

After Alex and John were treated and given some medication for pain,

John took Alexandra's hand. He had a bandage on his head and looked a little worse for the wear but he smiled at her.

"Hey, kid…you did good back there. You need to rest. I guess now, we wait."

Alex broke into tears again and John pulled her to him. He wasn't sure where to begin to comfort her. He knew that she was still in shock. He handed her a tissue and assured her that Nick and Mac would be fine. He could usually handle girls but he wasn't sure what to say to Alex.

The doctors finally cleared both Alex and John from the E.R. and checked them into the hospital. They said they wanted them to stay a night or two for observation until their test results were back. They were admitted to separate rooms, close to each other and on the same floor.

Alex had pleaded with her doctor to see Nicholas from the time they brought her in. Her doctor could see that she wasn't going to rest unless he agreed, so he told her that she could go in to see Mr. Stewart if she only stayed a short while—and if she would rest! She promised the doctor that she would rest, if she could only see Nick.

A nurse finally wheeled Alex to the room where Nicholas was sleeping. When she entered, she saw that he was hooked up to an I.V. and a heart monitor. He had other tubes that seemed to be going everywhere. Alex didn't know what they were for but she knew Nick's condition was more serious than the doctor had let on. His face was bruised and he had a black eye. His leg was either sprained or fractured and his x-rays had not yet been returned. He looked so pale to her!

Alex went over to him. This man had given up everything for her and he was hurt…so hurt. She just wanted him to wake up so she could tell him how much she loved him. She sat in her wheelchair, beside his bed and took his hand.

"Nicholas?"

When he didn't respond, Alex got up, holding onto the bed for support. She bent over his face and whispered that she loved him. She stayed there for what seemed ages but it was only a few minutes.

"Lord, you know this good man. Please be with him. His child needs him, Father. I need him."

When she said this prayer, Alex felt a warmth and a peace that she could not explain. She looked back down at Nick.

Nicholas Stewart's eyes fluttered and as he struggled to wake up, he felt pain. His vision was blurry and the name, *Alexandra,* ran through his mind. He was spinning through a dense fog but he heard someone's voice.

"Nicholas, you have to wake up now. It's time."

It was an unknown voice but it commanded he listen and obey.

"Alexandra…Alex…where are you?"

Alex jumped. He was speaking!

"Right here, darling. I'm right here." Alex squeezed his hand.

The light in the room was so bright. Nick's eyes couldn't focus but he saw a woman sitting near him.

"You have to be an angel," he whispered.

"Oh, Nick, try and wake up. Come back to me, Nicholas. I love you."

Tears were cascading down her face. Alex kissed his forehead and held on tight to his hand. He was woozy but he had spoken. She laid her face, close to his. The wetness of her tears mingled with bruises and bandages.

"Alex?"

Nick Stewart began to come out of a very deep sleep.

"Yes, darling. It's Alex. I'm here."

Nick Stewart tried to focus.

"Nick, we're in a hospital. You're going to be all right. Do you remember anything? It was so close. We were in a car and we crashed."

"Crash?" Nick remembered being in the car. "Quentin…I remember Quentin. Alex, are you all right?"

Nick remembered hitting a wall with the car. He was trying to hold onto Alex.

"I'm fine, Nick. I'm fine now that you're awake."

"You're so beautiful."

He reached for her face with his hand and grimaced with pain, as he tried to move his arm.

"Don't try and move, darling."

"How are John and Mac?" he asked.

"John's okay. He should be here any minute to see you. He's in a room down the hall from mine. Nick, he was wonderful. He got all of us out, before the car exploded."

"The car…exploded? And Mac? What about Mac?"

Alex didn't want to tell him but knew he had to know. She would rather have him find out from her, than from a stranger.

"Mac was in surgery but he's in the Intensive Care Unit. They moved him there, after surgery. Nick, it's serious."

Nick wanted to see Mac…he struggled to get up but managed to tangle some of his medical tubing. It held him like a vice.

NICHOLAS AND ALEXANDRA: SOUL MATES

"I want to see him."

"Nick, they won't let you get up and they won't let anyone see him until morning. You have to rest."

He didn't have to be told again. As he tried to raise his head, he became dizzy. He couldn't see anything. His head felt like a truck had driven right through it. He had to lie back down. He didn't have a choice. Alex tried to get him to calm down. She told him to rest.

Nick's doctor came in to tell Alex it was time for her to leave. He was pleased that Nick was awake but saw that he was becoming very anxious and upset.

"I'll give him a shot to help him relax and sleep."

Alex resisted leaving at first but she saw that Nick had calmed down and was drifting off to sleep again.

"Ms. Andrews, you need to rest. He's going to sleep through the night. I gave him some strong pain medication. It should knock him out for hours."

Alexandra kissed Nick's hand and was returned to her room.

John Cabe had already given a report to the local police about the incident and gave them a description of the man known as Quentin. When he finished, he started down the hall to see Alexandra. She told him about Nick...that Nick was resting. John told her that he spoke to police and they wanted a statement from her in the morning.

Alex looked so very tired. John gave her a hug and put her to bed. He tucked her in, as he would have a child and reassured her that he'd be right down the hall if she needed him.

"Thank you, John. Thank you for everything."

Alexandra was feeling her own pain. After the nurse came in and gave her something for it, she drifted off to sleep, with John watching over her.

The next morning, the sun came streaming through the window of Alex's hospital room. For an instant, she forgot everything about the day before. Then, the pain in her elbow brought it all thundering back to her.

She got up, depending on her one good arm to lift her. She was walking unsteadily but managed to get to bathroom. She wanted to take a shower, knowing it would help. As she called for a nurse to help her, she got into the shower and let the warm water run over her bruised body. It felt better than any pain medication.

By the time she got out, she remembered she had no clothes. Hers were ruined and the Hospital had taken them last night. She grabbed for a hospital gown and robe.

"We'll all need new clothes." She would ask John if he could order them some over the phone…but where were the credit cards? She lost her purse and Nick's cards had been left or destroyed. Surely, someone would have a charge account somewhere.

She collapsed on her bed, exhausted.

Such foolish things to think about, Lord. Thank You that we're all alive. Thank You so much, God.

A nurse brought in her breakfast tray. Following right behind her was a tall, lean man. He was dressed in a brown tweed suit and his graying hair accented what had once been thick, wavy and dark brown. He appeared to be someone the hospital staff knew.

"Miss Andrews? I'm sorry to interrupt breakfast. I'm Inspector Avery. I'm with the New Scotland Yard."

So, John had contacted Scotland Yard and not just local police.

"Yes, my friend told me someone would be here. May I see some I.D.?"

Inspector Daniel Avery showed her his identification. He looked at the young woman with some curiosity. She was pretty. Her blond hair was still wet from a shower. She had some cuts, along with some black and blue marks on her face and her arm was wrapped in a sling but she still managed to look appealing in the large terry robe that was at least three sizes too large for her.

"Can you tell me what happened? Let's have some tea together and you can go from the very beginning."

The inspector proved to be a gentleman. He poured both of them tea and offered Alex some sugar and lemon.

"Don't leave out anything. All right?"

Alex nibbled on a piece of toast and sipped the tea, as she told the inspector everything. She was glad to finally get this nightmare out in the open and talk to police. She said she didn't know where the map or the picture was. She told the lieutenant that they were probably burned up in the car.

Inspector Avery told Alex that he needed to speak to Nick Stewart but the doctor wouldn't allow it. He said that talking to Mr. Timmons was out of the question, too.

"Both of them are very ill, Inspector."

Alex found herself very protective of Nick and Mac. She was glad that Scotland Yard hadn't had a chance to speak to Nick yet. She didn't know how he would feel about giving up his investigation. She was concerned about that.

NICHOLAS AND ALEXANDRA: SOUL MATES

After Alex finished her story, she told the Inspector she would get in touch with him if she remembered anything else. She excused herself. Inspector Avery knew she was still in pain. He gave her his card and left.

Alexandra just wanted to see Nick and she wanted to know how Mac was. She was wheeled to the nurses' station, where she asked about Mac. Alex knew that Nick would want to know.

It seemed that John Cabe beat her to the front desk. He had showered and shaved and looking better. He was also flirting with a pretty young nurse.

"Hey, beautiful," he greeted Alex with a hug, "how are you feeling this morning?"

"I'm better, very sore. John, you look as if you're a lot better. Have you heard any news about Mac, yet?"

"Same as you. He made it through surgery. But, he's still in Intensive Care Unit. He still can't have any visitors. Doc said it's touch-and-go for the next twenty-four hours. I was just waiting for the doctor to get out of Nick's room so I could stop in and see how he is doing. I know you're on the way. Do you mind if I tag along?"

"No, I know you haven't seen him, yet. I wondered how we were going to tell him about Inspector Avery."

John looked away. He knew that the decision he made might upset Nick. He would have talked to Nick about it first, if the situation hadn't been so critical. He was a little worried, too.

"I know," he said. "Maybe we can wait and see how he is first."

"My thoughts exactly, John. But, we can't wait too long. Inspector Avery wants to talk to him. By the way, Avery asked me about the picture and map. I told him I had no clue where they are. They may have ended up in ashes. Do you remember?"

"No, last time I saw them was on the train."

They walked to Nick's room and knocked. The doctor was just getting ready to leave. He walked over to Alex and told her that she would be pleased at how much better Mr. Stewart was this morning. Both John and Alex entered. Alex saw that Nicholas had been up, at least to shower and shave. He did look better. He had color in his cheeks and a smile on his face when he saw Alexandra and John.

"Hey, John, did I hear you were my hero?"

John hugged Nick and told him how good it was to see him.

"You give me too much credit. I could never have pulled you and Mac out without Alex."

101

"Hi, beautiful," Nick said, looking at her like he did the first time he saw her.

"Do you two read from the same script?" asked Alex.

Nick looked puzzled as Alex bent over and kissed him.

"John just called me by the same nickname," she explained. "I'm glad you look better. How do you feel?"

She sat on the side of the bed and gave him the breakfast tray that was on a side table.

"Here. Keep up your strength."

Nick sipped on the English tea and ate a piece of toast while John and Alex told him about Mac. Then, Alex looked at John and John nodded. She decided it was time to let Nick know about Scotland Yard being contacted.

When he heard, Nick didn't react at all. He just nodded. He thanked John and he said something about how he would have done the same thing.

"Quentin has to be stopped!" he said.

He was very worried about Mac.

"Can I see him?"

"You can ask the doctor. I don't think they're letting anyone in but you're like a son to him. Maybe they'd let you sit with him."

Alex buzzed for the nurse. She asked her if Nick could speak to Mac's physician. The nurse was young and pretty and she told them she was a fan of Nicholas Stewart. She also told them she would find Mac's doctor right away. If anything could be done, she'd make sure to let Nick and Alex know.

Alex thanked her but the nurse was looking at Nicholas. He grinned that famous grin. Although he was bruised and had a black eye, Alex could see her melt right then and there. As the nurse left, Alex rolled her eyes at Nick.

"Aah, the famous Nick Stewart charm," she smiled.

"You're not jealous, are you?"

He smiled at her and once again, she too melted. She loved him so much. John Cabe looked down at them both and grinned.

"Gee, I'd tell you two to get a room but you already have two!"

They all laughed as Nick pulled Alex to him and kissed her cheek.

"By the way, Nick, Inspector Avery asked about the map and where it might be. Do you know if it was in the car when it went over the cliff?"

"I think it's still in my jacket. My jacket's hanging in the closet over there. Look and see if the envelope is still there."

John walked over to the closet and pulled out the ripped jacket. In the pocket, he found the map and the picture.

"Good, it's still there. I don't want the police, not even Scotland Yard to have it yet," said Nick.

"You're still planning on going on to the airstrip, aren't you?" asked John. He was a little shocked as he glanced over at Alex.

"Nick, no!" exclaimed Alex. "You're not well enough. You don't know who is still waiting for us out there."

"Look, babe, I thought about it. I may be the only one that knows what to look for. I don't plan to drive. I was hoping to take a helicopter and have plenty of company with me. I'm not going until they release the three of us."

"Why not Scotland Yard, then?"

Nick couldn't explain. John thought he was being unreasonable. Alex told him she would "never speak to him again" if he did this but he knew she didn't mean it. He saw, however, that they were very worried for him. He couldn't put them through this and he gave in.

"Okay, Scotland Yard can know but I insist going with this Inspector Avery to the site."

"Only if we go, too," chimed in Alex and John at the same time.

This broke the tension in the room. All three of them grinned and grabbed each other's hands.

"All for one...and one for all!" said John.

"I'm going to ICU. Do we all want to go there?" asked Nick.

"Yes," the other two answered at the same time.

The three of them started down the hall, with Alex and John on either side of Nick. John helped Nick walk on the crutches the nurse had provided. They got to ICU and were stopped by another nurse.

"I'm sorry but, you can't come in here without a doctor's permit," she said.

Then, she recognized Nick Stewart and apologized.

"I guess you're pretty worried about your friend."

"Can I just go in and sit with him?"

The nurse phoned Mac's doctor and got permission for one person to see Mac. The nurse said they could only stay five minutes and she cautioned that they could speak to him but not to expect an answer. Alex and John watched, as Nick limped on the crutches, into Mac's room. When the five minutes were up, he came out. He had tears in his eyes.

"I didn't know he was that bad."

"Nick, he's going to be all right. It's going to take time. I know how much you love him. He loves you too and that's what will make him fight to get back to us."

Alex took Nick's hand and held it to her lips. He was trying to conceal the tears. Her heart was breaking for him. She wanted to wrap her arms around him.

"Shhh…I know, I know…."

It was too much for John. His own eyes were wet, just watching Nick. He had to turn away. Alex went with Nicholas back to his room, motioning John to wait for her outside.

"Let's get you back to bed," she said to him.

Alex pulled back the covers and Nick climbed back in his bed.

"I'm sorry. It was such a shock seeing him like that. God, he just can't die, Alex. He can't."

"He's not going to die. We have to believe that. We have to pray he'll be well and strong again. I know God answered my prayer when we were stuck on that cliff and he hears us now. Nick, you have to realize that you've been in a trauma, yourself. We all have. We can't deal with all of this without each other, or without God. You're on some pretty strong pain pills and our emotions are raw right now. Give yourself a break and get some rest. We're not going anywhere today."

"I know. I am tired. I love you, Alex. I trust you."

She hadn't thought about his trust before. She had been so selfish, thinking only about her own issues.

"I trust you too, Nick, and I love you very much. Now, I'm going to go back to my room and get some rest, too. Will you be all right?"

"Sure, babe," he promised. "I'll come see you in a couple of hours. We can have, what the hospital calls lunch, together."

"It's a date!"

Alex kissed him and went back to her room, where John was waiting for her.

"How is he?"

"He will be fine. We all will be fine. John, you and I both need to get some rest. It's up to us to keep this company on its toes. And, we can't do that unless we're good, right?"

"Right, beautiful. I promise to lie down and take a nap if you'll do the same."

"I promise. Now, get out of here and go get some rest."

John grinned at her and went down the hall to his room. Alex was suddenly exhausted. She didn't know that she was so tired. She ached everywhere and her arm was throbbing.

She buzzed for the nurse and asked for some more pain medication. She was able to stand up for an instant, just long enough to get back into bed. The nurse returned a little later and gave her some capsules. Alex raised the head of her bed and was almost asleep before her head hit the coolness of the feather pillow.

Chapter Eleven

Alex woke up to a room filled with flowers. A small table covered with a cloth had been rolled into her room. It held a dinner for two and candles flickered in the center of table, beside a small bouquet of yellow roses.

"No hospital food here!" she exclaimed.

Where was Nicholas? He just had to be in charge of this.

She heard a soft knock, as Nick entered her room and said, "Wow!"

"Nick, how did you manage this?"

"I hate to disappoint you, but I had nothing to do with this. My bet's on John. He's a real romantic at heart."

"John Cabe—what a sweet man."

John peeked his head in the room just then and told them to enjoy. He disappeared before Alex could even whisper a thank-you. Nick went over to her and kissed her. She flinched slightly when his arm went around her waist.

"Does that hurt, Alex?"

"Just a little sore. I have a couple of cracked ribs. Please don't stop. It's fine."

He sat on her bed with her, moved his arms so she was comfortable and just held her, his head resting on top of hers. He kissed her again, brushing the bruises on her face with his lips, kissing each one, as if hoping to make them well.

"Alex, I'm so sorry you were hurt. I promised to keep you safe and look what happened."

"Don't you dare blame yourself. There's no way in the world you could have prevented this. None of us could have."

Alex moved slowly from the bed over to the table, where she bent down and gently touched the flowers.

"These are lovely."

"Yes. John outdid himself."

Nick limped over to where she stood, picked up the dinner cover and smiled.

"Guess what it is, Alex?"

"What?"

"Spaghetti, just like Mama Rita's."

Nicholas pulled over a chair and helped Alex into it. Then, he sat across from her, his face serious—no great grin, just those turquoise-blue eyes peering into Alex's soul again. He took her hands and told her how much he loved her. She squeezed his hand and then poured each of them a glass of juice.

"I'm sure the doctor would approve. A little of this shouldn't be too bad for us."

"Alex, if we weren't both so sore and stiff, I'd take you in my arms again, right here in the hospital room but I'm thinking we better wait."

Nick was better. She felt his need to be close. They had almost lost each other. She wished she could thank John Cabe for this private time.

She dreaded bringing up the subject but she asked Nick if Scotland Yard had contacted him. He said they hadn't, not yet.

Nick told her he had slept well, especially after seeing her. After lunch, they agreed that both of them needed to go and see how Mac was. Alex silently hoped that Mac was better, for Nick's sake as much as Mac's.

They finished their lunch and Alex let Nick use her wheelchair, while she managed walking behind him, holding onto the chair. They went back to the ICU where John Cabe was waiting for them.

He stopped them at the entrance and told them Mac's vitals were better and that he had been able to go in for a minute. John told them that Mac was getting his color back but he was still unconscious.

Nick squeezed Alex's hand and left her with John, while he went in to sit with Mac for a while.

"I hope he's okay this time. I hate to see him that broken up," she whispered to John.

"You have to understand, Alex. This is a father-son relationship. Mac is not just a friend to Nicholas. If he loses him, it will be heart breaking for him. I'm glad you're here for him."

When Nicholas came out of ICU, he was sober but he managed a smile for both of them.

"He does look a little better. I wish he'd wake up."

"He will, Nick. It's probably just as well right now. He doesn't feel the pain."

As they were talking about Mac, Inspector Daniel Avery got off the elevator.

He joined them and introduced himself to Nick and then he and Nick went back to Nick's room, leaving Alexandra alone with John.

"Thank you for the flowers and the surprise lunch, John Cabe."

Alex gave him a kiss on the cheek and told him there was some spaghetti left, if he was interested.

"You bet. Come on."

John Cabe and Alexandra had become best friends when they were in that crash. They were connected before but this brought them closer together than ever. It was good to have a male friend. Alex didn't have many of those. Before, she had no respect for many of the male species. Now, she couldn't imagine her life without these three men—Nicholas, her soul mate—John Cabe, her friend—and Mac, now a father figure for her too.

Nicholas Stewart told the inspector all that he knew and disclosed that he still had the map and picture. He asked the inspector to make copies. He said he knew where the map pointed and he asked if he could accompany Scotland Yard there. Inspector Avery agreed to allow it. The inspector told him that he would find Quentin Smith, or whatever his name was, in his files.

"We'll get him, Mr. Stewart."

"I hope so. He's caused a lot of pain, although, he wasn't alone."

"We'll find out what group he's with. There is one thing, however. I want you and Miss Andrews to relocate to a safe house for a little while, when you get out of here. It will be safer for both of you."

"What about John and Mac?"

"Mr. Cabe refused to go to a house but he agreed to have us shadow him at a hotel that we picked out. We already have Mr. Timmons' room under surveillance. Can you make arrangements with your studio in the States to drop out of sight for a few days?"

"If it means that Alex will be safe, I'll do anything. But, do we still get to fly to the airstrip?"

"As soon as you're both released, we'll make arrangements to fly there and then get you to the safe house."

Nick didn't like it but he agreed to it.

"You're looking a little pale, Mr. Stewart. You get some rest. You'll be hearing from me, later. Good luck."

Nick sat down on the edge of the bed. He would have to wait and that was always hard for him. No need to leave a message for the movie studio yet. They thought he was on vacation. *Some vacation, huh?*

Three days later, the three of them were released from the hospital. Mac had awakened but was not going to be released for some time. Nick made arrangements for a specialist to see him and before checking out, he told Mac how he felt about him. This was the first time Nicholas had spoken the words. Mac told Nicholas that if he had a son, he would be like Nick.

Mac also spoke to John and to Alex.

"Alex, John, thank you for getting me out of there. Alexandra, take care of both my boys."

She promised him she would care for John and Nick until Mac could do it himself. Somehow, she loved this old man very much. It would be difficult to leave him, even for a few days. But, Nick told her what Scotland Yard was going to demand from them.

"As soon as Mac is better, we'll fly him home to California. The sun and the beaches will be better than any doctors," Nick said.

As they said good-bye, everyone's eyes were moist. Mac knew it might be a long time before he was out of the woods, although John promised to check on him daily and give him any report he had. That seemed to satisfy Mac.

John, Nick and Alex said their good-byes too. John was on his way to the hotel and Nick and Alex were on their way to an airstrip near Cambridge, along with the pilot and the inspector.

Chapter Twelve

The helicopter sailed over the countryside. Alex looked at the sunny day outside and felt better than she had in a long time. The country was really beautiful. She was glad to get out of the hospital; although being in a safe house alone would be awful, she would be with Nicholas and that satisfied her. But first, they had to check out the airstrip. Nick was counting on finding something there. She hoped he was right.

When they arrived near Cambridge, the helicopter circled the old English army camp and the airstrips surrounding it.

"There it is. Set the copter down over there."

The pilot followed the inspector's orders and the helicopter landed right in the center of the airstrip. Nick and Alex were assisted out of the plane. Nick was walking by himself, with a slight limp, but Alex could walk now and her arm was much better. It was still wrapped up but she could use it again.

Nick walked to the end of the strip. Grass had grown between the broken concrete.

"This is where our unit stood to have a picture made. I remember that. We were sent here to help clear some of the strips and ready them, in case they needed to use them for the war in Iraq."

He looked at the grounds near the place where the picture was taken. It was some time back. He stood here with Ed Percy and the man he believed to be Aaron White. The arrow on the map that he had since memorized pointed to something just beyond this place.

What was it he was looking for? Nick questioned if he could identify anything, even if he found it. Then, he saw it—on the broken concrete, straight ahead. Someone had scratched out a message.

Nick leaned over to read it. "Aaron is Quinton!…going to blow up…chemicals…world…have to STOP him!"

Then, there were some letters scratched out that he couldn't read and finally, the words…"the POINT."

Nick called Alex and the inspector over. He wasn't sure what it was that Quentin was going to blow up but Ed Percy made it clear it was something that had to be stopped. Nick wondered how long it took him to scratch these words into the rocks. He wondered what the words were that he couldn't read. The three of them stood there, trying to decipher the message.

"Do you think it might mean West Point?" Alex asked.

"I don't know. Why wouldn't he say that instead of just the point?"

"Well, we know a little more about Quentin. He belongs to a group that worked outside the CIA and they worked both sides of the fence, so to speak. Their latest plot involved the bombing of a missionary group they didn't like. Real nice fellows.... they call themselves *The Organization*," said Avery.

The name was out. John had been right. Nick and Alex finally knew who was trying to kill them.

"You have to find them. We don't know when this is to happen or for certain, where it is going to happen. Can you put West Point on alert, just in case?" asked Nick.

"We'll do that. Right now, we have to get the two of you to a safe place and give The Yard a chance to work."

The three of them returned to the helicopter and soon they landed in a field outside a country cottage—somewhere in England.

Chapter Thirteen

"You'll find everything you need inside the house but, if you don't, this is Lt. David Emory and Lt. Joshua Green."

The two Scotland Yard agents that awaited them nodded to Nick and Alexandra.

"They'll be right outside your door twenty-four hours a day. One of them can run errands if you need anything. Also, there's a cell phone for your use. If you have any kind of emergency and need to get hold of the Yard, just hit the number four on the phone."

Avery showed both of them inside. The cottage was neatly furnished and well stocked, with food and clothing for both of them. It had a large living area, kitchen and two bedrooms. David Emory and Joshua Green were outside the house when Inspector Avery left. Nick and Alex stood facing each other in the living room, as the front door was closed.

"We're finally alone," Alex said.

She was slightly anxious about this new living arrangement but she rushed over to Nicholas. He placed his arms around her, slightly leaning against her.

"I guess we better lock the front door and tell the two guys we don't want to be disturbed for awhile."

"You think? I'm a little nervous, Nick. I'm so glad to be here with you but…"

The sentence went unspoken, as he smiled down at her.

"Don't worry, Alex. I remember. We wait, right?"

Alex smiled up at him and knew she could trust him. While he went to the door, Alex went in to look at the clothing in her bedroom. Surprisingly, they were in her size and most were very stylish. It was good to have some new, clean clothes, finally.

Nick told the men that they needed to rest and they were going to lock the door. David and Joshua nodded, never moving from their station outside the cottage.

Nick locked the door and went to find Alex. She was just coming out of her bedroom. She had changed clothes and was wearing a t-shirt and jeans. She never looked more beautiful to him.

She walked to him. Their bruises from the crash hadn't quite faded but they were too much in love to notice, as they held onto each other.

"It would be so easy to forget our commitment to each other right now," he said.

"I know. For me too…but we made a decision," she whispered.

"I love you so much, Alex."

"It doesn't mean I don't feel the same. I love you too, Nicholas." Her eyes were moist.

"Alex, please don't cry. I never wanted to make you cry."

He gathered her into his arms more closely. Just holding her made him feel better, as he stroked her hair and kissed the top of her head. He ached for her more than life itself and he held her so tightly that she throbbed with pain from the cuts and bruises. But, that didn't matter.

When they reluctantly released each other, Alex got their medication and put Nick's into his hand. She went into the kitchen and poured two glasses of water. He watched her every move. There was no other woman that ever compared to her. He thought of her bravery and her kindness. When she brought him his water, he motioned for her to sit down with him.

"It's going to be difficult, being here together, especially at night," he told her.

"What can we do to make it easier?" she asked him.

"Pray for strength to abstain—and concentrate on why we're here. We can also talk about us—our weaknesses, our faith. I think it would help."

Alex agreed. They couldn't be in the same room together without wanting physical contact but here they were. Surely, God would give them strength to resist, until He joined them together.

They began talking, for hours. They told each other about their family history, their beliefs, why they believed what they did and why it was important to both of them to wait.

Nick told Alex that he had not taken another woman to bed since Meg. He didn't believe in that, unless it was a life long commitment. But, he also said that he was finding it difficult not to make love to her. It had been such a long time.

Alexandra told him she was sure the Lord wouldn't mind them kissing or holding each other. Of course, that very action taunted them into wanting more. They had to be careful because both of them knew how dangerous it was—their being alone, together.

The next day, after a long restless night for both of them, Nick had a plan—an idea of how he could exist in the same house with Alexandra and not go crazy! He opened the front door and asked Joshua if he could go and pick up something for him. He had ordered a surprise for Alex earlier this week from his hospital phone. It was time she received it.

Nick called to Alex to see if there was anything that she needed and she asked if Joshua could pick up some shampoo. After Joshua told David he was leaving, Nick closed the door.

"Hey, Alex, what are you doing in there?"

Alex had been in the bathroom much longer than usual and he wondered if something might be wrong. When she opened the door, she was wearing a sheet, much like the one in Paris. But, she had pinned it up to resemble an evening gown, draping it in layers in the front. Nick laughed at her. Only Alexandra could lighten things up.

"My lady," he started to say.

"Don't you dare make fun of me. Actually, this took some time to put together. I'm fixing a very special brunch for you. So, stay out of the kitchen for a while, O.K.?"

"You bet. But, just so you know, you look gorgeous in that gown. I mean it."

"Thanks, hon. Why don't you go read the newspaper and I'll bring you a cup of coffee."

She kissed his cheek and went into the kitchen and shut the door.

What else is she up to? She doesn't realize that I have quite a surprise for her. Her special "brunch" will work out just fine. It will keep her busy for a while.

Nicholas had his own plan in the making.

About an hour later, Joshua came back with the shampoo Alex had requested and with the package that Nick had ordered. Nicholas thanked him and went into the bedroom with the items.

He unwrapped his package and looked at the contents. He had done well. Now, for his surprise for Alex! He called to her from the living room.

"Alex?"

"It's almost ready," she answered.

"Okay but I'm getting pretty hungry."

She opened the door and Nick went into the dining area of the large kitchen. Alex had a fire going in the fireplace and something smelled wonderful! The table was set with candles and a bowl of fresh strawberries and cream sat on the sideboard.

She made him sit down as she brought a casserole to the table. It had sausages and eggs, with some type of peppers and onions in it. There were fresh loaves of homemade bread that she had baked. Alex poured their coffee and put the jam and butter on the table. Smiling at him, she finally sat down with him.

"Wow! Everything looks great and it smells wonderful, Alex. How did you do all this? What's the special occasion?"

"I have a wonderful surprise, Nicholas. I heard from Mac's doctor today when I phoned the hospital. He is doing so well, they think he will be out in another week. Isn't that the greatest news?"

"It couldn't be any better," he replied. "I'm so glad to hear that. I really miss him."

"And," Alex continued, "I spoke to John. They're letting him fly here to see us in the morning."

"You just made my day."

She put her napkin in her lap.

"I wanted to do something special for you. I hope you like this."

Nick took a bite of the bread and sighed.

"Wow, that's good. Mama Rita would have hired you if she knew you could bake."

They said grace and both of them ate heartily. Nick told her that it was the best food he had tasted for a while. When they had almost finished, he moved over next to Alex. He picked up one of the strawberries and offered it to her and then thanked her for the brunch. As he put his arm around her, he pulled out his wrapped gift with his other hand.

"This is your surprise, Alexandra," he said.

"Nick, is this what you sent Joshua to pick up?"

"It's something I ordered last week. I had it made just for you. I hope you like it."

Alex fumbled with the ribbon, opened the box lid and found another smaller box inside—a ring box. She looked at Nick, daring not to breathe. He took the smaller box out and opened it for her. Tears were beginning to glisten in her eyes.

"Marry me, Alexandra. You must know how much I love you."

Nick removed the ring from the box and she let him place it on her finger. It was an exquisite diamond set in platinum. Nick had ordered it from a jeweler a few days ago.

"It's beautiful. Oh, Nick, are you sure? Do you really want me?"

"I want you beside me forever. I could get down on one knee, if you want but it would really hurt."

Alex laughed at him, among the tears. "I'd love to marry you, Nicholas Stewart. Oh, darling, please kiss me."

And that is exactly what he did.

The cottage had a small but well-stocked wine cellar. Alex and Nick found it by accident. Lt. Avery never showed them that part of the house. Maybe, he just forgot. Nick went down and picked out a nice bottle of champagne. He brought it back to the kitchen so that he and Alex could invite Josh and David inside to toast this special event.

"Even though I can't drink this, they'll enjoy it."

"We'll really have something to tell John, won't we?"

"And Mac," she replied. "I can't wait."

Nick went to the door and invited David and Joshua inside for a toast. The men wished the couple well and exchanged stories of how they had proposed to their own wives. David said he had two young children and Joshua said that he couldn't wait to see his own wife, Marley. They talked and reminisced for a long time. Nick and Alex enjoyed the company for a change.

They asked if the men had any news of how much longer they might be at the cottage. Both replied they didn't know and hadn't heard anything yet but Avery said that he would be contacting them sometime tomorrow. After a leisurely afternoon, the men went back to their duty stations and Alex and Nick tackled the kitchen cleanup.

"I'll miss this place, Nick."

"I know. It's going to hold some memories for us and we don't even know where it is, actually."

"Well, maybe John can get some idea when he flies in. At least we may find out what town we're near. It has to be close to some place where you can get shampoo and a diamond ring. How did you manage that?"

"I ordered it over the phone from my hospital room. Boy, I'm glad it fits. Josh gave the jeweler the local P.O. number so we know there's a post office somewhere near. It looks great on you, by the way, babe. Are we going to spend this entire evening in the kitchen, Miss Andrews, or can I speak to you in the living room?" His grin lit up the room.

Alex pulled his face to hers, kissed him and left the last of the dishes in the sink. She walked with Nicholas into the living room, in front of the fire they just built. He had turned on some music and they sat there, listening to the soft sounds. Alex fell asleep later with her head in his lap. She looked like an angel to him. He picked her up and put her to bed, then went back into his room. Soon, he wouldn't have to leave her. Soon, she would be his wife.

Something strange, a sound like a loud pop, woke Nick up the next morning. He heard the noise and thought it might be John arriving. He went to look out the window and immediately, he knew something was wrong.

David wasn't at the front of the house and Josh's car was gone. He went to the front door and opened it ever so slightly. It was then that he saw David's body lying at the side of the door. Nick became cold with fear, closed and locked the door and then ran into Alexandra's room to awaken her.

Nick shook her and covered her mouth lightly with his hand.

"What is it? What's wrong?"

"Alex, I don't want to frighten you but I think David's dead. He's lying by the side of the stoop. Josh is nowhere in sight. We have to get out of here, now."

Nick took the cell phone and dialed four—the number that Inspector Avery told him about—in case of emergency. He told the Scotland Yard secretary what was going on. She told him that she would get in touch with Inspector Avery right away and she asked Nick to stay on the line while she called Avery from another phone.

Nick had the phone to his ear and was trying to put on some clothes at the same time. Alex grabbed her jeans and a shirt while slipping into her shoes. The inspector was finally on the line.

"Nick, you and Alex get downstairs, now! There's a wine cellar there and there's a panic room behind the wine rack. Do it NOW!" Avery began giving a torrent of instructions to Nick Stewart.

"You have to pull out the bottle of Bordeaux that's on the end of the right side. It unlocks the panic room. Go! I'll stay on the line."

Nick pulled Alex down the stairs to the cellar below. He found the fake wine bottle and when he pulled it out halfway, as Avery instructed, a door behind the rack slid open.

"It's the room, Alexandra. It's a panic room."

Nick shoved Alex inside.

"Okay, Avery, we found it. How do we lock the room?"

"There's a button on the left wall. It lights the room and turns on the air. It will also lock up the room and it will slide the wine bottle back into place. It won't unlock until you push the button once more, from the inside.

"I have you on a monitor right now. I can see you from my office computer. Nick, I have men flying there right now. Did you see anyone at all outside?"

"No, but I think David's dead. I'm not sure about Josh. His car's gone and he's nowhere in sight."

"Nick, look on the shelf in the room. There's a pistol and a rifle and some ammunition up there. Give one of the guns to Alex and you take the other, just in case you need them."

Nick turned around, saw the shelf and found the guns. He took them down off the shelf and loaded them. Alex didn't say anything. She was shivering and cold. She just took the pistol that he handed her.

Avery told Nick that the room was fireproof and that it had its own air system. "It's built for conditions like this," he said.

"What if they try to blow us up? Will it stand up to that?" asked Nick. He knew Quentin was an expert in bombs and explosives.

"Well," replied Avery, "it's supposed to hold up. Let's hope we don't have to find out."

"So, I guess we just wait, huh? Can you see the rest of the house with your monitors?"

"Yes, so far no one is around or in the house. My men should be there in a half hour or less. Wait—I see some movement at the back of the house."

Nick shuddered and he pulled Alex closer to him, as if everything would be all right if they were together.

Avery saw movement near the back door. Then, he saw the man known as Quentin lean down and break in the door.

"He's in the house, Nick."

"Can you see who it is? And where is he?"

"It's our boy, Quentin. He just broke in the back door."

Nick made sure the rifle he had was loaded and ready. If by any chance, Quentin got through the door, he would be ready for him.

"He *will* find this room. You know that, Avery."

"I know but he won't be able to get in."

Quentin was tired of all the waiting. He could not believe Nicholas Stewart and the girl survived that crash. He swore that they must have nine lives!

If they think they're getting away again, they're mistaken.

Quentin went through the back porch and into the kitchen, touching the skillet that still held part of an omelet. He checked his gun and walked into the living room. The other three men he brought were outside. They had taken care of one guard. And, the other one…well, he wouldn't worry about that one.

Quentin didn't see anyone. He looked in all of the closets and walked into the bedroom, where he searched through everything and then headed back into the living room. There wasn't any attic. Then, he saw a door.

He walked to it and slowly turned the knob, listening for any noise they would make. There were stairs, leading down to a cellar. Quentin smiled.

"He's on his way into the cellar, Nick," reported Avery. "Just be quiet down there."

Nick told Alex what was happening and motioned her to the back of the panic room. She was holding the pistol he had given her as if she had never fired one before. He guessed that might be the case but he wanted her to have it for protection anyway. Nick undid the lock position for her and showed her how to hold it. He took her hand and showed her where to point it. She looked up at him and nodded. Nick moved to the front, pointing the rifle at the center of the door.

"What's he doing now?" he whispered to Avery.

"He's just looking around. So far, he hasn't found the panic room. Remember, he can't open it."

This didn't make Nicholas Stewart feel much better. If he and Alex could find the door, so could Quentin. How in the world could he have known they were in this house? And where were Avery's men?

"He's over by the door, Nick. He's found it."

Nick's jaw tightened and his body became tense.

"What's he doing? Tell me everything. I want to know exactly where he is, center, right or middle!"

"He's feeling the crack around the opening of the door. Now, he's going to the other side of the cellar and he's bending over to get something out of his coat. It's not a gun. It's some type of…I can't see. He's in the way. He's getting up and moving to your door again. He's putting something on the door. It's a strip of…oh, my God."

"What, what is it?" Nick asked, hearing the urgency in Avery's voice.

Then he knew, without any reply from the inspector.

"It's plastic explosives, isn't it?"

"Sure looks like it."

"If he manages to blow through the door, it'll blow us all to Kingdom Come, won't it?"

Avery didn't answer.

Nick told him, "Okay, Avery. I'm not waiting for him to blow us to smithereens in here. You tell me exactly where he is. When he gets to the side of the door that slides open, I'm going to open it. I'm only going to have a minute of surprise to shoot him. You *have* to let me know when he's standing up on the right side of that door."

"Okay, Nick, if you think that's the only way. But, the explosive may not be able to blow through the door. It's seven inches of solid steel."

"Avery, exactly how many inches has Quentin blown up before? You and I both know he has the stuff to do it. I can't wait, Avery."

"All right, Nick but be careful! He has a gun, as well as the explosive."

"Where is he?" demanded Nick.

Alex had stopped breathing. She knew in a few minutes, someone would die. She wanted to run to Nick and stop him but she stood frozen where she was.

"He's putting the plastic on the bottom of the door," said Avery. "He's on the left-hand side. Now, he's moving to the right. He's standing but he's back over to the left at the top. He's moving to the right side. He's beginning to stick the explosive around that side. He's on the right side, holding the tape at the top and beginning to move it down."

"Now!" yelled Nick.

He pushed the button and the panic room door began to slide open. It surprised Quentin as he watched the door move by itself and he dropped the plastic explosive. He was reaching for his gun when he heard the shot.

Quentin looked down, as he felt something wet in his side. The sight of his own blood seemed to surprise him. He managed to grab his revolver from his coat but Nick was outside now, pointing the rifle directly at his head. Quentin shook his head in disbelief, pointed the revolver at Nick but Nicholas Stewart had already pulled the trigger!

Quentin fell to the floor and his gun fell to one side. Nicholas kicked the gun out of the way. He had hit Quentin in his forehead and blood was everywhere. He felt sick! It wasn't a movie part. He had killed a man!

Then, he remembered...Alexandra. Nick turned around to see her crouching in the back of the room, in tears. He went back inside and pulled her up to him.

"He's dead," Nick said to both Alex and to Avery.

Avery said, "Nick, remember there are two or three more men outside. I can only see one at the moment but if they heard the shot, they'll be inside. Stay ready. Go back inside the panic room and lock the door."

Nick and Alex couldn't seem to move at all. He had just shot a man. Alexandra was saddened that it had to come to this. She prayed for Nick and she prayed for Quentin.

Nick seemed to be in a trance but he managed to tell Avery they'd close the door again. He took Alex with him to the button and pushed it. The door slid shut, hiding Quentin's body from both of them. Nick Stewart had tears in his eyes, as he held the woman he loved. How could she ever forget this?

"Nick, I see a helicopter outside. It must be my men. Wait there until I can see."

Two of Quentin's men were heading from the woodsy area toward the house, when they saw the helicopter. The two men in the helicopter saw them and saw their rifles.

"Those aren't Avery's men," said the pilot. "Something's wrong down there. I see one of the inspector's men out cold…or dead by the front porch. What the…?"

His passenger grabbed a rifle.

"Get me lower," he said to the pilot.

The helicopter was lowered as much as it could be, without being a target. The passenger pointed his rifle at one of the men who was pointing at the helicopter and he fired. One of the gunmen went down.

"Good shot!" the pilot said. "I've got to get in touch with Avery and see what we've got ourselves into."

The pilot got on the radio and contacted Scotland Yard. He got Avery's secretary and told her where they were and what was going on.

"Patch me through to Avery, right now!" he insisted.

Inspector Avery was handling two phones now. He forgot about the other helicopter. He had sent one of his pilots to pick up John Cabe.

"Cabe shot one of them," the pilot reported.

"Good boy!" Avery replied. "If you can get Quentin's men to come out from hiding, that could save Nick and Alex. They're trapped in the cellar, where the panic room is. There are two other gunmen still out there. I don't see them inside the home, yet. I have my video monitor on and haven't seen movement. By the way, tell Cabe that his boy, Nicholas Stewart, killed Quentin."

"Gee, Inspector, what did we get ourselves into?"

"You just got there before the rest of my men did. I thank God you did. Try and keep anyone else you might see from going inside. By the way, do you see Joshua anywhere?"

"No but David's been shot, it appears. He's at the side of the front porch. Shouldn't we try and get to him?" asked the pilot.

"It's too dangerous," Avery replied. "When my other copter gets there, you can see about him then."

"Well, it looks as if they're here right now."

Cabe and his pilot saw the other helicopter heading to the field in front of the house. Cabe's pilot landed his helicopter close by. John jumped out and ran toward the house. He went inside, found the cellar door and kicked it open.

Nick Stewart heard the commotion above and he had his rifle ready. Avery yelled at Nick over the phone. He told him his men had arrived. So had his friend, John Cabe.

John ran down the stairs when he saw Quentin. He whistled a slow drawn-out sound. Then, Nick opened the door to the panic room and John saw Nick and Alex. He ran into the room and hugged them both. He breathed a sigh of relief until he saw Alex. She was white and she looked as if she might throw up.

"You got the bum, huh, Nick?"

Nick just nodded as John surveyed the scene.

They're both in shock. I need to get them out of here.

"Hey, beautiful," John smiled at Alex, "Why don't you come with me?"

John picked her up and lifted her out the door over Quentin's body and up the stairs, with Nick Stewart right behind him.

"John, we forgot you were coming. Avery said you shot one of the gunmen outside. You helped save our lives, again." Alexandra was rambling.

John felt her tremble. She was cold as ice. John put her down on the sofa and turned to Nick.

"Looks to me like your boyfriend here is the real hero," John replied, as he found a blanket and covered her with it.

"He is," said Alex. "He promised to protect me and he did."

Nick went over to Alex, kneeled before her and held her close, as it all came thundering home to them. They both wept. Alex knew it was horrible for him to have killed a man. She couldn't even imagine. It was horrible for her to watch…but now, maybe it was over. She looked directly into his eyes.

"Nick, I love you. I love you so much." And Alex held onto him.

"I had to do it," he told her. "I had to…I didn't have a choice."

He kissed her eyes, her cheeks and her mouth. She was safe. That was all that mattered to him.

John smiled at them from across the room, thinking that now, they were all going to be all right.

Scotland Yard detectives had combed the woods, the fields and the house. They didn't find the other two gunmen, nor did they find Joshua. David had been killed and when Nick and Alex were told about this for certain, Alex cried softly.

"He had a wife and two children," she said. "We just got acquainted with him and with Joshua. He died for us, Nick. He gave his life for us."

"Where is Josh?" Nick asked.

Joshua's car was gone. That was all they knew.

Avery got off the phones and sighed a huge sigh of relief for Stewart and Miss Andrews. He also knew that he would answer for what had happened. He was missing one agent; another was dead. How did they find the house or know about Nicholas Stewart and Alexandra Andrews? It was going to be messy, explaining all of this.

He went through the papers on his desk and picked up a copy of the map that Nick Stewart had given him. On the back of it were numbers that still didn't make sense.

He hated to tell them but you could bet that Nicholas Stewart and Alex Andrews were not safe. No one was safe until this mystery was solved. The Organization had other hit men...they were planning something big...something that they thought Nicholas Stewart and Alexandra knew. Avery would not be able to rest for a long time.

Alex, Nick and John were on their way back to London in the helicopter that flew John to them. Inspector Avery wanted to see all of them. He told them he was ready to share *all* of his information with them.

Chapter Fourteen

Inspector Daniel Avery sat in his office at Scotland Yard. His chief inspector wanted to see him. That wasn't good news and he knew it. He was awaiting the arrival of Nicholas Stewart, Alexandra Andrews and John Cabe. He had to tell them what he had found.

They might be under the delusion that everyone is safe now that Quentin Smith, was dead. That was far from the truth. True, Quentin was a big fish in the Organization but the plot was a lot bigger than that, at least the part that he knew.

He reached for his pipe and lit it. It was something that calmed him. He leaned back in his chair and closed his eyes for a moment.

Nick, Alex and John had been returned to London and had been debriefed. After they were given changes of clothing and given a bite to eat, they were brought to the inspector's office.

"Nick? I feel like I can call you by your first names. Alexandra? I hope you're all right. Mr. Cabe? I can't tell you how good it is to see you. You all did well."

The three of them nodded to him and sat down across from him. He offered them coffee. It was good to have coffee instead of the tea they had in the hospital. It had just been made and the aroma filled the office. It was hot and strong, exactly what they all needed.

"I want you to know what I have learned. The Organization has attempted these murders and they're not through yet."

Alex trembled. Nick reached across, took her coffee from her and sat it down on the table in front of her. She had been shaky ever since being trapped in the panic room. She moved closer to Nick.

"What is it, Avery?" asked Nick.

"Yeah, what is it that we don't know?" chimed in John Cabe.

"These groups of terrorists are suspected of doing these things...."

Avery went to his computer and turned it on. A movie screen descended from the ceiling and as Avery narrated, pictures of bombings, shootings and other terrorist activities were flashed on the screen. Many of the photos included Quentin.

The pictures appeared to be from all over the world. Nick and Alex recognized some landmarks but others were just grotesque pictures of people being tortured or shot. There was one of a school bombing, with nuns and children trying to run for cover.

"How horrible," gasped Alex.

Lt. Avery turned off the computer and relit his pipe. "Horrible, indeed," he said. "Now, I want you to know that this goes much deeper than your being targets of this outfit. The Organization is planning something really big. We think that it involves blowing up a National target of some type. It's going to be huge! Other groups have told us that these criminals want to kill a lot more people next time, not just hundreds but thousands. They're planning something bigger than what happened on 9-11."

Nick and John glanced at each other and John spoke. "And, we're supposed to know what it is…and we don't know a blasted thing!"

"We've got clues. You may know more than you think. The map told us about Quentin and that the bombing is going to blow up something that will affect the world. Maybe it's something connected with the Point. We've got West Point on alert. So far, they don't know anything. Now, I want you to think about the numbers on the back of the map. Mr. Cabe, I know you were trying to decode those. Any luck?"

John shook his head. Scotland Yard had gotten nowhere either.

"I think one of you may have seen these, somewhere. I want you to think hard about this."

Alex finally spoke up. She told them that she wasn't going to say anything until she remembered for certain but she thought she had seen those numbers or numbers like them somewhere. She couldn't remember where. It had been gnawing at her for days. The inspector's face lit up.

"So, you may have knowledge about them? But, you just don't remember?"

Alex nodded.

Avery asked her if she would submit to hypnosis. He told her it might help to jog her memory. She might remember where she had seen the numbers.

"I'll do anything to help."

The inspector told them that he also had to find them another place to stay. He said he hated to let them go but had no reason to keep them there.

"You can stay with me, at my hotel, tonight," John told them.

Avery said that they would put some extra men on duty to watch over them.

"It has two bedrooms," John said. " Nick and I can stay in one and Alex can take the other. It's a pretty nice apartment."

They all agreed and left with the security men.

It was good to get to a home, even if it wasn't their own. John poured them all coffee when they got to his apartment and Alex went to take a shower. She stood under the warm water a long time, trying to remember where she had seen that set of numbers. Try as she would, it still eluded her.

When she got out of the shower, she put on a robe that John lent her and she went back into the living room with the men.

"Better?" Nick asked her.

"Yes, dear, and I think you need to do the same thing. Go take a hot shower and try and relax."

"It does sound good." Nick yawned, kissed her and headed for the shower.

Alex took another sip of her coffee. She was feeling drowsy despite the caffeine. She asked John if he could think of anything that might help her remember.

John told her he thought that the hypnosis was a good idea and that it might be the thing to jog her memory. Other than that, he couldn't think of a thing. He told her she looked tired—and that's when he noticed her ring.

"Hey, isn't that new?" he exclaimed.

"Oh, John. We were going to surprise you with the news. I forgot all about it. Nick and I are engaged. Isn't it wonderful?"

"It is, Alex. No one deserves better than you and Nick. I know he loves you, Alexandra."

"And, I love him. We haven't had a chance to tell Mac yet. We were going to call him from the cottage but…"

"Well, we can call him right now, as soon as Nick gets out of the shower."John put on another pot of coffee and poured all of them another cup.

"This calls for a celebration! What say we order a pizza?"

Alex laughed at him. She was suddenly awake and hungry for pizza. It sounded good.

"Order it," she said, "We'll surprise Nick."

"One supreme pizza coming up!"

John went to the door and told the security man what they needed. The agent said he would take care of it. It reminded Alexandra of David and Josh.

Where could Joshua be? She hoped he wasn't dead but that was probably what had happened to him.

When Nick came out of the shower looking refreshed, Alex told him she had told John about their engagement. John went over and hugged Nick.

"She's a brave, beautiful woman you've got there, Nicholas," he said.

"I know. I don't deserve her," smiled Nick, "but I'm glad I have her."

"Hey, buddy, we just ordered pizza and I made a salad. Why don't we call Mac before it gets too late and you can let him know. He'll be tickled pink."

"Sounds like a plan," replied Nick.

He picked up the phone and called the hospital. When he reached Mac, he told him they were all fine and back in London.

"We'll see you tomorrow, Mac. I wanted to tell you something."

Nick told him he had asked Alex to marry him and that she had said, "Yes." Mac sounded delighted. He told Nick that he couldn't wait to see them and to give Alex a kiss. He congratulated Nick. Then, they chatted about going home...back to California.

Nick told Mac that it wouldn't be long now. He was going to make sure they returned home very soon, because it was important for Alex to meet the "other woman" in his life, his daughter, Sabrina.

Alexandra listened to Nick talk about his daughter. She knew that she wasn't anything like Sabrina's mother and she had a moment of stark terror! What if his little girl didn't like her? Alex tried to relax. She liked children. She was certain because Sabrina was a part of Nick, she would love her as much as he did.

She was anxious to go back to her home, too. She wanted to pick up Sandy and take him with her to California. She wasn't even sure if Nick liked dogs, but who wouldn't love Sandy?

Nick hung up the phone and planted a big kiss on her forehead.

"That's from Mac. He said he'd give you another one tomorrow when we go see him. He said to say hi to you too, John. He sounded good, almost his old self."

"We've really had it lately, haven't we?" said John.

No one answered. They all knew how much they had gone through. The doorbell rang and the pizza arrived. The large crust was oozing with cheese and meat.

"It reminds me of Mama Rita's and of New York."

The food and their weariness began to set in. Alex and Nick excused themselves. He saw her to her room and kissed her good-night. Soon, they wouldn't have to be in separate rooms. Nick told her that he wanted to marry her as soon as he could.

Alex fell asleep right away but Nick had difficulty. When he did sleep, he dreamed about seeing Quentin. He dreamed about a chase and numbers jumped from one place to another in his head.

He woke up in a cold sweat. He had never killed a man, not even in the war. Now, he knew what soldiers who had killed someone must have felt like. He got up and paced.

Alex awoke, hearing a noise coming from the living room. She got out of bed and went out to the living area where she saw Nick standing at the window, grim and tired. She went over to him, saying nothing. As she touched his sleeve, he pulled her to him and just held on. She knew he was thinking about the shooting.

She wished he could talk to Pastor Dan. Nick would like him. Nick Stewart was a strong person but under it all, he was so gentle and he had just killed a man...and he had done it for her.

The next morning, Alex commented to John that she wished she could go for a walk and just get some fresh air. Nick had fallen asleep early this morning and she didn't want to awaken him.

"It might clear the cobwebs," she said to John.

She knew she would not be allowed to go anywhere else until after her meeting with the psychiatrist this afternoon. He would put her under hypnosis and try and find out what she couldn't remember on her own.

"We have a small gym downstairs, Alex," said John. "I've been using it this past week. It isn't very big but there's a treadmill and bike and some weights. It helps. I can go with you, if you want."

"That sounds good to me, John."

"Security will have to go with us. I'll tell them. I think you'll find an old pair of sweats in my dresser that you can wear."

The two of them and a security man went downstairs to the small gym. They left a note for Nick, saying they would only be about a half hour.

Alex got on the treadmill, while John went to the weights. Walking was good, she thought. The exercise did help. She was still sore from the crash and this was an easy workout.

When she finished, she was sweating and asked John if there were any towels in the gym.

"There may be some in the lockers. They aren't locked."

What he said to her made Alex catch her breath. In fact, she couldn't breathe at all, for a minute. Her gasp scared John so much, he was ready to hit someone with a weight and the security man had pulled out his gun.

When she could finally speak, she cried out, "I remember. I remember! John, it was the lockers! The numbers were on the lockers in the gym in the high school…in Westville! I remember!"

Alex was ecstatic. John and the guard sighed with relief that she hadn't seen a gunman in the gym, or something worse.

"Quick, let's go back upstairs. I've got to tell Nicholas," she exclaimed, taking the stairs two at a time.

"Right. Upstairs, it is…" John was out of breath trying to catch up with her.

Nick was still asleep but Alex woke him up.

"This might make him feel better too," Alex told John.

She sat down on the bed and shook him gently. He mumbled something and tried to turn back over.

"Nick, darling, you've got to wake up. I have good news!"

"What…what is it?" he yawned.

"I remembered. I remember where I saw the numbers! It was in the gym of the high school in Westville. They were locker numbers, Nick….locker numbers!"

Nick Stewart was suddenly very much awake. It made sense. There were too many numbers for it to be anything else. He wondered if all of this would end up where it had begun…in Westville.

This afternoon, they would share the information with Inspector Daniel Avery. He hugged Alex and got out of bed.

Alex was glad she didn't have to undergo hypnosis. She shared the information with both Avery and his chief inspector.

"Now, we just have to figure out WHERE the lockers are that we're looking for…"

Alex hadn't thought about other lockers, except those at the high school. Now, she thought about it. It could mean the lockers could be anywhere…were they back to "square one," again?

Nick, John and Alex went to the hospital to see Mac as soon as they were finished with Avery. Mac was standing on crutches but looking much better than when they last saw him. Nick went over and hugged him, as did Alex and John.

"Now, for that kiss…" Mac grinned.

He planted another big one on Alex and she hugged him and kissed him back.

"You've got a good one here, Nicholas. You treat her good and keep her."

"Yes, sir," Nick replied. "I intend to do just that. I know how lucky I am."

The group chatted about going home. Nick told Mac that he could arrange any help or physical therapy that Mac needed. Nick felt they could do it at his home in California.

"Can Scotland Yard keep us in England?"

Surely, it made sense that if they contacted the FBI in the States; they could arrange for the group to go home. They would agree to being shadowed but Nick wanted to get back to his estate and said that he had to get back to work.

"I have security there," he said, "and an alarm system that puts some to shame. I could upgrade everything and hire extra men. The FBI could be our contacts as easily as Scotland Yard."

"Then, let's talk to Avery. He may be glad to get rid of us. Besides, it sounds like whatever is being planned is going to happen back in the States, not in Europe," said John.

It was exciting for them to think about. Nick was on the phone, arranging another meeting with the inspector.

When Nick came out of Avery's office, he almost burst with the news. He told the other members of his group, "Avery agreed to it. We're going home! We're going home in the morning!"

There was a small cheer in the halls of Scotland Yard. English agents stuck their heads out from behind closed doors, to see what was happening. John and Alex hugged each other and hugged Nick. The United States had never sounded so good to them.

Chapter Fifteen

Four weary travelers could hardly believe that they were on their way home. John and Mac grabbed seats on two recliners near the bar. Alex and Nick sat in the club chairs, near the front.

The only other passengers on the jet were two FBI agents, sent to fly back home with them. One manned the front of the plane and the other, the back. The jet was secured and inspected by both Scotland Yard and FBI before they left. They searched for any explosives or peculiar luggage. When it was cleared, the passengers and crew were allowed on board.

"This is nice," Alex whispered, "even with the armed guards. We're on our way home, Nick…home."

She squeezed his hand and he smiled at her.

"I can't wait for you to meet Sabrina," he said. "She's going to fall in love with you."

"I can't wait, either."

"Hey, guys," yelled John, "you want anything to drink?"

John and Mac had already made themselves at home. They found juice, soft drinks and coffee. John poured himself some orange juice. He held the cup up to toast them.

Alex said, "I'll have some juice too…"

"I'll get it for you." Nick walked back to where his friends sat.

"Hey, Nick," said Mac, "did you find out anything about the lockers?"

Nick didn't want to talk about this right now but he whispered to Mac and John.

"They're checking out both the Westville and West Point gym lockers. I don't want to have to go back to Westville but Avery told me that we going to have to go next week for a hearing. It's about our limo being attacked. Don't say anything to Alex. I don't want to spoil today for her. I'll let her know later."

He poured some juice and coffee and returned to his seat.

"Boy, it just doesn't stop, does it?" John said to Mac.

Mac replied, "My guess is that it never will until the Organization is destroyed. I also bet the CIA has been informed since we're traveling with FBI. The rest of the goons can't be far behind, either."

"You think there's something in one of the lockers? What could that be?" John wondered.

"Something is somewhere…in a place they don't want us to find. The puzzle just goes on and on. My guess is it's either a bomb or instructions about what's supposed to happen. And, it's got to be big, for all these agencies to get this involved."

Mac looked over his shoulder, to see one of the agents looking at all of them.

"Creepy," he said.

When the plane landed, the four passengers, along with the two FBI agents, were transported to the local FBI building. They were taken to a conference room and left to wait for an update and another interrogation. All that Nick could think of was taking Alex, John and Mac to his home.

An agent who identified himself as Tom McGee came in and sat down with them. He told them that he wouldn't keep them long and he would speak to Mac first, because he knew Mr. Timmons needed to rest. He took Mac out of the room, while the other three waited.

"Well, he wasn't too friendly, was he?" said Alex.

Nick was a little annoyed at the entire procedure. He got up and paced the room. John took out a pair of nail clippers and began to clip his nails. His feet rested on a coffee table and he appeared to be relaxed, compared to Nick.

"I'm tired of all of this," said Nick. "We're in our own country and we've just been through a living hell. Scotland Yard couldn't protect us. What does the FBI want from us? Surely, they were given the files from Scotland Yard."

"Boss, relax. At least they took Mac first so he can rest. That was kind of nice, wasn't it?"

Alex shook her head to John. She knew when Nick was in this mood, nothing they could say would make him sit down and take it easy. Alex was tired too. A little later, Agent McGee called Alex into another room. Mac had not returned from his interrogation and she asked McGee where he was.

"Oh, sorry. I offered to let him go and lie down. He didn't look strong…the hell that he's been through. If you want, you can see him. He's just down the hall. We have a room that has some beds. Some of us don't get a lot of sleep around here."

Alex reconsidered what she had said about Agent McGee. He was being very thoughtful and he seemed to be open and honest with her. He put her at ease and she thanked him for taking care of Mac.

"Now, Ms. Andrews, tell me all that you remember. I know it's a long story but try and remember the details; something you may not have remembered before."

He turned on the tape recorder and Alex started talking. It was another two hours before the group was finished. The four friends were brought back into the conference room, when Agent McGee came back.

"You've been very kind to repeat everything," said McGee. "Now, it's my turn to update you about what's going on, or what we think is going on."

The four of them looked at each other and leaned forward to listen.

"The group that's been trying to make sure none of you live is known only as the Organization. They're a fanatic bunch. You learned from Inspector Avery that they've killed a lot of people. They play whatever side the most money is on but they have no love for the United States.

"They think that your friend, Ed Percy, told you what they were up to, Mr. Stewart, and that you, Ms. Andrews, could identify what they did the night he was killed. Now, they think all four of you know too much. As for the map and the numbers, the lockers at West Point don't match the numbers, so we're left with Westville High.

"What's there that could be so important? It had to be something Percy hid. He was the only one who had gone undercover for the CIA, to find out what the group was into. The fact that he and Quentin both went to Westville was no accident. They were together, at one time. Then, things got ugly, somehow and Quentin found out Percy was betraying him.

"The Organization isn't finished until they find out what Percy hid. I don't think they know it has to do with the lockers, Ms. Andrews. We haven't found anything either. Now, the locker numbers were all odd numbers. We aren't sure why and we aren't sure what is hidden. We've scoured the gym and the lockers by an undercover man…he's their new janitor. I understand you still have a home there, Ms. Andrews? "

"Yes and my dog's there with some neighbors."

Nick interrupted.

"But she's moving here. She only has to get her dog flown out here."

"And my personal items," Alex concluded.

"I'd like you to go pick up your things yourself. Tell the neighbors you're coming back for the dog. This doesn't have to take place for a few days…give you all a chance to rest up. Mr. Stewart might be able to fly you there in his jet. It would make the town think the small town girl did well."

He paused. "It would also make you targets…something I know sounds terrible. But, if we can get them out in the open…"

"No, absolutely not!" exclaimed Nick. He had been shaking his head during most of Agent McGee's speech. "I won't have Alexandra placed in that position. Get someone else! We're not interested!"

McGee didn't look surprised at Nick's reaction. He understood what he was asking of them.

"Well, I'll give you time to think it over. We can't make you do anything but we'll be shadowing you here. I just thought Ms. Andrews might be able to slip in the high school and see if there's anything else that she remembers…anything out of place. I'll have a driver take you home now. My agents will accompany you and I've already arranged for the estate to be watched. With all of your own security, Mr. Stewart, you should be safe for awhile."

Agent McGee watched the group leave. He'd give them a few days but he wasn't about to let this drop…not with so much at stake.

Chapter Sixteen

A black Lincoln was waiting in the parking garage. Alex recognized the driver and the agent who opened the door for her, as the same two agents who had been on the plane with them. They drove off on their way to Nicholas Stewart's estate, just south of Los Angeles.

By the time they got to Nick's estate, it was dark. Alex couldn't see much from the window of the car. After they passed through some locked gates, they drove up a drive that seemed to go on for miles. Then, she saw the lights of his home. It was a large stucco house with a red tile roof. The estate rambled across acres of what she knew would be well-manicured lawns and hills. Flowers and shrubs ran up either side of the drive and the large carport ran the length of the front of the house. It truly was a mansion, she thought. Alex wondered how she would fit in this new setting. It seemed like another world.

Alex loved the small English cottage where they had been. She was a girl who loved hills and mountains, antiques and old things. She thought about her old house in Westville and briefly about Sandy, running through her home, sleeping at the foot of her bed. Where would he live if he were here?

But, she was also someone who loved Nicholas Stewart. Somehow, she had to make this work for both of them. The car stopped in front of two massive wooden doors. A manservant opened the doors as the group entered.

"Mr. Stewart, welcome back. We've missed you."

"Hello, Crawford." Nick handed his coat to the man and then gave him Alex's shawl.

"Crawford, this is Ms. Alexandra Andrews, my fiancee."

The man looked surprised but smiled at Alex.

"Miss Andrews, welcome," he said.

"Congratulations, sir," he said to Nicholas.

"I want you to take as good care of her as you've taken of me all these years, Crawford," Nick continued.

"That goes for both of us, too, Crawford," chimed in Mac, grinning at Crawford.

"Mr. Timmons, what happened to you? Oh, sir, can I get you something?" Crawford was not expecting Mac and John and certainly didn't expect Mac to be hurt.

"It's O.K., Crawford. They're getting me my own hospital staff. Right now, I just want a hot bath and a bed."

"And, Crawford," Nick interrupted, "Mac will be here in the main house with us, in the bedroom by the library. Mr. Cabe will have the room down the hall from him."

This evidently surprised all three of the men, since Mac and John had apartments in their own quarters, in back of the main house.

Nick looked at them and said, "Remember, all for one and one for all?"

They all joined in rather loud laughter. Then, Nick took Alex's hand and told Crawford she would be staying in his suite and to let her have the run of the house. He told Alex he wanted her to have his bedroom and he would take one just down the hall.

"I'll show you the rest of the estate tomorrow," he said.

Crawford told Nick he would have someone bring up their luggage and Nick told John and Mac that if they wanted anything, just call the kitchen staff.

He and Alex said good-night to John and Mac and told them that they would talk in the morning. He guided her up the curving stairway.

When Nick opened the door to his bedroom, Alex took in her breath. She could not imagine being here, let alone sleeping here. A terra cotta comforter, satin pillows and warm colors on the walls welcomed her. Plants were everywhere.

He noticed she had not moved into the master bedroom and was still standing in the doorway.

"It's only a room, Alex. I could carry you in," he grinned, trying to break the tension.

He wondered, if for a moment, that she doubted his intentions. He fully planned sleeping down the hall but he knew this was strange for her. It had to be and she still had said nothing.

"Alex?"

"Oh, Nick, I'm sorry. It's beautiful. I was just wishing…"

"What?" He took her hands and guided her inside the room. Then, he sat down and motioned her into one of the side chairs that was placed in front of a massive fireplace across from the bed.

"I was wishing I didn't have to ask you to leave. Oh, Nicholas, I don't think I should stay here. This isn't just hard anymore; it's impossible."

He knew how she felt. Perhaps, he should have gone to one of the apartments in back of the house. But, he knew he would still stay awake there, thinking about her.

"Tell you what. You get a shower and go to bed. I'll be here in the morning. We can talk about this then. We have to resolve this darling, soon."

He was kind, again. He kissed Alex good night and left. She was too tired to argue tonight. She fell onto the bed and fell asleep in her clothes.

Alexandra awoke with a warm California sun streaming through the French doors of the bedroom. She rolled over to find Nick sitting in the chair, next to her. He had been just watching her sleep.

"Nicholas. Hi. I have to say…this is the softest, most comfortable bed I've ever slept in. I could sleep all day. I don't know why I'm so tired."

Nick took her hand and kissed it.

"I love you," she continued. "I love you too much. It's too tempting, Nick. I have to live somewhere else. It's become too difficult."

"No, Alex, you're just wise. We are too close. But, I won't have you leave. I thought about it last night. I'm going to stay in the back in one of the apartments that I had fixed for John and Mac."

She started to object but he stopped her.

"It'll work, Alex. It will only be a short while. You see, Alexandra, I want you to marry me soon. I want you to marry me as quickly as you feel settled and at peace here."

Alex couldn't believe what he was proposing. It was as if the weight of the world had been lifted from her shoulders.

Nick got up from the chair, leaned over and kissed her.

"Come on, I have to show you a shower that's not only big enough for you, it's big enough for three or four people! You can lose yourself in it."

He pulled her up and toward the bathroom. She remembered how sore she had been and hoped for a shower massage, like back in the hospital. She remembered the tiny shower that they all had shared in Paris and smiled as she followed him into the dressing area that she had been too tired to look at last night.

There was a Roman bath, a giant dressing room and closet. Nick took her hand and turned the water on for her.

"Now, you relax. I'll be waiting for you. We'll have breakfast and then I can show you the rest of the house."

He left the room and Alex smiled. If this wasn't love, nothing was. She removed her clothing. Her arm was still stiff and she winced slightly as she touched one of the fading bruises.

The warmth of the water soothed away any leftover cuts and bruises she might have had. She stayed in the shower a long time. When she got out, she grabbed her robe and started back to the bedroom, where Nick was waiting for her.

Nick? When will I meet Sabrina?" Alex knew that would play an important part in deciding their wedding date.

"Soon, darling."

Then, he went over to the phone and ordered breakfast.

They had it served outside on the patio. Alex, for the first time, saw the magnificence of the green, rolling hills and the expanse of the estate. It was beautiful.

There was a grove of orange trees and there were gardens everywhere. Just below the patio, where they relaxed, she saw a rose garden. There was also another large patio, which led to an Olympic size swimming pool.

"Nicholas, it's beautiful. No wonder you missed it and wanted to come home."

"I'll show you around after breakfast. I want you to see everything. And, we'll go check on Mac and John, too. I want to make sure Mac's nurse got here. He was exhausted last night. Did you notice?"

"I did. I hope this sunshine will make him feel better. I know I do."

Alex took a bite of toast and sipped her orange juice.

"I could stay here on the patio and in this sunshine all day," she sighed.

"Well, I could arrange that, too," he smiled.

She was so beautiful and she had been through so much. Nick thought that the fresh air and the sun would do her good. He wanted to give her anything that she wanted. He was totally in love for the first time in a long time and he wanted everyone to know it.

Later, he showed Alexandra his house and the grounds. There was a stable, horses and some tennis courts. He even had his own private airstrip. Alex couldn't help but feel overwhelmed and just a little out of place. For the first time since she met him, she had doubts about how she would fit in his world.

When they returned to the house, they found Mac and John and Alex felt a little better, just seeing them. It seemed to ground her, being here, with them. She knew them and they had been through so much together. Nick took

Mac to meet his new nurse, while John and Alex walked over to the gazebo by the pool.

"A lot to take in, isn't it, Beautiful?"

"You could say that," Alex replied. "I guess I just wasn't prepared for all of this. It comes so comfortably to Nicholas. I just didn't think it would be so…so…big!"

John Cabe laughed at her and put his arm around her waist. He walked her over to the patio and into the rose garden.

"You know, Alex," he picked up a rose and gave it to her, "Nick was born in New York City on the wrong side of the tracks. When he made it big out here, he wanted to buy his mom and his family a house…a car…anything they wanted. He may not have told you that. He and his family weren't that close, until he became wealthy…except for his mom and she's no jewel, like he pretends.

"Everything he's earned, he's tried to give them more and more; in turn, they gave him less and less—less love, fewer family get-togethers. All they wanted from him was what he could buy them. So, he began buying things for them, even for his wife. Meg couldn't take the fakeness of the big parties and the life the Hollywood bigwigs wanted for Nick. He saw less and less of her and his child, until she got sick. When Meg died, I thought Nick would die too.

"He's changed, Alex. Last year, I saw it begin. He didn't care what anyone thought—not Hollywood, not any of the women he went out with…only Sabrina. He loves that little girl and she loves him. He started spending more time with her. He let a lot of scripts go by.

"He did the one movie that made the studio a lot of money and he only took that part because he really liked the script, not for the money. But, he still had a hole in his heart, Alex. You filled it.

"He'd sell all of this, Alex, just to be with you. He doesn't care about all of this. Don't you see that? He'd go and live in a shack if it was with you. You're his world now, not all of this."

Alex had tears in her eyes. She leaned down and picked another rose. Its scent was wonderful, just like Nick's love. It didn't matter where they lived. She was more important to him than anything…and it took John Cabe to let her know. She hugged him, to thank him and they walked through the garden and back to the house.

"Alex?" Nick was calling her. "Alex, come here. I want you to meet someone."

On the patio, standing with Nick, was a beautiful blue-eyed, dark-haired, little girl.

"You have to be Sabrina," said Alex.

She bent down and held her hand out to the child.

"Sabrina, this is Alex. She's a very good friend and I want you to meet her."

Nick didn't tell Sabrina that Alex was his fiancee and Alex was grateful for that.

It's too much, too soon. Let us get acquainted first, Nick, please.

"Hello," said Sabrina, "I'm glad you make my daddy smile."

It was an odd thing for a five-year-old to say, thought Alex.

"I'm sure you make your daddy smile, too, Sabrina. He says he loves you very much."

"He does. And I love him, too. I'm so glad you're home, Daddy," she said, turning her attention to Nick. He picked the child up and hugged her, telling her he had missed her too. He asked her to go up to her room and told her that she'd find a present from him.

"Really, Daddy, what is it? Want to come with me, Alex?" the child asked. She was tugging at Alex's skirt.

"Of course, I do, Sabrina…let's go!"

As Alex and Sabrina headed indoors, Nick looked at John. John just nodded. It looked "right," seeing them together that way and he knew Nick was thinking the same thing.

Alex and Sabrina found the present, tied with a large pink bow. Her room was filled with toys. Alex thought about what John had told her. Sabrina laughed with glee when she opened the box and found a large baby doll.

"It's a doll, Alex. Isn't she just beautiful?"

"Almost as pretty as you are, Sabrina."

"Let's have a tea party, O.K.?"

Alex spent a long time playing with the child. She was darling and she looked so much like her father. Alex wondered if Nick had given them this time by themselves just so they could get acquainted. It seemed to be working, she thought. The child was likeable and she seemed eager to please Alexandra.

"Alex, do you have a boyfriend?"

The question took Alex off-guard.

She asked God to forgive her and she lied, "Not right now. I have friends who are boys, if that's what you mean."

"My daddy could be your boyfriend if you wanted. I like you. You're the first lady that I've met that has talked to me, or played with me, besides my Nanny."

"I am?"

"Yes, the other ones I met usually just wanted to get rid of me. And, they didn't make my daddy smile, the way you do. I think he likes you, too. He's a real good person, Alex, so you might want to think about him being your boyfriend, O.K.?"

Alexandra smiled. This child was too bright for her own good. Alex promised that she would think about it and she agreed that Sabrina's dad was a really good person. That seemed to satisfy the child, for now. They played some more, until Nick, Mac and John interrupted.

"Sabrina, honey," said Nick, "we have to get you back to school. Uncle John will drive you there and I'll see you later this evening."

"O.K., Daddy. See you later, Alex!" Sabrina went over and hugged Alex first, then her father.

"Bye," she waved.

Alex moved over near Nick. She watched the child, until she was out of sight.

"Oh, Nick, she's adorable," Alex said, when Sabrina left. "Thank you for not telling her about us, yet. By the way, she wanted to know if I would think about having you for a boyfriend. And, she told me that I was a good playmate for her."

"I knew you two would get along."

Nick kissed Alex and led her downstairs into his study. He closed the door and pulled her next to him.

"You don't know how much you and Sabrina mean to me. I would do anything for both of you," he told her.

"I have some idea," she whispered.

Nick knew she was his future. He led her to a leather sofa and they sat down together. Alex fit in his arms perfectly and she would fit in his life too. He kissed her hair and her forehead. She looked up at him, as he found her mouth and pulled her closer to him. This was what he had wanted for such a long, long time.

"Nick? About that wedding date?"

He grinned at her.

"Next week too soon?"

She answered by kissing him again. "It may have to be tomorrow," she laughed.

They were interrupted by Mac's voice on the intercom.

"Nick...Alex...phone call for you. It's Agent McGee."

Nick picked up the flashing phone in the study. McGee just wanted to know how they were and to tell them that his agents had not seen anything suspicious. Nick told Alex and she breathed a sigh of relief. He didn't mention going to Westville and seemed to have dropped the subject, for now.

Nick and Alex went to the living area and told Mac what McGee had said. You could see the sense of relief on Mac's face, too. This evening, he would be able to enjoy dinner with Sabrina and with Alexandra, Nick thought. It was good to be home.

The evening went extremely well. After dinner, John treated them by playing the guitar. Sabrina practiced the piano and Alex and Sabrina sang, having the whole group applauding. It was probably the best evening they had in a long time—since all of this started.

Later, Sabrina said that she was very sleepy, and asked to be excused. She gave her dad a kiss and gave Alex a hug good-night. Alexandra couldn't help but believe that the relationship between her and Sabrina was going to be a very good one, indeed.

Mac and John asked to be excused and gave Alex a hug good-night. Mac hugged Nick, too. When they were saying good-night, Nick Stewart thought about his family. This small group *was* his family now and he cared more for them than he ever thought was possible.

The next morning, Nick was ready to go back to his studio. He had to film a retake on one of the scenes in his new movie. He asked Alex to go with him and watch the scene.

"It shouldn't take too long, Alex," he said, "and I'd like you to see the studio and meet some folks. Don't worry, I won't mention the engagement yet, if you don't want but you'll have to hide that ring."

Alex hated to take off her ring, so she hung it on a chain and put it around her neck, hidden under her blouse. She wore slacks and a light jacket over her shoulders. The color was a light aquamarine. Nick had picked out some clothing for her and had it delivered to the estate.

His taste was so much like hers; it was uncanny. She loved the color of the suit. It was slightly lighter than the color of Nick's eyes.

"You look beautiful," he told her. "You're going to wow them at the studio, gorgeous. I bet you'll be happy to go to a store, yourself and pick out your own clothes, again!"

"I was just thinking how much your taste is like my own. The suit's beautiful. I couldn't have picked out anything that I liked better. Thank you, darling."

"You are very welcome, Ms. Andrews. Let's get going…"

When they arrived at the film studio, Nick's crew greeted him with a lot of enthusiasm. They still believed he had been on vacation and kidded him about looking so rested.

Nick and Alex shared glances at that remark, thinking of all that they had been through. It was anything but restful. Alex noticed one of the FBI agents near the stage and felt safer. The studio thought Nick had hired some new security. This was the first time they had been out in the open in a long time.

Alexandra was invited to sit in a director's chair on the set. Everyone was polite and friendly to her but she felt like she was a little in the way. When the scene started, Alex settled down to watch. It was exciting to see Nick playing this scene. His director was telling the crew to get back to work. He was showing Nick how he wanted the lighting done.

Alex was sitting in a darkened area, watching the stage. She glanced behind her for just a second. At that moment, Nick thought he heard one of the stage lights explode. When he turned in the direction of the noise, he heard one of the studio staff scream! Alex was crumpled in her chair. Her light aquamarine suit was stained with dark, red, blood that was turning it an ugly reddish-brown.

"My God! Alex!" Nick yelled.

The studio was in a panic. There seemed to be more FBI agents coming out of nowhere. They had their guns pointed on the cast, warning everyone not to move. The shot had come from the back of the sound stage. Both studio police and FBI agents were running to see who had fired the gun.

Alexandra looked lifeless. Nick jumped over the cables and knocked over chairs to get to her.

"Alex, please…someone get help. Call an ambulance! Alex, oh, Alex…please answer me."

She didn't respond to his pleas. Nick tried to find a pulse but he didn't hear or feel one. He began CPR on her, and when the ambulance arrived, both Alex and Nick were put on board, along with two FBI agents and the emergency technicians from the hospital. They continued giving Alexandra CPR and placed an oxygen mask over her pale face.

"She's stopped breathing! Alex? Alex, it's Nick. Please hear me. I love you."

Nick was asked by the Emergency Technicians to get back out of the way and to let them work. Nick couldn't believe it. They were supposed to be safe! They were on a closed set, with all the protection he could think of and now Alex could die! He put his head in his hands and wept.

Alex was taken into the Emergency Room at the hospital. The FBI agents were at her door and the hospital wouldn't let Nick into the room with her. When the doctor did come out, he told Nick she would have to be taken to surgery to get the bleeding stopped and to get the bullet out of her.

Nick called John on his cell phone. He could barely speak. What seemed like hours later, John rushed into the hospital where he found Nick in a waiting area.

"What happened?" he shouted.

"I'm still not sure. Somebody shot her, right there on the set. God, John, she could die! She wasn't breathing. Now, she's in surgery. There was so much blood that she lost."

"She's not going to die. She's going to be all right. You have to believe that, brother. I mean it. We both have to believe it."

"She's been in surgery for over an hour," Nick told John. "Why don't we hear something?"

"Calm down, boss. I'll go see if I can find out something."

John didn't know what else to say. He was worried, too. It made no sense. All the protection in the world had not prevented this. What were they going to do? He tried to find a doctor, or nurse, who would tell them something.

No one knew anything. He looked for the FBI agents and found one who told him Alex was still in surgery. He said from what he had seen, the wound was near her heart and it was serious. That was all the doctor had told him. John thanked him and went to get some coffee for Nick and himself. How was he going to tell Nick what the agent said?

He saw the hospital chapel and went in. John Cabe wasn't usually a praying man, but he got on his knees and that is exactly what he did. He prayed for Alex and for Nick.

When he got back to the waiting room, he handed Nick a cup of black coffee. He kept the other and then told Nicholas what the agent had said to him. Nick looked up at him and John knew that Nick Stewart was saying his own prayer for the woman he loved.

Later, Nick went to the chapel. He always believed in God but he had put Him on the back burner recently. He knew that. He realized now that he had skipped a lot of church services since Meg died and he didn't have a pastor that he really knew, anymore.

If he thought that would save Alex, he'd go every Sunday and give away all his money to the church. But, he realized the only thing God wanted was for him to come back. He put his head down on the pew in front of him and cried. He cried for Meg and for his failure to forgive himself for her death and he prayed for Alexandra...his beautiful Alexandra...Was God going to take Alex now, too?

Just then, he felt a hand on his shoulder and he turned to see a physician. He could barely make out his features. The light behind him was so bright that he had difficulty seeing his face but what he did see calmed him.

"Nicholas?" the doctor asked

"Yes? Is there news about Alex?" he asked.

"Alexandra is going to be all right, Nicholas. I wanted you to know. I'm worried about you. Forgive yourself, Nicholas. I already have."

What a strange thing to say to him, thought Nicholas. He turned around to say something but the doctor was gone. For the first time in a long time, Nick tried to re-evaluate the past two years. He fell to his knees and prayed that he could forgive himself.

He prayed for Alex, Mac and John. He asked for a solution to be found for this situation that they were in—for strength and for courage. When he got up, Nick Stewart felt an enormous sense of peace.

He said, "Thank you, Lord," and he started down the hall, back to the waiting room. He knew in his heart that Alexandra would live.

Chapter Seventeen

Alex could hear faint noises and voices somewhere in the distance. She saw a bright light overhead and then—everything went black. She dreamed of Nicholas but he was in the distance. She couldn't get to him, no matter how hard she tried.

She seemed to be walking in a foggy place where she couldn't see anyone. She had to get out. She felt that someone was behind her and she knew she had to get away. Something was hurting her and she couldn't breathe! Then, a dark peace replaced the pain.

She knew she was safe. There was a voice that was talking to her, telling her that because she had honored Him, she was going to be all right. Then, there was a light so bright she saw nothing but white figures around her. She believed they were nurses, or angels and there was a doctor who had come to help her. She reached out...

Later, the pain returned to Alex. The voices kept telling her to breathe deeply but she couldn't. It hurt too much. Someone touched her toes and she saw a woman in white. She tried to speak but she couldn't. There was something in her mouth. She dozed off, again.

It must be morning. Alex was in a white, bright room and she dreamed that Nick and John were there. She reached out to touch Nicholas but something wouldn't let her arm move. She thought she saw Nick come over, close to her and she dreamed that she felt him take her hand.

"You scared us to death, babe," he whispered. "You're going to be all right."

She tried to talk but still couldn't. She wasn't sure he was really there.

"Don't try to talk. You've just had surgery. You're in a hospital. Alex, someone shot you."

Alex tried to focus. Nick was there! He had tears in his eyes. John Cabe was in the room, too and he came to the other side of her bed.

"You're still beautiful, kid. You've had a hard fight in surgery. You rest now. We aren't going to leave your side."

He squeezed her other hand and she tried to squeeze back.

A nurse came in, checked her vitals and turned on Alex's pain medication. She told Nick that Alex was going to be given the *strong stuff*.

She heard her tell them, "Ms. Andrews will sleep now."

Alex felt the blessed relief of the pain medication taking over. She turned to Nick and felt his fingers caressing her own. He leaned down and kissed her forehead and she fell asleep.

When Alex woke up, a doctor stood at her side. The room looked different to her. The walls were blue, not white and there were flowers on a bedside table. Her eyes couldn't seem to focus well and things looked fuzzy.

"Well, young lady, I'm glad to see you. I'm going to have the nurse remove a few tubes. We'll leave in your I.V. and the pain pump."

Alexandra couldn't seem to sort out what he was saying even though she listened intently.

"Tomorrow, I'm going to want you up for awhile and your friends can help you walk some. Today, it's sponge baths and a lot of sleep, I fear. Tomorrow, we're going to arrange for you to take a shower."

Alex tried to smile but she could not imagine being able to move from the bed. When they took the tube out of her nose, she was able to make a noise but her throat was so sore.

Then she saw Nick! He came closer to her and Alex pointed to Nick's pen and a notepad. She tried to say his name but he cautioned her not to speak just yet. He gave her a cup of ice to try and suck on as the doctor checked her left shoulder. The bullet had torn through her shoulder and had gone down through her lung.

The doctor told her that she was lucky. They were able to repair most of the damage. It had been close to her heart but had missed some major arteries.

"You're going to have a pretty long recovery with that shoulder and the lung injury. There'll be lots of physical therapy but I think it will heal well. I did my best, now the rest is up to you. You follow my instructions and we're going to get you well. O.K.?"

Alex nodded and grabbed his hand to say, "Thank you." He was a kind man and she needed kindness. She also needed the positive message he gave to her. Nick was talking to him but she couldn't listen any longer. She dozed off again, her body needing the healing rest.

Nick didn't tell John about what had happened to him in the chapel but he thought about it a lot. It was as if a heavy burden had been lifted from his shoulders. He knew Meg was at peace. He knew that she had forgiven him.

He also knew that Alex was going to be all right, eventually. The doctor looked familiar to him but he knew there was no doctor…that someone had come to him…perhaps, an angel? He wasn't certain John would believe him. Still, Nick had rededicated his life that night. He owed God nothing short of himself.

Nick asked John if he would get both of them some breakfast and bring it back to the room. The nurse in Alex's room told him that she would be glad to get it for them, to just tell her what they wanted.

He thanked her and gave her their list. It was evident to him that she was not just a nurse but an FBI agent, too. He saw part of a holster when she bent over to remove some of Alex's tubing. John went into the bathroom and asked if someone could bring some razors and a change of clothing too.

The nurse told him that they had placed some items for both men in the adjoining room. She opened the door to the room next door. It had been made up, just for them.

"Wish we had known that last night," said John. "One of us could have slept on a bed instead of that 'comfortable' chair."

He smiled at the nurse and she smiled back. Nick thought to himself that John could flirt with any woman, young or old and charm them. The nurse showed him where the toothpaste and razors were stored. There was a change of clothes for both men, hanging in the closet. John disappeared into the restroom. When he came out, he was close-shaven and freshly showered.

Breakfast was later brought to them and both men attacked the food as if they hadn't eaten in days. When Nick thought about it, they hadn't eaten in over two days, except for coffee and juices. Neither of them wanted anything until they knew Alex would be all right. When Nick finished eating, he went next door to shower.

"Call me if she wakes up," he told John.

John found a local newspaper that was shoved under their door. He picked it up and started to read. When he turned it over, he saw the headlines: "Nicholas Stewart Fired Upon—One Person Dead."

John groaned as he read the article. It was reported that "a young woman, Alexandra Andrews, was near death…after being hit by a bullet, fired by a woman who was hired as a prop girl at Mr. Stewart's studio. The woman, Mary Beth Williams, was reported dead after studio security went in pursuit and shot her."

"Nick, you've got to read this when you get out of the shower!" John yelled.

Nick came out of the shower, wearing a towel. He was looking for a robe, when John handed him the paper.

"Surely this can't be right. Did you know this woman?" asked John.

"No, never heard of her. I didn't see who it was who shot Alex. No one did, in all that confusion. I'm calling McGee! I'll try and see what's going on."

The paper reported Alexandra as "close to death." Lord, that part was so true.

Nick gave the paper back to John and dialed the FBI headquarters. He got McGee on the phone.

"McGee, what's going on? Why didn't you tell me that they had killed the shooter?"

McGee told Nick he was going to call him this morning, in fact, he was at the hospital entrance and would be up in their room in about three or four minutes. He wanted to wait until the doctors knew about Alexandra's condition. Nick hung up the phone and finished dressing.

"What did he say?" asked John.

"He's on the way up. He said he was just downstairs."

John looked over at Alex, who was still sleeping and motioned Nick into the adjoining room.

"We better talk in here," he said.

Nick grabbed some clothes and dressed as fast as he could. He just had gotten his shoes on, when there was a soft knock at the door. McGee entered, through Alexandra's door. He stared at the young woman who was still on an I.V. and a pain pump. He shook his head and went into the adjoining room.

"I'm so sorry this happened, Mr. Stewart. We couldn't even imagine anyone on that set was a part of the Organization."

"Who was this woman?" asked Nick. "I swear I never heard of her."

"She was cleared by studio security. She had been working at the studio about six months. She was the prop girl on your last set. She had no record...nothing. But, she's not dead, as was reported. We've got her. And, she will talk!"

"There's also that matter of Alexandra being reported close to death. That's what we want them to think. We believe it will only serve to protect her. Actually, Nick, we're going to plant another story tomorrow, reporting her condition has worsened and that she's gone into a coma."

"My God!" exclaimed Nick.

"It's for her safety. When she's strong enough to be moved, we're moving her to another hospital facility, one that's our own. It's in Nevada, just over the California line. Don't worry, we've told Mr. Timmons what we're doing. We've already let your staff go on vacation and our staff is in your home. Your staff thinks that you're mourning and waiting it out here, so they didn't object to leaving, all except for your main manservant."

Nick smiled. He knew his staff well and he knew Crawford would not want to leave. He knew they would do anything to help him. Then, he thought about Sabrina.

"What about my daughter? She's bound to be a target—"

"We've given your nanny a run down of some of the problem…not too much but she was packing when I left her. Sabrina, her nanny and an FBI agent are going to be flown to Bermuda for a few weeks. No one will know about it. She'll be safe."

"It's just getting bigger and bigger. It's affected all of our lives. I've thought of dropping out of sight but everyone knows my face. What's it going to take? Plastic surgery?"

Nick was becoming angrier by the minute. John spoke to McGee.

"What is it we need to do, McGee? We can't live like this, without some hope."

McGee told them that he would let them know. He said there had to be something Percy knew, or had hidden, that was still preventing what the Organization was planning.

"Like a computer disk, or something?"

"Maybe, we're looking for anything. He hid it well, at least. When Ms. Andrews is better, I want her to see the gym in Westville."

He saw Nick's face harden and he clarified, "I mean, via camera and computers. Since she can't return there yet, maybe she will see something out of place that we've missed. She was the only one in the gym to change clothing during rehearsals for your movie."

The next day, Alex's color was better. Her throat was still sore but she was able to whisper to Nick and John. They brought her some liquids and ice to sip but she was still nauseous and unable to eat anything.

When the nurse came in to sit her up for the first time, Alex thought she might faint. She had to dangle her feet off the bed for a while and she was so dizzy! Then, the nurse helped her up and over to a chair. She let Alex sit down to take a sponge bath. The warmth of the water seemed to make Alex relax.

The I.V. was disconnected the next day and Alex was allowed a shower. When Alex returned to bed on those first few days, she was exhausted. She felt like she had worked all day.

It was Nick who helped her get her feet back under the covers—Nick who pulled the warm, clean sheets and blankets up to her chin, tucking her in as he still did for Sabrina—Nick, who sat on the bed with her—Nick who caressed her forehead and told her not to worry—Nick who helped feed her.

Alex could only watch him and love him more. He looked so tired but each time, when she fell asleep, Nick was by her side.

The doctor visited Alex the next week and he told them that her vitals were much better. He reminded Nick and John that they would need to assist her every day and walk her a short way down the hall and back. He reminded them that the walking was to help prevent pneumonia and he gave them instructions.

Alex still needed some deep breathing treatments and they were difficult for her at first. As Nick and John helped Alexandra walk, they got on either side of her. Alex could barely move. She was so sore; the pain tore through her shoulder and both men believed that she was breathing too hard. Nick had to hold her around her waist. When he saw that she was out of breath, he motioned to John that they needed to return her to the room.

"You did good, babe," he whispered to her, each time.

Back in her room, he lifted her and put her back into bed. John always went into the adjoining room to watch some TV, while Nick sat with Alex.

Tonight, she wanted to talk to him.

"Nick, what are we going to do?" she whispered in a raspy voice.

He told her a little of what McGee had told her—about moving them again and about catching the shooter. He didn't tell her that the newspaper was going to report that she was getting worse and worse. He felt that she didn't need to know the whole story yet. He mentioned that they would see a video of the school in Westville, much later.

"It will be to see if you notice anything out of place."

That seemed to satisfy her. Alex couldn't keep her eyes open any longer. She squeezed Nick's hand and asked him to come closer. He leaned down and she told him she loved him and then he took her ring out of his pocket. The hospital had removed it when she was in surgery. He put it back on her finger and kissed her hand and then her mouth.

"Never take it off, again Alexandra," he pleaded.

"No, I never will," she promised.

It was almost two weeks since Alex had been admitted to surgery. She was improving day by day, according to her doctor. McGee had consulted with her surgeon and sent copies of her records to their hospital in Nevada.

The three of them, Nick, John and Alex, were taken from the California hospital by an ambulance to a well-hidden airstrip and flown to the new hospital in Nevada.

Chapter Eighteen

Alex was gazing out of the window of her new room. The only thing she could see for miles was desert. There were some cactus plants and desert flowers near the window and she noticed a bird that landed on one of the plants.

"At least there's sunshine here," she said to Nick and John, trying to sound more cheerful than she felt.

They had been at the new hospital for almost three days. Today, they were waiting to view the live video sent from Westville. McGee told them this would probably take a good eight hours for them to view all the lockers.

They had been asked to take breaks, eat lunch and just let them know whenever they wanted to stop the tape. They could resume viewing it, whenever they were ready. McGee told Alex he did not want to wear her out, so if she tired, to let him know.

They turned the lights down in the room and turned on the video. For Nick and Alex, it was like being in a time machine. They were sent back, in an instant, to Westville. It was like the day when they first met and it felt like yesterday to Alexandra.

She looked over at Nick. He was remembering it too—that pretty woman that he couldn't take his eyes off—now she was sitting in the same room with him. So much had happened since then but the one thing that hadn't changed was the excitement he felt when he was close to her. He put his arm around her and smiled at her.

The camera moved from the auditorium out into the hallway. The video and cameraman was moving through the halls and inside the door of the gymnasium. Then, the sound came on and a voice was speaking to Alex, bringing her back to the present day.

"Miss Andrews, I'm Matthew. I do the video and live connection. I'm going to be telling you where I am. There's a microphone on your connection. Just pick up your phone and you can talk directly to me. If you want me to move closer, or go anywhere with the camera, just say so. Do you understand?"

Alex picked up the phone and told Matthew she understood. The camera moved slowly from the gym into the hallway, where the door to the locker room began. Alex felt like she was back in Westville. It brought back all the memories of rehearsals and the actors she met. When the locker room door opened, Matthew started down the first row of lockers. The camera focused in on the first locker, A111.

Matthew pointed the camera to the outside of the locker and then opened the locker door, showing an empty locker. There were pictures attached to the inside. It was a teenage girl, in a swimsuit. There was a heart painted around it.

"Miss Andrews?" Matthew interrupted, "We've taken out all of the books, anything that could be sorted through. We've gone through everything that was inside the lockers and found nothing. We left all pictures, anything taped up, inside the lockers. I know this will take awhile. There are over 100 lockers in here. If you get tired, need a break, just holler at me."

"Thanks, Matthew," Alex replied. "Go on to the next locker."

This had gone on for almost an hour and forty-five minutes, when Alex called it off for a break.

"Matthew? I can't look anymore. I've got to lie down, for a while. Go take a break and I'll be back with you in an hour."

"Sure, Miss Andrews."

They had only gone through twenty-one lockers and were only up to A122. "The other numbers of the lockers are in the halls, not the gym. Are we going through those too?" she asked Nick and John.

"I think the only ones we're going to be viewing are the ones that you may have seen. Here, babe, here's a soda. Drink that and go lie down and rest."

Nick was worried about Alex. Her shoulder still lacked much range of motion. He knew she was still in a lot of pain. He longed to hold her at night but he was afraid he would hurt her. So, he slept in a bed next to hers, helping her in and out of her clothing, getting her water, anything to help.

She had lost a lot of weight and her appetite had only returned this week and the food at this smaller hospital was better than before.

He and John had wandered the halls. They agreed that most of the patients were probably FBI personnel or field agents. It was a small facility. From any window you saw desert. At least, one could see for miles. It would be difficult for any gunman to get close without being seen.

Alex was resting and Nick was thinking. What had he really noticed when he was at the school? He knew the answer—only Alexandra, from the time he first saw her, only Alex. He still believed that there had to be a reason that Ed Percy had moved to Westville. Something had to be there.

He wondered if what they were seeking had ended up at Ed's home and was now ashes? No, Ed was too smart not to make copies of important documents but why would he pick the high school to hide them? The town library made more sense. Ed would stand out at a school. He just didn't fit there.

Wait a minute. Ed knew Alex was in the movie and Alex was his next-door neighbor. How hard would it be to have hidden something in her bag, or hidden it in her clothing? Nick felt like he was on to something.

"Alex, what was your locker number? Where did you put your costume?"

"Oh, I think it was 151 or 153. No, it was C153. It's around the corner on the other side from where we've been looking. Why?"

"Did you put your costume in the locker or change clothing on the day of the bombing?"

" I changed and I put the costume back on the next day. You know, I left the costume in the locker and had to change at the school. Then later, when we stopped by my house, I changed clothes. The costume is still there, at my house."

When Matthew came back from his break, his phone was buzzing. It was Alex Andrews.

"Yes, Ms. Andrews?"

"Matthew, go to locker C153. It's around the corner. I want you to scan it up and down, very slowly—on the outside first. And Matthew, have they run fingerprints on these lockers?"

"I think so. I'll find out. Aaah, here we are, old C153."

Matthew started at the top with his camera and slowly focused on the plate where the letters and numbers were. The letters were scratched and almost non-existent.

"Matthew, stop. I want you to look closely at the plate. Is it loose?"

"Yeah, the screws that hold it on aren't in tight. There's something—wait, there's something stuck behind the plate."

Matthew looked around for a screwdriver, or something to loosen the plate. He put on his plastic gloves and then tried his nail clippers. He unscrewed one side and the plate fell down. He pulled it out slightly and saw a tiny fragment of what appeared to be microfilm taped to the back.

"Bingo!" he exclaimed. "It's microfilm! I've got to get this to Agent McGee right away!"

"Matthew? Wait. We'll call McGee from here. Don't use the telephone there. Someone wants that film badly enough to kill for it," Nick yelled into the receiver.

"Right! Is this Mr. Stewart?"

"Yes, this is Nick Stewart. Matthew, you may be holding the only piece of evidence we have. You got anymore agents there at the school?"

"The school is covered with us!" Matthew laughed. "Don't worry, I'll be careful. I won't use the phone but you need to have McGee call me right away, so I know what to do with this."

"Matthew, put it in your pocket. Don't mention this to anyone except McGee for right now."

"Matthew, this is Alexandra. I want you to go ahead and scan the rest of the locker. Put the plate back on the front of the locker, so no one knows we undid it."

The camera was filming again. The inside of the locker was clean. Matthew put the plate back on the locker and Nick called McGee and told him what had happened. He also asked McGee if the FBI had gone through Alex's home. McGee said they had gone over Alex's house but they had not found anything. Then, Nick asked him to find the high school costume and to contact Matthew immediately.

Nick and Alexandra both looked at each other. They were remembering David and Joshua. They wanted to be there, to protect Matthew. He was FBI but he sounded so very young. Alex hoped that he could get the microfilm to Agent McGee as soon as possible.

McGee phoned Matthew. After he talked to him, he told him to pick up Agent Ross and to go to the airport. Matthew knew this was important and he did exactly as McGee told him.

A helicopter was on the pad and ready to leave. The two agents met each other, got on the helicopter and flew to nearby Chicago. McGee was already there, waiting for them and finally, Matthew transferred the film to him.

Agent McGee went to the local FBI office and waited for the copy of what was on the microfilm. When he received it, he whistled a low, slow, "Whewww." There, on a paper copy, was a list of *everyone* who was a member of the Organization. There were names that he recognized and some he didn't. There were names from all over the world. But, at the top of the list, was the name of the man who was directing all of this. He couldn't believe his eyes!

The event that the Organization was trying to hide was not included in the information. He hoped that Alex Andrew's costume would provide some more information. In the meantime, he contacted Scotland Yard and asked to speak to Inspector Daniel Avery. Inspector Avery would be most interested in this.

"Avery, It's McGee. I have some news to share with you…."

Avery, a continent away, couldn't believe what he was hearing.

"Can you wire me the information as soon as possible?" he asked.

"Not only to you but all our agencies. I called you first," McGee said.

"I appreciate that. A lot happened when they were here. Now, I understand how the Organization found out where they were."

"What I'm wondering, is *how* they found out that Alexandra Andrews was on the movie set of Mr. Stewart's film? They had to have an undercover agent there, too," said McGee.

"How is Ms. Andrews, by the way?"

"She's reported to be at death's door," said McGee. "Fortunately, that's not the case."

"Good. I like those two young people. I hope this comes out good for them," said Avery.

"Me too, Avery," said McGee. "Me, too." Avery was thinking of the pretty young woman and the handsome actor. No one would believe what substance they had! They were as courageous as any of his agents—and they would die for one another, if needed.

When Agent McGee phoned Nick and Alex back, he told them he wanted to share what they had discovered but he was going to do it, in person.

"I'll be there in the morning," he said.

"By the way, did you find the uniform yet?" Nick asked.

"I'm bringing it with me. I want Alexandra to go over this with me. I haven't had time to look at it too closely. I don't see anything, just looking at it but she might."

Alex and Nick told John about what was going on. John was excited and told them he believed that the puzzle was going to be solved soon. He had seen what the stress was doing to all of them. They were touchy and fidgety. They had put their lives on hold. John Cabe was ready for all of it to end, too.

Chapter Nineteen

Alexandra was ready for some type of diversion. She wanted to celebrate, after the progress they had made today. Her physical therapy was every day now and it was difficult. She realized Nick had barely touched her the past few weeks because he was afraid of hurting her.

He was right. She did hurt. She could barely move her left arm. She could write with her good hand, or use a computer with one hand. She still had to have help buttoning her buttons, zipping up and even eating her food. She was sick and tired of it and was ready for something radical! She sent another prayer up that she was doing the right thing.

"Nick," she called out, knowing he wasn't there. "Please, God, we've been through so much. Please let this be an answer. Don't let him tell me no."

Alex waited for Nick and John to take their daily walk around the hospital and she grabbed the female agent that watched her door most of the time.

Kathy Ross had been with the FBI about two years. She was attractive and knew her job. When she was assigned to guard Nicholas Stewart and his fiancee, she was excited but when she heard all of the details, she reminded herself that the entire world might be dependent on what they found out.

She had gone to Westville earlier and was there when Alex saw the microfilm. She flew back to Nevada when McGee went to Chicago. Kathy would give her life for these people, if it called for that.

She also knew Nick Stewart was handsome but was not prepared for just how good-looking he was in person and Alexandra Andrews should have been a model or an actress herself. Kathy thought that she was absolutely beautiful.

She was also someone Kathy admired after she read their file. She could not imagine going through all the terror that Alex and Nick had gone through. So, when Alex grabbed her in the hallway, she was ready to listen to what she proposed.

"Look, Agent Ross," Alex said, "you have to help me. That means giving us some privacy this evening and keeping out the rest of the staff, except for this one. She pointed to the name. You'll see why. I need to have someone pick up all these items and bring them here, without Nick or John seeing them."

The young woman agent looked down at the list and then she smiled at Alex. She admired her bravery and she knew *why* she was frustrated. She saw no harm in what Alex requested and nothing that would place them in danger, so she told Alex that she would help her.

Alex managed to send Nick and John on several errands that afternoon. She asked them to use the computer in the hospital library and look up several things for her. They thought that she was on to something about the investigation, so they dutifully did what she requested.

Later, she had one of the pretty young nurses take John in hand and ask him to have dinner with her. She gave her a note to give to him. The nurse had flirted regularly with John, before now and Alex figured that John Cabe would be delighted with this arrangement. The nurse later reported to Alex that John would be ready if and when she needed him. It was all coming into place.

Alex had to give credit to the female FBI agent. Kathy Ross couldn't help but smile. She handed Alex the food and other items that she had picked out. The two hospital beds were moved out of the hospital room and a sofa and a few chairs replaced them, along with a single double bed.

Alex ordered flowers and candles. Kathy found a small C.D. player and some music that Alex requested. She shooed away the male FBI agents and told Alex that she, herself, would patrol the hall and that *no one* would disturb them, except who she had asked for

Alex was given her medication in a small cup, to take later, so that the night nurse would not come in either. This was one assignment that Agent Ross thoroughly enjoyed planning.

She wished Alex luck and then handed her the last package that she had ordered.

"I hope it fits," she smiled. "I think it's beautiful, Alexandra."

"It's perfect. Thank you, Kathy," Alex said as she hugged the agent.

When Nick finished the computer work, it was dinnertime. He picked up a couple of sodas that Alex had requested and started back to her room. He was tired and ready to relax but he wasn't prepared for what he found when he opened the door to Alex's room.

Alex was changing her clothes in the bathroom, when she heard Nick walk in.

"What the. :.?" she heard him say. "Alexandra Andrews, are you in here?"

When she walked out in a shell pink gown with shoes to match, she saw that famous half-grin appear on his face.

"Wow!"

Nick looked at Alex and then at the room.

Flowers were everywhere and soft music was playing. Candles were lit, sharing their soft, flickering lights with the couple that was there. Then, Nick saw the tuxedo, laid out on the bed.

"Hi there, sweetheart," Alex whispered to Nick.

She walked over to him and kissed him.

"You look beautiful, Alex. What's going on? Not that I mind. I'm just surprised. The dress—It reminds me of another evening." He was thinking of New York.

She stammered. This was the hardest thing she had ever done.

"Nick, Nicholas…you said you wanted to marry me?"

"Of course."

"Nick, there's a chaplain here, at the hospital. We're in Nevada. I've given more blood for a blood test than they will ever need for a license and so have you. Nick, marry me—tonight. We can always have a big wedding later. Right now, all I want is you."

He couldn't speak. Why hadn't he thought of this? Because she had been so hurt—marry her? Of course, he wanted to marry her!

"Nick?" Alex was worried. He hadn't answered.

Nick walked over to her and took her in his arms.

"Of course, I'll marry you. Right here, right now. I love you Alex."

John Cabe was waiting for the phone to ring.

Come on, Nick. Don't blow this! he thought.

When he finally got the call from his friend, he told him he would be right there. John Cabe was dressed for a wedding. The nurse had told him of Alex's plan. Alex had rented a tux for each of the men. She had talked to the Chaplain and with Agent Ross's help, her room was turned into a chapel. John couldn't believe all they had done.

Then, at last, Agent Kathy Ross knocked on his door. She was dressed up in a cream colored suit.

"Ready?" she smiled at John.

"You don't look half bad, Agent Ross—for an FBI agent. Let's go!" John grinned at her.

The chaplain of the hospital smiled as he looked at the young couple. "Alexandra…Nicholas? Are we ready?"

Nick Stewart looked into Alex's eyes and said, "We're more than ready, sir."

John Cabe was Nick's best man. Agent Ross was Alexandra's bridesmaid and witness. It was a small, private wedding. No one would find out about it, until later. Right now, all that mattered to the two who were being married was that God had blessed them. He had let them both miraculously live to see this day. They had a new faith…in Him and in each other.

As they said their vows, Nick told Alexandra that they could be stronger now, that they were one. He told her how much he loved her…his soul mate.

He surprised her once again when he gave her a wedding ring. He had bought it when he got her engagement ring. He had it and his matching ring with him. He told her he had carried them with him, as a reminder of where their future was heading. It had helped him through some very dark days.

Alex had tears in her eyes, as she told him she had always loved him.

At last, they were married. John Cabe and Agent Ross congratulated them and toasted the couple and the chaplain gave them both a hug.

The music continued to play. The guests had gone. Nick leaned down, finding Alexandra's mouth. His breathing slowed and mixed with hers. For a minute, neither of them could say anything. Nick just held on to her and pulled her even closer.

"I love you Mrs. Stewart."

She snuggled in, close to him, as they listened to the music and while he ran his fingers through her hair and kissed her.

"I never want this night to end, Nicholas."

"It won't darling. This time, it won't."

He didn't have to leave her ever again. She belonged to him and he belonged to her and tonight there were no nightmares—just two people in love.

Chapter Twenty

Alex yawned, stretched, looked over at her husband and smiled. Nick's dark hair was buried in the pillows and somewhat tousled. As he woke up and saw her, he leaned over and kissed her. His turquoise-blue eyes had brightened again and Alexandra saw a life in him that she had not seen in awhile, not since she had been shot.

"I love you, Mrs. Stewart. I love you so very much."

She moved back into his arms again, reaching for his face with her fingers.

"I'll have to see that Agent Ross gets a very special gift before we leave here," he grinned, as he kissed his new wife. "How about some breakfast, Mrs. Stewart? This time, it's my treat. You just stay in bed. I'll get us something."

Alexandra hated the thought of leaving the warmth of the bed but she knew they still had to look forward to a visit from Agent McGee this morning.

"Just coffee, darling."

Just then, Alex and Nick were interrupted by a knock at their door. When they looked at the clock, they both noticed that it was nearly 9:00 a.m. and their meeting was scheduled for 9:30!

Alex grabbed her robe and hurried into the shower, while Nick answered the door. A male FBI agent told them that Agent McGee would be arriving in about thirty minutes. Nick thanked him and yelled at Alex.

"We have to hurry, Alex."

Candles had burned down and rose petals were on the floor. They hurriedly dressed, as there was another knock. John Cabe was waiting in the hall.

"Hmmm. Quite some party, I'd say," he grinned. "I thought you all might need some coffee."

He handed Nick two cups of coffee from the cafeteria and grinned again.

"You're a lifesaver, John. No time for breakfast. Thanks, bud!"

Alex soon joined them, saying "hi" to John and thanking him for the coffee. Nick and Alex tried to appear casual as they watched John look around the room and then burst out laughing.

"Let's get out of here and into the conference room before McGee walks in too," Nick said.

As the three of them left, a nurse walked up and gave Alex her pain medication for the morning, along with a glass of water. Alex didn't have the nerve to tell her that she had forgotten all about the pain medication last night.

She downed the pills, as they continued to walk to the small conference room, where Agent McGee was waiting for them.

"Morning, Nick. Hello, Alexandra. You're looking much better! Mr. Cabe? How are you?"

Nick smiled at Alexandra and held onto her hand, as they were seated. They looked back at McGee in suspense.

"What did you find on the microfilm?" Nick asked.

McGee handed them a paper with a list of names from the Organization. It went from the top to the very least of their group. There were hundreds of names, some that they knew very well.

"Wow," Nick said. "Look at this. Some of these guys are heads of corporations, politicians, attorneys and thugs."

Alex pointed out the first name. "How can this be right?"

McGee answered, "His name is Joshua Gruber, German citizen—alias Joshua Wright, industrialist and owner of a plant that manufactured chemicals for third world countries—alias Scotland Yard's own Joshua Green—new face and new credentials. How he got by with it, we may never know. We also found out that the girl who shot you knows Mr. Green very well. He knew you were going to be at the studio that day, Alex. He ordered the hit, or so she says."

"But, he was in our cottage. We spoke to him. He guarded us. Why didn't he kill us then?" she asked.

"Gruber likes playing games. And, he doesn't do his own dirty work. He was just waiting to give the signal to Quentin and his boys to do away with you. He's still alive, Alex and he's dangerous as hell. We've heard he's in the States somewhere, maybe with another new identity."

"Did you find anything else?" asked Alex.

"Oh, your costume, uniform—whatever you call it. I brought it with me. I thought you might look it over. See if you see anything unusual. Look really closely."

McGee handed it to Alexandra, as Nick looked at the costume also and touched the blouse. It reminded him of the first time he saw Alex, wearing that short skirt and noticing her long legs. When he looked into her face back then, his world stopped—and nothing had been the same for him since.

He watched Alex, as she felt the pocket in the shirt, the high school letter on the sweater and touched the label inside. Then, she took the skirt and ran her hands down each and every pleat. She turned it over and ran her fingers over the hem. She stopped, noticing a staple that held up part of the hem.

"I don't remember this," she said.

"What? What's that?" asked McGee.

"The staple. Sometimes, you don't have time to hem up a loose thread. I've done it myself—stapled or taped the hem. I don't remember doing it on this skirt." The skirt was heavy wool and it was difficult taking out the stitches but she pulled the stitches out, one by one.

As she pulled out the last stitch, a tiny vial, no larger than a small needle, fell out, along with a tiny rolled up paper. McGee grabbed the flask and held onto it, while Alex unrolled the paper.

There was a scrawled note that said, "Get this to the FBI. They're going to use this at the U.N. Don't break it open. It's deadly! This is not a joke! Edward Percy."

Alex handed the note to McGee.

"I think this explains why they wanted Percy dead."

McGee looked somber and placed a call from his cell phone.

He said, "We've got it, Mr. President. I'm getting it to the lab right now."

He looked at them and said, "I don't have to tell you to be quiet about this. I'll be in touch."

McGee hurried out of the room and the three friends walked back to Alex's room. They had become very quiet. Alex suggested they have some coffee or iced tea to drink and she went to the kitchen. She wanted to be busy. If what she found was true, they now had a place for an explosion that could change the world.

They had the name of every member in the Organization. She remembered the words that were scratched into the rock—some of them missing. They still didn't know what the point meant.

"Blow up the point," Alex pondered. "What did he mean, or was it a mistake?"

Alex poured some iced tea. She also made some more coffee and returned to Nick and John and asked them once more what they thought Ed meant.

None of them could know that it meant they were still in more *danger* than they realized.

"That had to be some kind of chemical. It couldn't be an explosive, could it?" asked John.

"Who knows? With all of the new germs and all the new explosives, who knows?" replied Nick. "The only thing that made sense was that I knew the guys in the picture and found the map. The map led to that goofy message and the numbers led to the locker. I think Ed hid the stuff in that locker, knowing somehow that Alex and I would be led back to it. The rest of it has quit making sense to me. We know there's a madman out there still wanting us dead. And why? So we wouldn't give the information that we just discovered to the FBI. He doesn't know we already did that and, what's the point of all of it? I don't know. If he had said blow up the U.N., it would have made more sense. Perhaps, some of the words that were scratched out on the rocks would have told us more but we couldn't read them."

It was obvious to Alex they were getting nowhere. They'd just have to wait for McGee's next move and see what he finds out. They just hoped that he would tell them.

"Ed spoke in code a lot, didn't he?" Alex asked.

"I guess. He was an expert in that," replied Nick.

"Well, maybe he didn't want anyone else to know what he meant, if they found the message. So, he used the word point to mean something else," suggested Alex.

"What's another word for point?" asked Nick.

"Tip…uh…We need a thesaurus," said John.

"Exactly," said Alex, "a thesaurus. There's one on the computer."

Alex ran to the library and turned on the computer.

"Look at this," she exclaimed. "One of the words for point is summit."

"A summit at the U.N.!" yelled out John. "Now that's the first time, it's made any sense at all."

"We have to let McGee know," said Alex.

"We can leave a message for him to call us. I'll tell Agent Ross."

Nick got up. He went into the hall to find the woman who had helped give Alex and him one of the best nights of his life, since Alexandra was shot. He thought of Alex. They shouldn't have to think about any of this now. He went back into the library and got his new wife.

"I'll find Ross later, Alex. John, will you call McGee? We're going back to our room."

He just wanted to make her forget all of this—just for a little while longer.

Chapter Twenty-One

McGee was waiting for lab results later in the day, when he received a call from John Cabe. He gave him the information that he had concerning the word "summit."

McGee agreed that it could be the meaning of the word, "point," but he was also following up on some other leads. When he hung up, he thought about the upcoming Summit that was going to be held this summer at the U.N. The Secretary of Defense and the President of the United States were scheduled to speak, along with a lot of dignitaries of other countries. Mr. Cabe, Nick and Alex could be right in their suspicions.

With something that big, only Joshua Gruber would want to claim responsibility. The last time Alex and Nick saw him, he was posing as an agent from Scotland Yard. He had gone to a great deal of trouble changing his looks and identity. He was a genius, *a mad genius* and a danger to all of them. He could look entirely different now.

The only thing Nick and Alex might remember would be his body build, his height and his voice. Other than that, he could probably walk into any room in any building, even their hospital, if he had proper I.D.

It made McGee very uneasy to think about it. He was glad they had to fingerprint the personnel at the hospital. They had established other safeguards, especially since Gruber had managed to fool Scotland Yard. McGee knew that Gruber had to be exposed. His entire organization counted on his anonymity.

If they could just get him to show himself, he could be put away for a long, long time. McGee sat at his large oak desk and leaned back in his chair and thought. He had to find a way to bring Gruber out into the open but how?

Nick wished that he knew where Sabrina and her Nanny had been relocated. He would like to talk to his child, first to comfort her and secondly to hear her voice. It would cheer him up to be able to tell her about Alex but they decided to keep their wedding a secret and have a larger wedding later with all their friends and family.

He decided to phone Mac, who was still living at his estate. He could see Mac wondering how he, John and Alex were doing. His call was answered by a click. Nicholas knew he was being recorded.

"Mac? It's Nick. Just wanted to check on you. How are you doing?"

Mac told Nick he missed them all but had found an agent who enjoyed chess and that was how he was spending most of his time at the estate. He told Nick the studio had called and that he might want to call them, just to let them know how much longer he might be gone.

Nick told him he would try and get permission to call them but that Mac was the only one he could phone right now, due to all the sensitive information coming and going. Mac asked about Alex and Nick told him she was much better and had sent him her love. He wanted so much to share his news with Mac.

"You hold on to that one, Nick," Mac joked.

"I'm trying my best, Mac. We've been through a lot but I think we're closer than ever."

Nick almost laughed. He had to tell Mac about the wedding but he knew the phone was bugged. He'd have to wait until he saw him in person.

McGee had an idea on how to force Gruber out of hiding. Other than his ego, there was something that Gruber couldn't resist. That was a dare. He had to talk this over with Alex Andrews and Nicholas Stewart. He only hoped they would see that this might be the only way to catch Gruber.

The next day, McGee drove his car to the hospital. He was slightly nervous about presenting this plan to them. If they said no, there was little else he could do about it. McGee parked the car and walked into the hospital. He hoped he could sell this plan to the Stewart clan.

Alex paced. She couldn't imagine what could be so important. McGee entered the room, flashing a smile to all of them. Nick shook his hand and John nodded to the agent.

"Well, I've got something to propose to you," he began. "I know this may sound strange but it's not going to put you in any danger. Beside, I think it just may work to bring out the elusive Mr. Gruber. If we can catch him and find out where his chemicals are stocked, his organization will tumble. Are you interested in getting your lives back?"

They all looked at each other. Nothing had sounded so good to them in weeks.

"First, we move you all to an apartment. We will post Agent Ross and some others there to guard you…even you, Mr. Cabe. You can have one nearby them, just for a few days."

"Tell us more," said Nick.

"Okay, the first thing that we tell everybody is that Alex died."

"What? What in the world are you talking about, Man?" asked John Cabe.

"It's only 'pretend', John. We can correct the story to the newspapers later. The only way that Joshua Gruber is going to come back out of hiding is, if he thinks he's in no danger. And, he would be prime for a dare from you, Nick."

"Go on," said Nick. He was already beginning to think McGee had lost it.

"Well, like I said, we run an article that says Alex died of her wounds. Then, we give information about where Alex's funeral and graveside service will be held."

"Do you really think he is going to show up? Just for that?" asked Alex, taking her own "death" like it was nothing.

"No, no. There's more." McGee sounded flustered.

"Of course. There always is," John said.

"Alex's funeral and services will be listed in the obituary column—and right under that, is going to be a note to Gruber, from Nicholas Stewart."

"And, what am I saying to this slime ball?" asked Nick.

"You're going to say something like, 'I know who you are, Gruber. You're a coward. You killed my fiancee. Now, come and meet me face to face! Signed, N.S.' Believe me, Nick, he'll never run from the challenge."

"I thought you said this wouldn't put us in any danger. I won't let Nick do it," said Alex.

"The people at the funeral and graveside won't be either one of you, Alexandra. You'll both be at home, watching all of this on T.V.," smirked McGee.

"Oh, I like that better already," said Alex.

"You're going to have a closed casket, Alex. So, they're never going to see you. Nick is going to be played by one of our FBI agents. He's going to look like you, Nick, and he's going to be mourning his lost love. But, inside his jacket is going to be a small revolver and your pallbearers will have high scope rifles hidden under their overcoats. All of the mourners will be more agents. Even Scotland Yard has offered to be there. They don't take kindly to one of their lieutenants being killed."

"Sounds like a good movie script," said John, "if they can pull it off. How are they going to know who Gruber is, if he doesn't look like himself?"

"That's where Alex and Nick come in," said McGee.

"How?"

"Because you saw him last. You may be able to identify his movement, the build of his body, his voice—something. He may even come up to our phony Nick and tell him he's ready for a duel or something. I believe, even if he's changed his face, you might recognize him. Is it a deal?"

"Well, right now, it's the only game in town. I guess we'd be O.K. doing this."Nick looked at Alex and she nodded. Even John told them it sounded good.

"He may try to kill the fake Nick, you know. And, if he doesn't look exactly like Nick, he'll run," said Alex.

"We know. We'll let you see Mr. Stewart's double before we do this." McGee was very proud that he was able to pull this part off. He took a long breath.

"When does this happen?" asked Nick.

"Four days from now. We move you today. Alex "dies" tomorrow and that release will go to all the papers first. Then, the funeral arrangements will be disclosed the next day. The funeral will be two days from then."

"That's on Friday," said Alex.

"Yep," said McGee. "Maybe, we'll have a really good weekend coming up!"

He thanked them, shook hands and told them he would be back tomorrow.

Nick woke up the next morning in the new apartment, where he and Alex had spent the night. When he went to the door to ask for the newspaper, Agent Ross was standing guard and she handed him her copy.

"You won't like it, much," she said.

Nick brought the paper into the kitchen. Alex was still asleep. He decided not to wake her up. He made coffee and set out a couple of cereal bowls. As he sat down with the coffee, he unfolded the paper.

The article on the front page showed a picture of Alexandra and Nick together. It was taken at the movie set, right before the shooting. He didn't know who took the picture but Alex looked beautiful.

The headlines read, "Nicholas Stewart Mourns Death of Lover."

Boy, Hollywood couldn't have played it up sappier, he thought.

The article went on:

Alexandra Andrews, latest love interest of actor Nicholas Stewart, was shot by a crazed prop girl last month. Since then, Ms. Andrews has been in critical condition.

Hospital officials reported her death early this morning at 4:00 a.m., June 1. Mr. Stewart, it was reported, was in isolation while mourning her death. His press agent gave a statement that said, "Mr. Stewart reported that Ms. Andrews was a remarkable woman. She was the head of a P.R. firm out of Chicago. She was a dear friend to Mr. Stewart and his family and will be sorely missed."

A grandmother, Martha Andrews and an aunt, Victoria Williams, both of El Toro, CA, survive her.

She was visiting relatives and had gone to see Nick Stewart on his soundstage. The prop person, evidently in a jealous rage, shot toward the chair where Miss Andrews was sitting. Her name is being withheld during the investigation. She was captured and shot.

Funeral arrangements for Miss Andrews are unknown at this time. Mr. Stewart plans not only attending but is in charge of making final arrangements. He told this reporter he intends seeing that justice will be done in this case. It is rumored he planned to marry the pretty young executive later in the year.

Nick put the paper down on the kitchen table. It could have happened that way, he thought. Alex had come so close to being killed. It sobered him up. He hoped the article wouldn't upset her too much. It was strange, seeing your name in print, especially when it said you died.

He wondered what tomorrow's obituary would say. He rang John and asked him to come to their room as soon as he could. He went to the kitchen, fixed some breakfast and took a cup of coffee outside to agent Ross.

"You okay?" she asked.

He nodded to her and told her he was expecting John Cabe. She smiled at him and thanked him for the coffee.

"I never got to thank you for what you did. I just want you to know it meant the world to us, Agent Ross."

"It was my pleasure, Mr. Stewart."

Nick knew Alexandra liked omelets, so he put the cereal away and decided to gather the ingredients for a Western omelet. At least the FBI had been generous with supplies and food. He was in the middle of dicing the ham for it, when John knocked on the door.

"Hi, come on in," said Nick.

Nick handed the paper to John and he put the plates on the table. John poured himself a cup of coffee and sat down. He began to read the article.

"Whoa…that's grim," he said

Nick nodded.

"I don't know how Alex is going to take this," he said as he sat down again.

"She's not up, yet?"

"No, I thought I'd let her sleep. I'll go wake her for breakfast. I'm glad you're here for some moral support. Help yourself to part of that omelet. "

John put some bread in the toaster and then sat the butter and jelly on the table. He served the omelet on the three plates as Nick woke Alexandra. She came out to the dining area wearing a robe that was too large. She was still drowsy from a peaceful rest.

"Something smells good," she said.

Nick poured some coffee for her, kissed her and helped her into her chair. John took the toast out of the toaster and put it on a plate, then brought it to the table and sat down.

"Hey, beautiful, breakfast is served…just for you…"

He passed her the toast and Alex took a bite of the omelet.

"I can't believe you made this," she said to Nick. "Thanks, darling. I feel so pampered."

"Enjoy. Hope it tastes okay."

"It's wonderful. I see you have the paper. Don't worry," Alex smiled, "I'm not going to fall apart."

Nick handed her the paper and watched her reaction. She read the article, folded the paper and put it back on the table.

"How about some more coffee?" she asked.

"Babe, you O.K.?" Nick asked, as he poured her coffee.

"Fine. I'm not going to let this spoil the day. I'm trying to think that we're one day closer to living a normal life. If this helps, I'm all for it. Where'd they get the picture? It's pretty good of you and me."

Nick and John were amazed at Alex's reaction. They had expected something else—anger, screaming, a little shouting—but not this. This Alex was beyond cool.

Nick was still on guard in case she started to scream or throw something. John had expected a few tears, at the least. He just quit eating and watched Alex. John looked at Nick. Nick shrugged his shoulders, as if to say he didn't know what was going on and Alex continued to eat.

"What's with you guys?" Alex asked, "Come on, guys. I'm really okay. Eat, will you?"

Nick sat down and ate a piece of toast and John finished his eggs.

"Well, I guess I'll go on back to my room," said John. "Thanks for breakfast."

As John got up to leave, he told Nick he thought he'd be able to handle it from here on. Nick nodded and grinned at him.

"She never ceases to amaze me, and I mean never!" said Nick. He patted John on his back and showed him out.

Nick walked back into the kitchen, leaned over and kissed Alex on her forehead. Then, he sat down across the table from her and he couldn't help but stare. Her fingers were curled around both sides of the coffee cup and a lock of her hair had fallen down her forehead. She wore a terry robe that was two sizes too large and fuzzy slippers that looked ridiculous. She was reading the cartoon section of the paper, smiling now and again. He could sit here and watch her all day. Just then, she felt his stare and looked up at him. She smiled at him.

"Hey, love," she almost whispered, "I really am okay."

She put the paper down and walked around the table to him. As he turned toward her, she sat down in his lap and put her arms around his neck.

"I love you so much," she said as she kissed him.

"I love you too. That's why I don't want anything to hurt you, not even words."

He held her close and put his chin on top of her head.

"I know," she said.

They sat there, just holding on to each other. Finally, Alex got up and said something about a shower. She headed for the bathroom and Nick told her he'd clean up the kitchen. She turned, walked back to him and took his hand.

"You can do that later, love."

Later that morning, McGee telephoned them. He asked if they had seen the article and Nick replied that they had.

"Your note will appear tomorrow, right under the obituary," McGee reminded him.

"I know and you think he will show up at the funeral?"

"He will either be there...or at the graveside service. My bet's on that service, since it's outside—more places to hide. *Our boy Nick* will be wearing a bulletproof vest. He's a sharpshooter, Nicholas. Gruber won't get away."

"Anything else we should know?" Nick asked.

"Yes, the lab report showed the vial contained a new explosive so powerful that the small sample we got in the vial could take out all of New York City."

"So, do we know where the rest of it is?" asked Nick.

"No. I think Gruber's got it stocked in one of those plants he has. We plan to hit those while he's here in California. But, we won't know that for sure until we can grill him," answered McGee.

"McGee, you've got to find it! What if he's already planted it in the U.N. somewhere?"

"We've notified everyone there. We'll find it."

McGee sounded so certain that Nick quit asking questions. He told Nick that he would talk to him tomorrow and to continue to "lay low." When Nick repeated the conversation to Alex, she had that worried look for an instant and then told him they needed to stay busy.

She threw him a kitchen towel and he dried the breakfast dishes that she was washing.

The obituary appeared in the newspaper the next day, along with the note to Gruber from Nick. Alex and Nick could do nothing now but wait...

Chapter Twenty-Two

Just as McGee had promised, the funeral was going to be televised. It was going to take place at one of the missions just south of Los Angeles. The time passed slowly for Nick and Alex. They sat on the sofa, reading anything they could find and drinking too much coffee. When they turned on the T.V., the plan for Alex's funeral was playing on the news. The phony Nick was shown.

"He's good," Alex said, speaking of the actor who was portraying Nick, "but I'd know he wasn't you."

Nick smiled at her. He had a double at the studio that didn't look as much like him as this guy. He told Alex the studio might want to hire him and he tried to make light of the situation.

Alex told him she usually cried at funerals, so not to worry if she got carried away with her own. Nicholas moved to the sofa, sat down and put his arm around her shoulders. When the phone rang, they both jumped. It was McGee.

"We've got a problem," he said.

By the tone of his voice, Nick knew it was a big one. McGee told him that the actor that was to play Nick had been put in the hospital with an emergency appendectomy. He wasn't going to be able to be there.

"But he's the one person we *have* to have there!" shouted Nick.

Alex looked up from her magazine and got up from the sofa. She walked over to Nick. She knew by the tone of his voice that something was wrong.

"Everything depends on this. We can't back out now. The funeral's been scheduled. The paper has all the details. Gruber will have read it and in my bones, McGee, I know that he'll be there! We have to catch him!"

Nick was sweating. He tried to tell Alex some of what happened. Now, she was hanging on his every word.

"What are they going to do?" she asked.

McGee told Nick there was only one way he could think of that would work but he knew it was dangerous. McGee then dropped the bomb. Nick knew in his heart that it was the only way they had to catch Joshua Gruber.

McGee said, "Nick, you could do it. I didn't want to ask after all you and Alex have been through but you would be wearing a bulletproof vest and have ten to twelve sharpshooters there. I can only ask you to think about it. If it were me, I don't know for sure what my own answer would be."

McGee was leaving him a way out but what about Alexandra? He wasn't sure she could take much more, emotionally. He wasn't sure he wanted to put himself in that position either. He told McGee he would have to talk it over with Alex and he'd call him back.

McGee reminded him, "Nick, we don't have much time."

"I know."

Nick turned to Alexandra. The look in his eyes told her that something was very wrong and she knew, instinctively, what McGee had asked of Nicholas.

McGee was watching the funeral from a seat in the back of the Mission Chapel. He didn't see anyone except his own agents. He had a tiny microphone in his ear and he could speak to his FBI agents and to Nick. Alex was plugged in from the apartment home and could hear what McGee was saying. If she needed to talk to him, she could also transmit.

McGee knew he was running a pretty dangerous game, putting in Nick Stewart at the last minute and he couldn't believe that Nick was able to talk Alexandra into it.

"See anyone that looks like him, yet?" he asked them.

"No, no one, not yet," they agreed.

"Cut in anytime if you do," he said.

The priest gave a eulogy for Alexandra and Nicholas Stewart played the part of his life. He went up to the front, where the closed casket was and fell to his knees. He kissed the casket and cried. One of the pallbearers had to help him back to his seat.

"This should have brought all his fans to tears," said McGee.

Alexandra looked on from her TV at home and took a deep breath.

"It could really have been me in that casket, McGee," she whispered, "and Nick is feeling it. I just hope he's careful of everyone around him."

McGee didn't answer. Finally, the funeral ended and the procession of cars was lined up to go to the graveside services.

"Still no one?" McGee asked over the speaker.

"Still no one," was their answer.

The funeral procession headed out. McGee was in one of the last cars. Alex saw Inspector Avery get into one of the cars near the middle of the procession.

"McGee!" she exclaimed. "If Josh sees Avery, he won't try this at all. He will think that Avery can I.D. him. You have to prevent Avery from getting out of the car at the graveside. If I can see him, so will Joshua. He could ruin everything. You have to keep him in the car."

"Don't worry, Alex. Joshua Gruber would take this as just one more challenge. But, if it makes you feel better, I'll notify Avery's driver. He can back us up from his limo."

Alex thought to herself, "If I were Gruber, I would never show up at this event."

Nick was thinking about Gruber being too smart to fall for this too but he said nothing.

As they drove to the graveside services, he looked out the window of the limo. A small bird had made a nest in one of the bushes. He didn't recognize its species but watched it fly back and forth, bringing different grasses into the nest.

It's June. It's the month for weddings and brides. We should be preparing for a honeymoon, not a funeral.

He thought of Alex and how she had reacted when he told her that he would have to be the decoy. She had pulled her turtleneck sweater up to her face, like she was trying to hide and walked out of the room without saying anything to him.

He knew it had just about killed her. After giving her a little time alone, he entered the bedroom where she had disappeared and had found her staring out of the window. He had walked over to her and pulled her close to him. He could still hear her sobs.

There was no comfort for that and he just wanting to take her pain away. He knew it wouldn't stop, until this was over. He had to do this, for them.

"Alex," he had told her, "I have to. We've come too far. I promise you…."

"Stop! Don't promise me you'll be all right. You can't promise that, Nick. What if I lose you?"

But, she couldn't ask him not to go. He had kissed her and held her the rest of the night. This morning, they spoke little about what had to be done.

Alex pulled her chair closer to the screen and asked McGee if he could turn up the sound on the service.

"Now, that's something," chimed in McGee, "trying to hear some of the good things they're saying about you?" He joked, trying to get her to relax a little. "Alex, he's okay. Try not to worry."

Alex noticed something. She asked for the camera to be pointed to the speaker who was reading the benediction. Nick and the agents looked more closely at the speaker.

There were two priests, the one who spoke at the funeral and the one speaking now. Nick listened to the voice too and he froze. He spoke into his microphone to McGee.

"McGee, something about that voice is familiar."

"Get a close-up, McGee," Alex almost screamed, " I want to see the priest who is reading, right now!"

Alex's voice sounded urgent. The camera was brought in for a close shot of the priest.

"I can't see his eyes. I need to see his eyes," said Alex.

"Do you think that could be Gruber?" asked McGee.

"His stance is the same and his body is about the right size. It's his voice that is just like Josh Green's voice. It could be him. I can't tell unless I see him in person. What does Nick think?"

McGee told Alex that Nick also thought the voice was familiar. They'd let this play out and hope he would try something.

"But, if it doesn't, I'll have him picked up anyway and brought to our headquarters."

"You won't have any reason to hold him if he doesn't do something, will you?" asked Alex.

McGee didn't reply.

"I think there's too many FBI agents around for him to try anything. He must know some of their faces. I think he's playing with us, McGee," said Nick.

"We'll get him—one way or another. We'll get him." McGee had his hand on the door handle of his sedan.

"This is so frustrating," Alex said and for a moment she turned away from the screen.

Then she yelled, "The monster wants to make sure I'm in the ground!"

She threw a pillow at the TV monitor. The graveside service was being dismissed. Nick had walked to the other side of the casket, had put flowers on it and was waiting for it to be lowered. The priest who they suspected might be Gruber, came over and put his arm on Nick's arm, as if to comfort the grieving man.

"What's this?" whispered McGee, expecting something to happen any minute.

Alex leaned forward, entranced. Then, the priest blessed the ground and disappeared to the back of the crowd.

The graveside crowd started for their cars. Nick stood up, watching him. The priest turned suddenly, took something from his hand and looked directly at Nicholas Stewart.

He smiled and started to throw something—a small vial—but one of the agents blocked him and threw him to the ground.

"Get him!" ordered McGee to his men. "Get him now and get that vial before someone steps on it or breaks it!"

The service turned to chaos. Two FBI agents took both the priests into custody. The one that Alex and Nick suspected of being Joshua Gruber went voluntarily.

He was being put into a car when Inspector Avery stepped out of his limo and stopped right in front of him. He scrutinized him, looking at his face, back and eyes. The man stared back at Avery, as if he had never seen him before. Avery motioned for the agent to go ahead and put him in the car.

"What does Avery think?" asked Alex of McGee.

"I don't think he knows for sure. He says it 'could be' him but he's not positive."

"Don't you have any recent prints? What about DNA?" interrupted Nick.

"He would have had his fingerprints changed when he changed his looks. DNA will take awhile. I don't know if we have the time. We're on it, though. We have the vial. Don't know what that is but I can guess. My guess is that it would have taken out this entire section of the state!

"Alex, we're coming to pick you up. I want you both brought to our headquarters to see this guy. Get your things and be ready to fly."

Chapter Twenty-Three

Alexandra rang up John on the phone. He had just seen what had happened on his own T.V. and told her that he was going to the agency with her. Alex was grateful to have some company. More than that, she was overwhelmed. It all came crashing down on her—Nick was safe. The tears she had held inside all this while flooded her eyes and ran down her cheeks and neck.

McGee gave permission for John Cabe to come with Alex, as if anything could have prevented him. John knew what this was doing to Alexandra and to Nick too.

He was getting good at letting Alex cry it out. He held her hand and hoped that Nick would be waiting for her. *He* was the only one she wanted to see right now and even though she knew Nick was all right, she would need to touch him and make sure he was.

McGee told Alex that only she and Nick would be allowed into the room to identify Gruber.

"That's fine," Alex told McGee. Soon, she and John Cabe were dressed and packed and waiting at the apartment's entrance, where Agent Ross met them.

They all knew that Alex's shoulder had still not regained full range of motion and that she was still not fully recovered. Ross was not just an agent but also an RN, sent by the FBI, which would be helpful in case Alexandra needed something. Ross assured them she would stay out of their way. Alex told her that she was glad another female was going to be with them. She and Ross had bonded after that surprise evening that they had planned for Nick.

John Cabe was pleased there was another female on the plane. Maybe Alex could talk to Ross. He let the two of them sit together and he sat across the aisle, smiling at Alex whenever she looked his way. Finally, the plane arrived in Los Angeles and they were driven to see McGee—and his newest prisoner.

179

McGee and Inspector Avery were together in McGee's office. Avery shook hands with Alexandra and then kissed her cheek, which surprised both of them. He then asked an agent to have Nick Stewart brought in.

Alex just stood there, as he walked over to her and took her in his arms. They didn't have to say anything to each other. He held her like that for some time, while the two detectives made small talk with each other. They had earned this moment together and everyone in the room knew it.

Finally Avery said, "Glad to see the both of you together. God knows it's been bloody awful for the two of you. I'm sorry to say I couldn't make a positive identification of Gruber but it could be him. He looks different, changed his face. If there's anyway you can tell us for sure, we can hold him. We've taken evidence for DNA. It may be awhile before we get that back but it should be a positive I.D. We just need evidence that he is the same person as Joshua Green. We know that he's connected somehow to the bombing of Ed Percy and for the plan to blow up the people at the peace treaty signing."

McGee reminded Nick that he and Alex had to see Gruber one at a time.

"May I go in first?" Alex asked. "I want to be close enough to really see him."

She said that she needed to sit across the table from him in order to see his eyes. McGee agreed but only if there was an agent in the back of the room with her. She nodded, squeezed Nick's hand and took a deep breath. Then, she went into a small, brightly lit room. It had one table with two chairs pulled up to it, facing each other. She sat down in one of the chairs—and waited.

After what seemed like a long time, a guard brought in a young man in priest's clothing. He sat down on the cold metal chair, directly across from Alex. Except for the same body type, he looked *nothing* like Joshua Green.

When the priest saw Alexandra, he couldn't believe it.

So, she didn't die after all. This is quite a scheme.

He tried to hide his surprise.

"Josh?" Alex asked.

He smiled at her.

"My name's Father Litton. I'm sorry, but I don't know anyone named Josh."

The voice had not changed. Alex shivered. It was Joshua Green's voice and she recognized it. Alexandra remembered how charming Joshua Green had seemed to her. He had a nice smile, good teeth and he had green eyes.

He had told her about his engagement to his wife. What was her name? *Marley...that was it...Marley Green.*

They spent an entire evening together, celebrating her engagement to Nick. She had to recognize some of his mannerisms. If this was Gruber, she had to play along—get him to relax and somehow lose his guard.

"I'm sorry, Father." She sounded apologetic. "I just thought you were someone I knew. I believed he might have died and I was hoping that you might be...I'm afraid I may have been mistaken."

"Oh, I'm sorry to hear that."

He almost reached across the table, as if to console her but stopped.

"Is there anything I can do?"

Alex noticed his left hand. The white flesh, where a ring had been, was now bare. It was obvious to her that he had been wearing a wedding band. Joshua Green had a wedding band. Now, there was only a white ring around the "father's" fourth finger.

Alex went on to ask if she could get him something to drink—something to make him more comfortable. Inside, she was sick at her stomach. He had ordered her killed! He had tried to kill Nick and John—and Mac, dear Mac...

"No, my dear. Thank you. Aren't you the pretty young thing? You know, you look a lot like the picture of the girl I just buried. Was she a relative?"

Alex looked directly into his eyes—his green, cold eyes and she knew it was Gruber.

"You might say that she was very close to me. And you, Father, did you know her? You gave such a moving speech."

She was playing with him, now. Somehow, she knew that he wanted her to identify him.

"I knew her briefly. It was some time ago. She was a beautiful woman, very much in love, as I remember."

Gruber was toying with her—daring her to expose him. He wasn't scared of her at all—like a cat playing with a bird.

"Yes, she was in love. So were my friends, David and Joshua. David had a family and his friend Joshua, told me how he had proposed to his wife. Her name was, let's see. I think I remember. It was Marley...yes, that's it...it was Marley! I thought that he too, was very much in love."

His eyes and mouth hardened just for an instant. She had caught him by surprise and she knew it. He had not expected her to remember Marley Green.

"Yes, her name was Marley Green and if I remember, she lived in New York City. I'd be willing to bet that she still does."

"I wouldn't know, my dear. So, tell me more about yourself."

Alex was through with the games. She turned off her smile and glared at Gruber.

"You liar!" she screamed. "Don't even try and pull this off. How could you do this, Joshua? You said you loved your wife and I believed you. You killed David, too, didn't you? And now, you're planning this? How can you do it? Does your Marley know who you really are? I think we need to tell her...."

Gruber's face quit smiling. He scowled and slammed his fist on the table. "Shut up, you silly woman!"

Gruber knew he had given himself away and had lost control. But then, he reverted to calmness. He was smiling at her again.

"Alexandra, I'm so glad to see you're still alive. If you hadn't met Nick first, you and I may have been more than friends."

"We were never friends, Josh. Friends don't try to have each other killed. And what about poor David? He had a wife and two young children!"

"I didn't kill David and you can't prove anything. In fact, Alexandra, you have nothing on me. You might have Ed Percy's fingerprints on something but you won't find mine. I was never fond of violence and I've always tried to live a quiet peaceful life."

He infuriated Alex. He was so sure of himself. Then, she decided she was getting nowhere. It was time to go back to what seemed to set him off in the first place.

"Tell me about your Marley, Joshua. What's she like? How can she stand living with you? Do you have any children? How close do you live from the U.N.? Aren't you afraid the explosion may kill everyone within a three- to four-state radius? I'd better tell Agent McGee to warn your Marley, or don't you care at all about her?"

Gruber glowered at her.

"She doesn't know anything! You leave her out of this!"

I hit a nerve, didn't I, Gruber? He thinks he really loves her. Marley may be the key.

Alex told the guard she wanted out.

"No, wait!" said Gruber.

"Tell us where the chemical is, Joshua."

"Now, Alexandra, you know I can't do that."

"Then, we have nothing more to say to each other."

Alex got up and left the room. She couldn't believe that she still called Gruber "Joshua." It was too intimate for a mad man, she thought.

McGee and Nicholas were waiting for her, as was Inspector Avery. Nick caught her, as she almost fell into his arms.

"You got his goat! Good for you, Alexandra. We have him identified, at least."

"But, we need to find the chemicals," said Alexandra. "And, he's never going to tell us. We need to find his wife. We need to bring her here."

"Let me see him first," interrupted Nick.

As Nick watched Gruber with Alexandra, it took all his self-control to not bust through the door and beat up the slime. That crack about Alex and Gruber being more than friends was just for his benefit but Nick had an idea.

"Gruber thinks he's got the upper hand. He likes to brag about how good he is and that's a big weakness. That ego of his just may hang him."

"Are you sure you want to see him right now?" McGee asked Nick.

"Yeah, I'm sure."

Nick took a deep breath and readied himself. He walked to the door of the interrogation room. McGee knocked on the door and told the guard that he had one more visitor.

"Mr. Stewart, I thought you'd be dead by now," greeted Gruber.

Nick said nothing, just glared and sat down across from him.

"You think we're not close to knowing all about your plans, Gruber? How do you explain how we identified you, anyway?" challenged Nick.

Gruber didn't answer. He hated this self-righteous pig.

"Think about it, Gruber. We have the map, the locker numbers, the sample of the chemicals and more."

Nick didn't want to give away too much.

"So?" said Gruber. "It could be staring you right in the face and you wouldn't know *where* it is!"

"Think so? Well, I'm sure we'll figure it out—without your help," said Nick.

It took all his acting skill just to stay on track with this maniac. "We're this close to the point."

"The point, huh?" laughed Gruber. "Oh, that's right. You think it's a place!" He chuckled to himself and Nick noticed how hardened his face had become.

"You're sick, Gruber," said Nick. "You think your wife's going to think you're a hero, after this happens?"

"Leave her out of this! She doesn't know anything!" yelled Gruber.

Alex had been right. She had hit a nerve and so had he. Gruber's ego made him brag to Nick about the point. Now, they knew it didn't mean a place at all.

"Well, Gruber, your wife's about to find out just who and what you are! Get me out of here, guard!" Nick demanded.

183

Gruber was taken back to his cell and Lt. Avery congratulated Alex and Nick.

"We're closer," he said. "Now, we know he is Joshua Green alias Joshua Gruber and we know that the point isn't a place. But, if it's not a place, what is it? We still know this is going to happen at the U.N. at the summit. Now, we have to find the rest of those chemicals!"

"The point," mused Alex. "We thought we had it all figured out and we were wrong all the time. What were some of the other synonyms we went over?"

John stood by, watching the procedure and saying nothing.

Now, he interjected with, "Tip…that was one of the words…tip."

"That could mean anything," said Nick. "We know there is going to be a summit meeting and even if point isn't the meaning for that, we know the date it's going to happen. We know it's at the United Nations, when the President and the Prime Minister sign a short-term peace treaty with third-world countries. Everyone knows about it. Gruber must have his demolition team lined up. The chemical has to have been stocked and ready to go, for him to be so sure. It could already be inside the building, for all we know. He's so cocky! I'd like to have an hour alone with him."

Nick hadn't been this angry in quite awhile. He was having feelings of wanting to kill Gruber and making him pay for all that he had put Alex and his friends through. He shuddered, thinking about what Gruber would have done to Alex, if she and Gruber had ever been alone together.

How could they have been so fooled by Joshua Green and why hadn't he gone ahead and killed them then? He knew the answer. Gruber himself had told him that he didn't like violence. He didn't want to get his own hands dirty but he could order thousands of persons killed without a thought.

"What a piece of work," said Nick.

Chapter Twenty-Four

McGee had a pick-up order for Mrs. Marley Green. They had found her name and address listed in the New York City phonebook.

"Guess he didn't count on you remembering her name," said McGee to Alex.

"I almost didn't. I was so giddy that night," reported Alex.

"Do you think she knows about him?" asked Nick.

"He would have to be pretty careful not to make her suspicious," said Alex.

"Or, it's something else. I've never seen anyone that cool about everything else blow up the way he did about her," noted McGee.

"Yeah, he was pretty out of it," replied Nick.

"I wonder if he has kids, too?" asked Alex.

"I hope not!" said Nick. "Nothing like having the devil himself for your dad."

"Well, you two did very, very good today. Let me take you out of here— with security of course," McGee laughed, "and let me buy you folks a steak dinner at one of the best restaurants in California. Of course, you may be their only guests tonight. I've cleared it just for our group, if that's okay?"

Nick, Alexandra and John gladly accepted. They hadn't had a night away from a hospital in weeks! John perked up even more when he found out that Agent Ross was coming. McGee had asked Avery to tag along and even Avery agreed to come.

Marley Green would be at headquarters tomorrow if they were lucky and that meant spending the night in Los Angeles. Alex believed if anyone spied Nick they would probably recognize him. Then, she smiled. If they saw her, they would think that they had seen a ghost raised from the dead.

The restaurant that McGee had chosen was dimly lit. McGee kept a piano player, the chef and a couple of waiters. The white linen tablecloths were decorated with flowers and the candlelight would have added a romantic effect if the group hadn't known what had brought them together.

McGee wasn't kidding about treating them well, however. They were offered anything on the menu. John purposely sat next to Agent Ross and while they were waiting for their main course, he asked her to dance with him. Alex and Nick noticed that Ross seemed to be enjoying his attention and decided if John could treat this like a special occasion so could they. In fact, this would be the first time they danced together since their secret wedding.

Alexandra glanced at Nick as he got up and held out his hand, inviting her to dance with him. Being in his arms again, she dreamed of another night when he had held her and danced so close. She closed her eyes and he pulled her to him, guiding her to the music. This night would end differently than the one in New York City, where they were so miserable to be apart from each other.

John and Ross were laughing and joking with each other and seemed to be having a good time. Nick just wanted to take Alex back home—home to his own house—home to Sabrina and to Sandy.

When the music ended and the couples sat back down, Nick leaned over and kissed Alexandra, right in front of everyone! He didn't care who saw them. John and Agent Ross just grinned at each other, sharing their secret.

After steak and baked potatoes, the entire group was feeling better and they were all in a good humor. Inspector Avery had even danced with Alexandra and he surprised her by being a very good partner.

Later, they were sipping coffee and talking about Gruber again. The bill was brought to McGee and he started to sign the ticket. The waiter's pen wouldn't write. McGee shook it and tried again to make it work and then asked the waiter for another.

It was at that moment that Alex gasped. "Oh!" she screamed…a small, pitiful sound that had Ross drawing her gun and Nick pulling her down under the table.

But Alexandra wasn't hurt. In fact, she was ecstatic! She was laughing and crying all at the same time.

"What's wrong with her?" asked McGee, thinking she had gone over the edge this time.

"Alex, what is it?" asked Nick, who was still holding her close to him.

John Cabe had seen this behavior before—when she remembered the numbers!

"She knows something!" John said.

"I'm sorry, I'm sorry but I think I know what the point is!" she exclaimed.

"What? What did you say?" asked Nick.

186

"I know what the point is," repeated Alex.

McGee walked closer to her and helped her up.

"It came to me when you signed our ticket," she said.

"What came to you?" McGee asked.

"It's in the pens! It's the tip of the pen—the pen point. It has to be it. They're signing a peace treaty. How long before the liquid oozes onto the paper and explodes? How many signatures before the entire U.N. is nothing but ashes?"

Alex's head was throbbing. She didn't know if it was the excitement of the knowing, or thinking, of what might happen.

"I tell you, I've done public relations before. They always have a special pen that's used. Then, one is given to each one who signs the treaty to keep as a souvenir. Who knows how many countries could end up with one of those pens in their Embassy or in an airplane? It would be easy for one of Gruber's companies to have made the lowest bid and put the chemical in all the pens that are going into that room that day. John was right! It's the tip, the tip of the pen—the pen point they're using to sign the agreement!"

Alex squeezed Nick's hand and walked over to John Cabe and gave him a big kiss, right on the lips. He couldn't say anything. For once in his life, John Cabe was speechless.

Avery and McGee smiled at each other. The agents in the room began clapping, then cheering! They had him! They had Joshua Gruber!

"Let's get back to the headquarters," said McGee. "I have some phone calls to make."

He knew the Organization's fall wasn't far behind.

The next day, Nick, Alex, John and McGee were watching from the observation room when Marley Green went in to see her husband. They now understood why Joshua Green had been so adamant for them not to tell her.

Alexandra felt sorry for what was about to happen. She felt that Marley Green didn't deserve this, finding out about her husband this way. This was Joshua Gruber's real payback, she thought.

She grabbed for Nick's hand as he stood looking through the glass. He was very sober. John Cabe muttered something about how he was glad he wasn't in Gruber's place today.

It seemed that Marley Green was not only blind, she was also in a wheelchair. She couldn't move her hands, feet, or her legs. Marley Green was *totally incapacitated* except for her hearing and speaking. She had a nurse who had to take total care of her.

Gruber was prevented from going over to sit next to her. He was handcuffed and his feet were shackled. He had to sit across the table from his wife and tell her what was happening. She didn't understand, of course. Alex watched as those cold, green eyes gathered tears in them.

McGee couldn't watch and told the guard to stop this procedure. He would tell Mrs. Green about her husband. Gruber watched Marley as she was wheeled out. He aimed his fist at the glass, to those he knew were watching them. When Gruber turned to leave, he looked like a beaten man.

"Does he know we know about the pens?" asked Alex.

"Oh, yeah. He knows."

"And?"

"All of the pens that were passed out were picked up this morning. The chemical was found in all of one box, the box made in Joshua Gruber's factory," said McGee.

He told Alexandra and Nick that they would have to testify and that he would be placing heavy security around them. Then, he told them they could go to Mr. Stewart's estate until the hearing, if that was all right with them.

John cheered. Nick picked up Alex and swung her so high, her feet left the floor. Alex cried and laughed at the same time. Home—home! They were finally going home.

Chapter Twenty-Five

It was December before the hearings of Joshua Gruber ended. He was found guilty of espionage and other crimes. He was sentenced to death.

As predicted, other members of the Organization, who were scattered throughout the world, were being picked up. Other countries were trying them in other courts and were finding them guilty.

The fatal chemical that had been exposed by the FBI and Scotland Yard was turned over to the United States government. It was said that it had been totally disposed of and destroyed. Nicholas Stewart had his doubts about that. The Organization had been worldwide. If there were any of the chemicals remaining, anywhere else…but he couldn't think about that now.

It was in the hands of the nations of the world now and he was glad that his country was a sane one and that they would strive to find any madman who might have future plans to take over the world. That was what Joshua Gruber wanted. Nick was sure of it. He had dreams of taking over the world. He wanted to be another Adolph Hitler or some other maniac.

And now, he had gotten what he deserved. Justice had finally prevailed for Joshua Gruber and his Organization.

Epilogue

Nick looked out the window of his new home in Colorado and saw that a light snow was falling. After more than one year since he and Alex met, this was the home that they had picked out together. Everyday life had not lessened their love, the love that they had found in the excitement and rush of the prior months.

If anything, he loved Alexandra Andrews more today than he had back then, if that were possible. They had learned to argue over a tube of toothpaste, squeezing it on each other, ending up in laughter and a kiss.

Crawford thought Nick was crazy when he let Sandy, Alex's dog, into the mansion in California, to romp through it with Sabrina and Alexandra. She had made that place a home too but they both loved it here, in Colorado. This was their sanctuary. They had found a new church home—one they attended as a family.

Today, even with the snow, Nick noticed a blue jay under the eaves of the porch. He watched while Sandy chased a squirrel and then tried to catch snow with his mouth. He was barking at it like it was the enemy.

"Another protector in the family," he grinned.

The new movie was finally finished and his life had been almost normal recently. Nick told the studio that he was only going to accept one movie every other year.

He had other business dealings that were making more than enough money for his family. Life was too short to work all the time. Besides, he didn't need to do that anymore. He wanted to live his new life with Alex.

Now that she had recovered, they were beginning to learn again what it was to have fun. They laughed a lot—and they loved a lot. His thoughts were interrupted by a knock at the door.

"You ready, buddy?" asked John.

"Never been as ready as this!" replied Nick.

They walked to the large living area, where a group of friends were waiting for them.

190

"Have you got the ring?" Nick asked John.

John checked his pocket and nodded. He had never been comfortable in a tuxedo but this was different. It was Nick and Alex's wedding day and he was the best man—again. No one but he and Agent Ross had been told their secret, except for Mac and Sabrina.

The house had been decorated and there were flowers everywhere. Still, with the snow, a warm fire was burning in the massive stone fireplace. A bevy of ceramic angels graced the hall table and candles were everywhere.

The music started and Sabrina came in. Nick watched her as she scattered flowers from her basket. She made a beautiful flower girl, wearing a light pink dress with a matching jacket that was darker in color. Her new shoes made a light tapping noise as she walked down the aisle to her father.

Nick watched Sabrina's dark curls bounce as she tossed rose petals up in the air and to the side. She grinned widely when she saw her father.

"Hi, Daddy," she said and waved at him.

"Hi, precious girl," Nick waved back.

The group of friends laughed and Sabrina went to stand beside her dad. He leaned down and gave her a kiss and took her hand.

Then, Mac came in with Alexandra on his arm. Nick swallowed hard when he saw her. He thought she looked beautiful the first time they married. Now, she was stunning! She wore an ivory satin gown that wrapped around her curves and fell to the floor in folds.

She had only a single strand of pearls around her neck. Her strawberry-blond hair touched her bare shoulders. She carried a simple bouquet of burgundy roses, sprinkled with pink carnations and white baby's breath. Mac was smiling at Nick and John as he led her down the short aisle.

When Mac was asked, "Who gives this woman?" he answered, "I do." He kissed Alex and whispered to her, "I love you, Alex. Take good care of him."

John managed to find the rings, again, when he was asked for them and he breathed a sigh of relief.

Nick and Alex had written their own vows. They each talked about meeting their soul mates and risking everything for their love and most of the people there knew exactly what they meant.

Agent McGee, Inspector Avery and Agent Ross were all guests of the bride and groom. Nick's mother sat in the front row, beaming. Alex had managed to smooth over hurt feelings, even with her.

When Nick kissed his new bride, the small crowd stood up and clapped. Sabrina came over and kissed her new mother and her father.

"My family," said Sabrina.

"And mine," answered Nick.

After Mr. and Mrs. Stewart were introduced to their guests, the guests were told the reception would be in the large dining room. As the small crowd dispersed, the bride and groom disappeared for a few minutes.

While the guests were being seated and served, Nick took his wife outside for a moment, onto the patio. He kissed her, held her close to him and pointed out the fresh snow. She was shivering but it wasn't because of the cold. Alex felt the closeness of her soul mate, her husband. These vows had renewed their love for each other. She thought about the wait. It had been worth it.

Nick handed her a small gift before they went back inside.

"Darling, you've already given me so much."

When she opened it, she found a small globe, with a cityscape of New York, along with two reservations to a hotel they both remembered. Nick grinned at her and looked at her with those sparkling blue eyes she loved so much.

"We've had to wait, again, Alexandra. The honeymoon's my gift, Mrs. Stewart," he said.

Alex smiled. She had already reserved a carriage ride through Central Park and a gift certificate from Mama Rita's. It was her gift to him. She would tell him about that later.

She looked up at him and replied, "As far as I'm concerned, we've been on a honeymoon since the day I met you, my love, and it's been quite a ride. And just think, it's only the beginning!"

He picked her up, carrying her over the threshold and then put her down inside their home, close to him. As he kissed her once more, he thought about their future together and he smiled.

The End

Printed in the United States
71410LV00005B/142-189